The Barbarian's Vow

Also by Keira Andrews

The Barbarian's Vow

Barbarian Duet Book Two

BY KEIRA ANDREWS

Barbarian's Vow: Barbarian Duet Book Two
Written and published by Keira Andrews
Cover by Dar Albert
Formatting by BB eBooks
© 2021 by Keira Andrews
Print Edition

ISBN: 978-1-988260-63-1

This is a work of fiction. Names, characters, businesses, places, events and incidents are either the products of the author's imagination or used in a fictitious manner. No persons, living or dead, were harmed by the writing of this book. Any resemblance to any actual persons, living or dead, or actual events is purely coincidental.

Chapter One

T HERE WAS INDEED a worse fate than crossing the damn
sea—doing it in the stinking heat.

Cador's pitifully empty stomach heaved as the ship rocked
over the white-foamed waves. Sweat stung his eyes, and he
gripped the bow rail with slick palms.

After weeks with only the water and sky in sight, now he
blinked at mainland Onan huddled on the horizon, growing
bigger by the hour. The temperature soared seemingly by the
minute. At least the cursed sun was behind them now as it bore
down mercilessly, prickling his reddened neck.

Though he'd stripped down to only his vest and trousers, his
face was flushed and his throat constantly dry. He'd trimmed
his beard and scraped his face clean with a razor, yet his
stubborn hair grew back to a thick stubble too quickly. He toyed
again with removing his boots, but he was so rarely barefoot
he'd felt strangely unguarded and exposed when he'd tried it.

The sea spray stung his chapped lips, but at least it was cool.
His pale skin burned easily, but he couldn't stand covering his
arms. He wore the damn vest so he didn't roast his back. He
could only manage sips of water or his stomach rebelled.

The very worst part was that he'd suffer it all gladly if Jem
would so much as *look* at him.

Jem owed him nothing—least of all forgiveness. Cador reminded himself of this daily. Hourly. He had only himself to

blame. He'd agreed to his tas's plan to marry Jem and plot his eventual kidnapping.

It was almost impossible to believe now he'd cared so little for Jem's fate. Jem had only been a burden. A means to an end. Jem had been *nothing*. Now he was everything, and he hated Cador. Perhaps that was the punishment Cador fucking deserved.

A terrible scream split the air.

He jolted, immediately shamed to be grumbling about the heat and wallowing in self-pity. He hurried to the ship's rear, passing Jem and Jory, their dice game abandoned for the moment. No matter how he tried to ignore it, to walk so close by Jem and feel as though they were strangers was a dagger twisting in his gut.

All eyes were on Hedrok. Or at least what they could see of him on a pallet under the sunshade of boar skin strung tight. Cador's sister, Delen, watched from her usual position by the helm, staying close to Creeda and Hedrok, but not too close.

Creeda knelt by her son, leaning over him, muttering her prayers and assurances. She clutched a bound bundle of twigs from the old sevel trees. Her dark hair was knotted tightly as usual, copper skin largely untouched by the sun since she rarely left Hedrok's side. Her cheekbones stood out even more sharply, her muscled body taut and too thin.

As much as Cador despised being at sea, there were indeed many things far, far worse. The deadly wasting disease that struck only Ergh's children, including his nephew, had claimed too many victims.

"Can I help?" he asked, his fingers twitching.

Creeda didn't spare him a glance, eyes locked on Hedrok's pale face twisted in agony. "More water."

He hurried to fill the small pail. Leaving the helm, Meraud joined him by the water barrel. Her small, trusted crew accompanied them on this unexpected journey, along with a few hunters who were ignorant of the scheme to kidnap Jem. And Bryok's secret scheme to murder him.

"Getting low," Meraud murmured. Her graying curls hung past her shoulders, tied back at her neck.

Indeed, Cador had to lean in, the pail thudding the barrel's bottom as he filled it. "Enough?"

She squinted toward Onan. "Just. I expected more rain."

"Should I tell Creeda to make this last?"

"No. Let him have as much as he needs."

Another of Hedrok's screams carried on the wind. Cador nodded. "I'll give up my share."

Meraud laughed softly, the wrinkles around her eyes deepening. "You can barely keep it down anyway." She nudged him affectionately. "You and that poor horse will be glad to know we should make land before morning."

They had brought only one mount since the voyage was hard enough for people, let alone horses who needed to roam. The unfortunate gray beast, Lusow, stood in a makeshift stall they'd quickly nailed together at the stern, though Jory walked him about the deck for hours a day.

At first, Lusow had stamped and snorted and bucked when Hedrok screamed or wailed. Even the horse had become inured to the boy's cries. Though Jory had gone to him, feeding him a carrot and brushing his back soothingly.

Jory had chosen Lusow for speed and would ride ahead to the Holy Place to send for more horses and provisions, then south to Neuvella with the news for Tas that Bryok was dead and their convoy would be arriving soon. Part of Cador had wanted to bring Massen, his faithful stallion, but he would not subject him to the journey needlessly.

Hedrok thrashed on his pallet, legs unmoving beneath a thin blanket. Cador returned with the water, hovering uselessly as Creeda encouraged Hedrok to drink. He shivered, sweat dampening his hair. He pushed at the blanket tucked around his waist.

"It's too hot to be covered up," Cador said.

Creeda glared up at him, her brown eyes narrowing. "Go on, then. Remove the blanket."

The challenge had been issued, and Cador crouched, pretending it didn't bother him at all. It *shouldn't* have bothered him to see the evidence of the disease. He didn't allow himself to flinch as he uncovered Hedrok's spindly bare legs.

At his feet, the dried husks of bone and dead flesh were a dark color that got lighter as it spread higher, Hedrok's long tunic bunched at his hips. The blistered, violent rash that spiderwebbed to the tops of Hedrok's thighs was blood red. Cador forced his gaze to remain on Hedrok's writhing body, hating the way his legs remained motionless.

Creeda dampened a cloth, wiping Hedrok's brow as Cador uselessly asked, "Are you sure it was wise to bring him?" before he could school himself.

She gave him a withering look. "As I told you, Hedrok suffers whether he's here or home. He suffers every hour of every day. Your prince promises the Neuvellan healers will try to help, and sevels are plentiful there. If the lack of sevels truly caused this, I will feed them to him until his dying breath. We have nothing left to lose."

Cador nodded. They'd considered bringing all the afflicted children, but if they declared war with Ebrenn in the West, the children could be put in more danger. There was no good answer. Who the fuck knew the right thing to do?

"And here, we are closer to the gods," Creeda said. "The clerics will help. I pray and pray, and perhaps the gods will finally heed my cries."

"Mmm." He could say no more in favor of the gods or the clerics. Were the clerics truly pious and good, or did they crave power like everyone else? Tas certainly believed the clerics would worm their way into control of Ergh if given a chance.

As Hedrok whimpered, Cador tried to soothe him without getting in Creeda's way. Her other words echoed. *My prince.* If only it were true.

He asked, "Is this new? Has he been fevered before?" He should know the answer. He should have visited his nephew daily. Should have been there for Bryok and Creeda and their little ones left on Ergh who showed no signs of the sickness yet. Yet.

Gaze locked on her son, Creeda muttered, "It's happened before. Not for this long. Bryok said—" Stroking Hedrok's hair, she sighed.

"What?" Cador was suddenly desperate to know. His brother was sunk in the depths of the Askorn Sea, where he belonged. Still, he was eager to hear this unknown thought. Bryok's death had left Creeda a widow, and he wondered if she mourned him or if there was simply no space left for it.

"He thought more heat would burn out the sickness. That perhaps the mainland weather would help."

Squirming, Hedrok rasped, "No fire." He'd reached ten years, yet seemed so small and young.

"No fire," Creeda agreed. When Hedrok stilled, she muttered to Cador, "Your mad brother almost burned down the house trying to torch the sickness free." She curled her lip. "He'd have been the end of us all."

No, it didn't seem Creeda grieved her husband. Cador couldn't blame her. He wasn't sure he grieved Bryok either. He was aware of Delen inching closer and sensed his sister's worry. When he turned to give her a reassuring nod, he found Jem's honey eyes on him too.

Jem jerked around on his low stool, facing the sun that moved steadily west. He closed his eyes, basking in it as he had often in these days of sunshine as they neared the mainland. Would he ever want to leave again?

There was so much to grieve, yet the thing Cador mourned most was the loss of his husband. He'd have sailed a thousand days sweating under the pitiless sun if Jem would only forgive him. He had to be patient.

Fuck, he hated patience. Action had always been the better way.

He settled beside Hedrok, relieved when Creeda allowed it. The sticky heat lingered in the shade, but at least there was relief from the glare. Hedrok mercifully dozed as Creeda sang lullabies, the bundle of sevel twigs tight in her grasp. Cador had always known her to be serious—severe, even, and it still surprised him how light and sweet her voice was when she sang.

Midship, Jem sat alone. He threw the dice over and over in a strangely compulsive way, pausing to scratch his head. It gladdened Cador that he didn't hide below-decks in a miserable huddle as he had during their voyage to Onan after their wedding. Yet each scant, precious word Jem spoke to another made his complete silence with Cador all the more torturous.

Creeda had been willing to see Jem's head delivered to his mother the queen to spark war, yet Jem appeared to hold no grudge against her, wholeheartedly offering Neuvella's help to fight the disease that ravaged her son. Of course he did, for he was *good*.

If only he would give Cador a sliver of attention or sign he cared. That Cador hadn't destroyed every bit of affection and love and desire that had grown like fire between them…

If Jem *had* loved him, he didn't now. That precious, unexpected bloom was as dead as the sevel trees that would no longer grow on Ergh. Cador had ruined it all. He'd deceived his husband from the moment Jem had been forced to stand at the altar with him and have their palms branded. He turned his left hand, peering down at the bird's curving wings imprinted forever on his flesh.

Sometimes, he almost expected the brand to have vanished. To wake up alone under his furs in his plain cottage. To ride Massen into the forest and join Bryok on the hunt, trying to make his brother proud. Spear a boar, feast and fuck, and do it all again the next day, and the next. His life had been simple. He couldn't recognize it now.

He held Hedrok's small, clammy hand. He'd never hunt with Bryok again. His brother had been crazed—yes, with grief for his dying son, but he'd wanted power most of all. Cador would never forget the sight of Bryok's body disappearing into the black from atop the Cliffs of Glaw. Yet it was the vision of Jem's leap that truly haunted him.

In his nightmares, he saw Bryok rushing at Jem with his sword high to sever his head. Watched Jem vanish off the cliff's edge, hearing his own raw scream, boots somehow mired in quicksand, making him helpless to do anything but watch again and again and again.

Cador wasn't asleep now, but he saw it all unfold in his

Cador had always thought so. He'd basked in Tas's affection and approval since he was a boy. He'd never questioned him—not even when Tas arranged Cador's marriage to Jem and planned to use Jem so cruelly. He understood Tas's fear of the clerics getting their hooks into Ergh and changing everything. The fear of revealing weakness to the mainland and losing their way of life.

But was it fair to plot and deceive? Was it right to help their sick children at any cost?

He refocused on Delen. If Cador didn't know her so well, he'd think her not bothered, but he could hear the note of tension in her voice as she answered his question.

"We can't exactly tell Tas in a letter that his son is dead with no other details. It would be too hideous." She grimaced. "Not that it will be much better face-to-face."

"No," Cador agreed. He dreaded it beyond the telling.

Jem was silent, still looking at his feet.

Delen swiftly said, "It's done and he must face it as we have. Bryok is dead, and Tas has a new heir."

Absurdly, Cador almost asked who. He blinked at her. It truly hadn't even flickered across his mind.

Delen frowned. "You're the second oldest. You'll be chieftain now."

"But I don't want to be chieftain!" He sounded like a ridiculous child. He could imagine Bryok berating him for moping over Jem and now this. He must regain control. Regain his dignity. He was a mighty hunter of Ergh, and if he was to be chieftain, he must accept it.

He discovered Jem watched him now. Was that sympathy? His heart leapt as Jem tightened his jaw, standing straighter and clasping his hands behind his back.

To Delen, Jem said, "We are in agreement on the contents of the message."

She held out the scroll. "Would you like to read it before it is sealed?"

Jem took it and scanned the short missive before nodding and handing it back.

Delen said, "We should only have to camp a night before provisions from the Holy Place arrive. Jory is our best rider, and he will be quick about it. We will travel light, aside from—" her gaze flitted to the ship's bow where Creeda hovered over Hedrok. "Well, the cart will be slower, but we can go ahead to speak to our parents. Now, as for what precisely to tell them."

"The truth," Jem said sharply.

She nodded. "Of course. But will you permit us to speak to our tas before telling your mother the...details?"

Jem's face could have been carved from stone. "By 'details,' do you mean Kenver's initial plot to kidnap me and sever my hand so it could be sent to my mother to incite a war with Ebrenn?"

Delen grimaced. "Yes, as much as we truly regret it. I'm sure our tas regrets it too."

"You can't speak for Kenver." Jem clenched his jaw. "He concocted the scheme to begin with."

She nodded. "You're right. I hope you know—"

"Don't." Jem held up a hand. "It's done and cannot be undone. Regret is useless."

In the tense silence, Cador knew the truth of those words. He'd never known such regret, and it would change nothing. He shielded his eyes from the sun, which at least was setting now.

Needing to say *something*, he blurted, "Is it always this blasted hot in summer?"

For a moment, he thought Jem would refuse to answer. Finally, he said, "No, actually. I was always told it was more temperate this far north. But it's certainly better than all that gray in Ergh."

"That's a matter of opinion," Cador grumbled.

Delen quickly said, "Let's stay focused. Prince Jowan, may we speak to our tas before confessing to the queen? I propose that Cador and I meet with him privately to discuss Bryok. Then the three of us will join you in explaining the truth to your parents. We must be united in our cause. The children are more important than anything else. Whatever our grievances may be—whatever our sins—we must stand together."

Jem seemed to consider this. "And we'll tell them the whole truth?"

"I swear it," Delen pledged solemnly.

Jem nodded.

"We'll be on land again soon, at least," she said. "You must be eager to return home, Prince Jowan."

"An understatement if ever I heard one. Yes, I am very eager to return to Neuvella permanently." Jem turned on his heel, leaving them at the bow.

Cador had no desire for small talk either, and Delen fell silent beside him. Jem rejoined Jory, picking up the dice.

Jory cast a worried look to Cador, his ginger hair wilder than ever in the sea wind and brushing his shoulders now. Cador nodded and tried to smile. Jory was a loyal friend who was completely innocent of any plotting, and at least Jem was willing to game with him. Even if it made Cador ridiculously jealous.

As the sun blessedly set, painting the sky an eerie pink, he looked to Creeda at the bow praying by Hedrok. The boy appeared to sleep, at least. Delen watched too, the pinch of her expression melting into tender concern.

Creeda had forgiven her for killing Bryok, apparently understanding that his hunger for power had surpassed redemption and Delen had only wielded her spear in necessity.

Before he could bite his tongue, Cador said, "Sometimes I think you love her."

Delen jolted, narrowing her gaze at him. "What?"

He might as well say it. "Sometimes I think you've loved her for a long time."

"And?" Her hands were fists, ready for a battle in a blink.

"And nothing." He frowned in confusion at her anger.

She glanced around and hissed, "You think I killed him for my own gain?"

It was Cador's turn to stiffen in surprise. "No!" He grasped her arm. "*Never.*"

Delen exhaled loudly, the sudden fight disappearing. She nodded, looking to Creeda again. "I shouldn't," she murmured.

"Why?" He had to admit he didn't understand the appeal. But Creeda and Delen had been friends since they were girls. Perhaps there was another side to her as sweet as her singing.

Delen shook off his hand. "You know why."

"But—"

"Shall we speak of your love? How long will you shrink away and let Jem's anger fester?"

"He deserves to be angry."

"That may be, but the longer this separation lasts, the deeper the chasm between you. This talk of him never leaving Neuvella again—"

"How can you blame him after what we've done?"

Delen sighed. "I don't blame him a bit. But as I said, we must be united in our cause. You and he must be united most of all or we don't stand a chance."

"We will be."

"See to it." She gave a curt nod and strode off, disappearing into the hold.

His gaze returned to Jem as it always did. Small hands cupped, Jem tossed the dice. No secrets there. From those first moments in the Holy Place when their impending marriage was announced, Jem had revealed all.

Although he'd often tried to conceal his emotions, they were plain as day. Now it was all hurt and fury, and Cador longed to once again see his shy smiles of delight.

Resolutely, Cador faced the endless sea. He watched the waves swell, capped with frothy white as the wind increased. He inhaled the briny air that was still far too hot to be refreshing and longed to see his breath cloud in the frigid air of home. He tried to think of any damn thing but Jem.

Oh, to hear Jem's cries of passion and kiss his sweet lips. Bury his prick inside him and bring them both to ecstasy. To return to the cottage and those heady days of exploration and fucking. Even to just bake bread with him and tend the goats—perhaps nurse another hatchling like Derwa.

He never thought he would miss a bird.

In the wee hours, he rose from his pallet to piss off the rear of the ship. Meraud's second nodded to him from the helm. Snores and the sea's wet slaps on the hull were the only other sounds, the waves mercifully flattened. A breeze sent welcome goosebumps over his bare arms as he wandered to the bow.

A half moon shone high above, glinting silver on the water's surface. His heart leapt to his throat when he realized Jem was at the rail. Cador kept several feet between them but couldn't make himself leave Jem be.

For long minutes, they stood together yet apart, watching the dark horizon. It felt like an eternity as Cador waited for him to speak. To cry, to scream, to pummel him with his fists. Anything but this terrible silence.

When he could take it no longer, he pleaded in a hoarse whisper. "If you could only understand…"

"I do."

Holding his breath, Cador waited once more, a tendril of hope—

"But I hate you for it."

Cador dug his blunt fingernails into the worn rail, wanting to wrench the wood loose and smash it to smithereens. Jem was silent again, which was a relief after the ice in his voice. He was silent so long that if Cador hadn't watched him from the corner of his eye, he'd have thought himself alone. As he deserved.

"Strange how I can no longer see the stars," Jem muttered.

Cador glanced around, pathetically glad when he confirmed that, yes, Jem was speaking to him. He squinted toward Onan. The shadow of the land did indeed blend into the sky where earlier the stars had carpeted the heavens.

"Perhaps a storm approaches? Or merely clouds. We can rarely see the stars on Ergh."

"But…" Jem leaned forward, going up on his tiptoes. Cador could just make out his nose wrinkling in the remaining moonlight. "Is that…"

"What?" Then it reached Cador in the same instant, an acrid waft.

Jem reared back so suddenly he almost toppled onto his arse. Cador reached for him, Jem jerking away. But he met Cador's gaze and spoke with a tense new tremor.

"Smoke."

near here." He squinted west. "Long ago there was a large fire toward Ebrenn."

"Tan is making her displeasure known."

As one, they turned to Creeda where she knelt by Hedrok's pallet at the foot of the mast. They'd shifted the poor boy closer in preparation of disembarking. After what seemed like hours of sobbing but was likely only some minutes, he slept fitfully again.

Eyes closed, Creeda clutched her bundle of sevel twigs. Her low voice seemed scraped raw. "Tan punishes the mainland for its greed. The clerics have warned of this."

The clerics had been warning of any number of catastrophes for as long as Jem could remember. He rocked nervously on his bare feet. The deck was still warm, the air hot even in deepest night.

The wafts of smoke seemed to heat the wind. He wondered how far away this fire was. They were days from Neuvella, so surely his home was safe. The fist of dread in his chest tightened nevertheless.

No one responded to Creeda, for what could they say? She fell silent, lips moving in a wordless prayer as she stroked the twigs in a repeating pattern. It made Jem's skin crawl. He wanted to tear the bundle from her hands and hurl it into the sea.

Atop the Cliffs of Glaw, Creeda and her cohorts had spread a circle of gnarled sevel branches, an altar for their offering to the gods. He touched his throat, remembering her and her husband's plan to sacrifice him by severing his head. He sincerely hoped Creeda's gods craved something less blood-thirsty now.

Shifting his weight back and forth, he scratched his nails over his scalp, wincing as he loosened a scab. Over the weeks of the voyage, he'd developed the nervous habit. It had started merely as touching his head whenever he struggled to fall asleep—which was every night now—and running his fingers through his hair, laughing mockingly at himself.

Yes, your head is still attached.

It was comforting at first, making him think of lazy childhood days by the lake, his beloved sibling Santo indulging him by playing with his hair. It wasn't until he woke one morning with blood crusted under his fingernails that he realized he'd been scratching too hard.

His hair was so thick that no one could tell what he'd done, and he'd vowed to stop. Yet this new habit was strangely hard to break.

In his nightmares, cruel hands grabbed him, and he suffocated in darkness, a rough sack over his head as he thrashed. He often woke kicking, relieved at least that he didn't cry out in his sleep. He couldn't appear weak in front of the Erghians ever again.

The only way he'd feel safe was if the conspirators were locked away. He couldn't give in to the temptation to forgive Cador. He wouldn't give in to his weakness. They thought him soft and spoiled and *nothing*. They were wrong.

He glanced around the deck. Delen had assured him the people accompanying them back to the mainland hadn't been party to the plot against him aside from Creeda. But perhaps he should have them all locked up. How could he believe a word from Delen or Cador?

He could leave it to his mother to decide. The thought was undeniably reassuring. When he returned home, Mother would take charge. He wouldn't have to worry. He wouldn't have to be afraid.

Shoving his hands in his pockets after catching himself scratching his head, Jem spread his toes, pretending he felt the sand of the southern beaches of home. He would stand fast.

Lusow whinnied and side-stepped, Jory rubbing him and speaking softly. Jem didn't envy the task. Truth be told, he didn't envy Cador and the other hunters who helped him with the pulleys to lower the horse to the barge. One of them, Kensa, had joined in the dice sometimes.

He knew she and Cador had lain together in the past. Not that it mattered now. Cador could dally with her day and night for all Jem cared. Her dark hair was cropped short like all the hunters, and the muscles in her neck stood out as she heaved with the others, tawny skin shining with sweat. Along with smoke, hints of ash now hung in the air, dusting Kensa's vest.

Lusow thrashed his legs fruitlessly once he was airborne, Jory not stopping in his assurances that were practically shouted now. In his leather trousers and vest, Cador's muscles looked even starker than usual, straining as he pulled on the ropes.

Gods, he was still the most handsome man Jem had ever seen.

He hated him.

Cador had married him knowing he'd be kidnapped and maimed. He hadn't cared. No matter that he'd vowed from his knees atop the Cliffs of Glaw that he regretted plotting against him. No matter that he'd called Jem his love.

Jem had heard over and over on Ergh that the mainlanders were silly and weak. He would not prove them right. How could he respect himself if he forgave such a violation of trust? Wasn't he worth more?

When he'd journeyed to Ergh, he'd been afraid of everything. Then he'd thought himself brave when he gave his heart and body freely—joyfully. But this wasn't one of the romantic adventures in the pages of his fantastical books. He should have known better. He should have known Cador was only using him. What a fool he'd been.

Even if the original plan was to only—*only!*—sever his hand and not his head, Cador and Delen had agreed to it. Cador had vowed to the clerics, the gods, and Jem's mother that Jem would have his protection. He'd taken his virginity. He'd kissed and held him and proved himself shockingly gentle and tender for a barbarian. Now all those memories were like the ash drifting on the wind.

Had Cador actually ever desired him? How could Jem believe he truly had? After so many attractive, muscled lovers, why would Cador want puny him? It had seemed so real, but now he questioned everything.

Though he had to acknowledge that Cador hadn't faked pumping his seed into Jem's body. He'd felt it. Tasted it. A thrill rippled through him now to remember their frenzied coupling before he schooled himself. He couldn't allow lust to cloud his judgment. Even if he believed Cador was truly sorry, to trust him again?

Impossible.

When Jem had agreed to allow Delen and Cador to meet with Kenver first, of course he'd lied. What choice did he have? He'd meant it when he told Cador he understood. Yes, he did understand why Cador had agreed to his father's plan—the children's suffering was unbearable.

But in Ergh's boots, Jem would have simply approached the mainland with the truth and asked for help. And that surely made him naïve, but no more than his own mother had been when she'd trusted the empty promises of the Erghians.

None of them were safe against such people. It was why, though he hated Cador for his betrayal, he was grateful for the vile lesson in it too. He'd learned well.

But really, weren't Cador and his sister naïve too? They seemed to trust that they wouldn't be punished for their treachery. It was Jem's word they believed, yet he couldn't allow any guilt for his deception. He *wouldn't*. He forced himself to lie and do the opposite of his instincts.

It was the only way to survive.

Hedrok whimpered and thrashed suddenly. Jem thought of Austol, wondering how his young sister Eseld fared. The disease was claiming her too, and Jem could only imagine how Austol suffered caring for her helplessly. He could even understand why Austol had been willing to do anything to save her, even if it cost Jem his head.

But he couldn't forgive it.

He'd believed Austol a true friend, and in Jem's life he'd had precious few other than Santo, his favorite sibling. Growing up, he'd been content on his own, nursing injured birds in his aviary and getting lost in his books. He thought of his favorite heroine, Morvoren, with a fond pang. She had been a loyal friend who never betrayed or disappointed him.

Because she isn't real, you pathetic boy.

Austol was all too real. All too flawed. Not that Jem thought himself perfect by any means, but had any of it been genuine? Austol had given him advice and taught him to ride, and Jem had never suspected for a moment his friend would be capable of turning him over to Bryok and the people who would see him beheaded for their cause.

How could Jem trust any of them? He ate with Jory and played dice. He kept quiet and was polite to all aboard, even

Creeda, knowing he was completely outnumbered.

Once he was home, the odds would be in his favor. Then they'd see what real justice looked like.

His gaze found Cador, as it always did. Thick legs braced, Cador's jaw was clenched tight as he led the team lowering Lusow to the barge. Jem could see his palms would be scoured by the rope and wanted to tell him to use more care—surely there was some material around to act as buffer.

He forced himself to look away, peering into the southern darkness again. Gods, he just wanted to get *home*. He was determined to help Ergh's innocent children. The last thing he wanted was a war. He was a Neuvellan prince married to the future chieftain of Ergh, whether he liked it or not. He would do his duty. What was right. He would seek justice, and if that meant locking up his husband, so be it.

And so let Cador burn his hands on the rope as well! And let Jem not care if he did! Yet his heart ached like an arrow dug relentlessly into it. He rubbed at his breastbone with his fist.

What he wouldn't give to be back in his aviary by the lake near the castle. *His* lake, with a honeysuckle breeze rustling the leaves and a sweet cake sticky in his pocket. Were there hatchlings who needed his help? It seemed so long ago that was his biggest worry in life.

His mind drifted to the forest around Cador's cottage with its evergreens and carpet of pine needles. The tiny buds of white flowers would have blossomed by now. Did Derwa flit from branch to branch with the other askells?

She was probably eaten by a hawk.

Sudden tears pricked his eyes, but at least he could blame it on the smoke.

Soon, the hunters rowed Jory and Lusow ashore before

With a deep pang, Jem missed his mother. Were she and the rest of his family well and safe? What of this smoke? He told himself again to stop fretting. A wildfire in summer. Nothing to worry about. Soon, he'd be home, and they could fix…everything. His mother would know what to do.

The barge was rowed to shore, and Cador lifted Hedrok carefully, easing him to the rocky beach and keeping the boy cradled on his lap while Creeda soothed him. Feeling useless, Jem approached Jory and a still-skittish Lusow.

"You're all right after your unexpected dip?" Jory asked.

Jem ran a hand over his wet curls, careful not to touch his sensitive scalp. "I'm fine. Hedrok is safe, so that's what matters."

"Mmm. Cador is safe as well."

He shrugged carelessly. His wet clothes stuck to his skin, but it was warm enough that he didn't mind. Nearing Lusow, he reached out tentatively, gratified when Lusow turned his snout into Jem's hand. Jem pet his white-speckled head.

He'd spent too many years fearing horses after being kicked by one. Now he knew they were good, loyal beasts, even if they could be intimidatingly enormous.

Jory smoothed his palm over Lusow's flanks rhythmically. "Now that we're back on the mainland, you must be eager to see your family."

"Very much so." Everything would be easier at home. Everything would be all right and he wouldn't be alone. He mostly believed Jory was a good man who meant what he said, but he was Erghian first and foremost.

Cador marched over and asked Jory, "Shouldn't you wait for dawn to ride?"

Wait? There could be no waiting! "You have to go now!" Jem's family might be in danger. From Kenver, from fire, from gods knew what.

"And risk Lusow breaking an ankle in a rut in this darkness?" Cador asked.

He swallowed his frustration. "Of course not. I wouldn't want Lusow to be hurt."

Jory gave him a smile. "It's all right. Sunset isn't too far off. We can keep a slower pace at first and ease Lusow back into it. At dawn, we run." He regarded Jem seriously. "I'll find out as much as I can about the fire and send back word with the provisions and horses."

He nodded. The orange glow to the west didn't seem any closer at least. "Thank you. Tell—" There's so much Jem wanted to say and so much he didn't. "Tell my mother I miss her and will see her and the others soon."

Jory nodded solemnly. He and Cador clasped arms, Jory muttering something softly that Jem couldn't make out. Then he was gone, walking ahead of Lusow until they left the rocky beach and he mounted. Jem had considered many times begging Jory to bring him along, but his extra weight would burden Lusow and slow them.

Jem turned to find Cador's gaze on him, heavy-lidded and— despite everything—thrilling. Jem stiffened and went to ask Creeda if she or Hedrok required assistance. It wouldn't be long until he no longer had to make nice with the woman who'd plotted his death, but her son was innocent in all of that and shouldn't have to suffer if Jem could help at all.

Soon enough, Meraud and her small crew waved them off, waiting on the ship for further instructions. Jem pulled on his thin boots and shouldered a pack heavy with food. His trunk remained aboard, and they'd send someone back for it and anything else too heavy.

They had only brought two hand-pulled carts, one holding Hedrok on a bed of furs, the other an impressive collection of spears and more food. Everyone carried a pack as well. They hoped provisions from the Holy Place would find them in a day or two, but there were no guarantees. Especially now.

Cador wore his sword on his back and carried his short spear as their small group walked south. His boots had to be sodden, yet he clomped along in them. Once they were off the rocks on the winding dirt path, the sky in the east growing gray and light, Jem had to speak.

"Wouldn't it be smarter to walk barefoot and dry your boots?"

No reply. Kensa walked between Jem and Cador, Delen pulling Hedrok's cart with Creeda alongside, the other few hunters hauling the other cart. Kensa elbowed Cador. "He's talking to you."

"I didn't want to assume," Cador muttered.

Irritation lashed at Jem. "You're the only one with wet boots."

"I've dealt with wet boots before."

"Fine."

"I've found a good spanking helps when he's sulking," Kensa said cheerfully.

Jem could only sputter and order his mind to think of anything else, and Cador barked, "Bullshit!" as Kensa grinned.

A haze hung over the horizon, and as the brilliant sun rose, it was clear this wasn't dewy dawn mist that would burn off. Jem belatedly realized the breeze must have turned since smoke no longer tickled his nostrils. He chose to take it as a good sign.

The day's journey was long and sweltering. The land was brittle, and the distant sky remained unnaturally orange. When they finally reached the forest-ringed fields where they'd camped months ago on their way north, Jem was exhausted and his feet throbbed.

He gratefully sat and yanked off his boots. There were hours of summer daylight remaining, but at least they could rest for a time before continuing.

Delen announced, "There were byghan in these woods last time. We'll hunt and settle in."

Settle in? Jem glanced around. Cador and Kensa were going through the spears, the others gently lowering Hedrok to the short grass on his furs.

"But we're going to keep going," Jem said. "It's not like Ergh—it will be light for hours. We might meet travelers with news."

Delen frowned at him. "We're waiting here until we have horses. There's a creek for water. This is far enough."

"But we can't just sit here!" Jem pushed to his feet. "I need to get home. I have to find out what's going on. What if this—" he gestured at the smoke-orange sky "—isn't from a wild fire? What if war's broken out? What if it's smoke from a battle?"

"Then you're better off here with us," Delen said firmly. She looked to Cador. "Don't you agree?"

Cador grunted his accord.

The *nerve* of them both. "He doesn't get a say!" Hands fisting, Jem dug his toes into the grass and dry earth.

This certainly caught the attention of everyone else, the hunters frowning. Jem reminded himself they didn't know the truth about the kidnapping schemes. And they only saw him as Prince Jowan, Cador's forced husband who must be subservient since he was a weak mainlander.

His cheeks flared as his mind very unhelpfully supplied

memories of all the times he'd eagerly submitted to Cador, taking his cock and begging to be mastered. That was different. That had nothing to do with this.

To his surprise, Cador didn't huff and puff and stamp his wet foot down. He quietly said, "There was nothing between us and the Holy Place that I recall. It makes sense to camp here and rest. Jory will not let us down. He'll ride like the wind and send us horses soon."

Of course he'd praise Jory.

Jem grimaced at the petty thought. Jory had been nothing but kind—although if a choice had to be made, he would undoubtedly take Cador's side. Jem had been churlish and jealous of him from the start since Jory and Cador had been lovers in the past. Cador had probably been with half of Ergh. And he could do so again!

Except Cador would soon be rotting in the castle dungeon, so perhaps he'd never lie with *anyone* ever again. Served him right, the betraying bastard.

"I can't sit here waiting and doing nothing," Jem admitted.

"Waiting is not easily borne," Creeda said. On her knees, she didn't look up from Hedrok's sleeping form. "Why do you think we're here?"

Horror prickled Jem's skin. Creeda had proven how far beyond *waiting* she would go to help her son. As had Austol for his sister. He felt for their years of agony. Creeda had surely been twisted by the pain of waiting while her child suffered.

Yet how could she even *look* at him after planning to behead him? Much less dare to offer him advice on the difficulty of waiting. He couldn't find an adequate response aside from the roar of resentment and fury he choked down. He remained silent.

Creeda spoke again. "We can pray." She held out the bundle of twisted twigs to him.

He bit back the instinct to deny the gods and tell her he didn't believe. This woman had wanted to see him beheaded to satisfy her vicious idea of these so-called gods, yet now she suggested he pray to them? She offered her sacred talisman?

Despite his revulsion, he couldn't bring himself to refuse in the face of Hedrok's ravaged form. A strange anxiety gripped him. He didn't believe the gods could be real, but what if he was wrong? What if praying now could possibly help this suffering child? And all the children?

He forced his feet to move and knelt close enough to her to take the charm. The gnarled sticks were surprisingly smooth to the touch, surely worn down by her fervent movements. It was only dead wood. There was no magic in it. No malevolence.

Holding the twigs, he bowed his head dutifully as Creeda recited a prayer to Tan, Glaw, Hwytha, and Dor, the gods of fire, water, wind, and earth. Her low, worshipful tone should have been a comfort, yet it made Jem sick. Reminded him of the sack over his head, the twine digging into his neck. The thought of staying the night and a whole day—and likely another night— near Creeda and her pitiful son was unbearable.

Eyes closed, he was helpless against the flashes of memory: Austol's pinched face, the suffocating sack, bruises and pain, Bryok's fevered fury in torchlight, the dark fall to the dred nest, clawing his way back up...

He was clawing at his head before he knew what he was doing. The moment Creeda's prayer ended, Jem thrust the talisman back to her and escaped into the trees as though he had to relieve himself. Heart thumping painfully, he leaned against an oak and tried to catch his breath.

A familiar chirping reached him. He opened his eyes to spot a female dillywig flutter from one branch to another. Her feathers were mottled brown, and she was absolutely beautiful. Tears filled Jem's eyes, and he wiped them with his knuckles, scoffing at himself.

He'd returned to Onan in one piece, and now he just had to get back to Neuvella. He brushed away the line of blood under his fingernails and straightened his unruly hair. He must go on ahead. He'd move much faster without Hedrok slowing them down. Not that it was the poor boy's fault, but his cries grated at Jem's ragged nerves.

Creeda had her prayers, but Jem had to know what was happening in his homeland, dread building with each moment and fearing the worst. He wasn't even sure what the worst could be. His life in Neuvella had been pampered and safe, and now he feared nothing, no one, and nowhere was safe anymore.

There might be other travelers or a farm he hadn't noticed on the way north. Surely there must be! If not, he'd meet the servants on their way from the Holy Place and be that much closer to ride south. He could ride on his own now. Austol had taught him well before—

Shutting out the creeping black thoughts, Jem returned to the camp and made sure his pack contained his fair share of food and a flask of water.

When darkness finally fell, the distant sky remained an unnatural orange long after sunset. He ate stringy byghan meat and watched Cador across the small campfire.

After, when Cador handed him a sleeping fur to make a bed, their fingers touched, and the enraging urge to feel more was as strong as ever. He hated that as much as he hated Cador.

Reminding himself this barbarian was as much a stranger as

the day Jem had been forced to marry him, he laid out his fur and wrapped himself in it. Quietly, he watched and waited until everyone else was bedded down or otherwise distracted—even now with Hedrok's occasional cries of agony, the barbarians didn't hold back from debauchery.

They were as shameless as ever, coupling—or more—right out in the open. Yet on this journey, Jem was no longer an innocent virgin. Now, he could imagine much more clearly the acts accompanying the sucking and slapping noises. Memories invaded, and he jammed his fingers in his ears before his cock swelled completely.

Once all was quiet and he could make out by the campfire's gleam Cador's chest moving up and down in long, sleeping breaths, he crept out from his fur. Anxiety balled in his gut, but he took a cleansing breath and firmed his jaw and his resolve.

As an owl hooted in the forest, Jem made his move.

Chapter Three

"H E'S STILL FUSSY about pissing in front of anyone," Delen said with a dismissive wave. "He'll be back."

Cador paced, eyes locked on the forest's edge, brittle grass making his bare feet itch. He hated not wearing his boots, but they'd remained uncomfortably wet. The fur he'd given Jem after dinner now lay abandoned, and worry grew with every moment.

His heart leapt at distant movement in the forest, plummeting when Kensa appeared. He strode across the clearing. Fuck waiting.

"Is Jem in there?" he demanded.

Kensa's eyebrows shot up. "Good morning to you too."

"Is he?"

She frowned. "Not that I saw. But you know how dainty he is. Those mainlanders—"

Cador marched past her. In the long shadows of the trees, he shouted, "Jem!"

Nothing. A faint breeze rustled leaves and birds called merrily. Were these the dillywigs Jem loved so much?

"Jem! Are you here?" Something scurried in the dry underbrush, and he whirled. Nothing. "Jem!" His heart thudded. "Answer me!" *Please.* "Damn it, answer!"

He's not here.

Instinct repeated it again and again. Gone. Jem was gone.

He strode back to camp, barking, "He's not here! If he's been taken…"

"Taken?" Delen stood from where she'd been speaking with Creeda, Hedrok still sleeping. "By who? Margh saw nothing on watch."

"Which is a fucking problem! Whatever happened, Margh should have seen it!"

Delen held up her hands. "Agreed. But it's hot, and we're all tired, and there were no threats here last time."

"That doesn't mean there can't be new threats! Onan wasn't on fire last time either!" His fingers itched for his spear. "And we think we're prepared to fight a war? Can't even keep watch over one tiny mainlander!"

Cador should have stayed awake. He should have made Jem stay by his side whether Jem liked it or not. He'd insisted Jem have a fur, so why hadn't he stopped him from sleeping off on his own?

"I'm sure he's fine," Delen said. "If he slipped away, we can hardly blame him for wanting some distance. When we get to the Holy Place, he'll be waiting. There's nowhere else for him to go around here. Now have some tea—"

"*Tea*? You think I'm going to sit around drinking fucking tea? I'm going after him." As Delen opened her mouth, he snapped, "No discussion. If I'm to be chieftain, you'll have to get used to following my orders."

After a stunned moment, she smiled thinly. "All right, brother. Off with you. But I'm keeping our map of the mainland."

"Fine." He yanked on his boots, annoyed to find they were still vaguely damp. How was that possible when the sun was barely up and it was so fucking hot already? He cursed and

Tregereth of Neuvella."

"That is our destination. The castle."

The woman nodded. "Going by way of Gwels is a longer route to Neuvella, but safer. If your people are traveling slowly with the ill child, it is wise to stay as far from the fires as possible. And you must want to get the child to a healer soon."

"Agreed. Where is Jem? Didn't you give him one of the horses?"

The woman's brow furrowed, and she shared a glance with her companions. "Who?"

His heart skipped. Ah, but this woman would be a stranger to Jem and wouldn't know his nickname. "Prince Jowan."

Her frown only deepened. "Prince Jowan of Neuvella? Your husband?"

"Do you know another?" he demanded. "Did you give him a horse?" His sword pointed at the dusty ground, and his fingers flexed around the handle. If something had happened to Jem, if someone had hurt him, if…

"Your…er, grace, we have not seen Prince Jowan since he left for Ergh months ago."

Fuck. Fuck! He breathed through the flare of fear that seared before settling in his gut like an icy fist. "He walked ahead of me. Some hours—I'm not sure how many. No more than seven. You should have met him. Is there another path?"

She was still frowning. "Not south. There's only the road we came on and the road we will take east."

"Maybe he hid from you." He'd be skittish after what had happened.

The riders all looked bewildered. The woman said, "I can't see why."

"It doesn't matter. Give me a horse." He marched over to

the extra mounts and eyed a large brown animal. "Fast?"

"Er, yes. The saddle is—"

Cador had already taken the reins and unfastened the restraining rope from the horse's bridle. He launched onto its back, patting its neck as it flicked its mane and sidestepped. "No need."

"But you should come with us and stay with your people." The woman nodded to one of her companions. "Steren will find Prince Jowan. He knows this area well."

Yes, it was the logical thing to do, but the thought of giving up and returning to Delen and the others without knowing Jem was safe made him want to howl like he'd been gored by a boar's tusks.

"I'll find him. Get my people safely to this elder healer and then to Neuvella." He belatedly added, "Please."

She opened her mouth before sighing. "All right. Continue on this road and you'll reach the Holy Place. If Prince Jowan hasn't made it, there are still enough servants to launch a search."

"Thank you. And what's causing the fires? Jem—Prince Jowan—said this isn't normal?"

The woman shook her head grimly. "The spring rains didn't come as expected. I've never known it to be this hot. We have seen the western skies alight for weeks. Of course we pray that the rain will come and all will be well."

"No rumors of battles that might have caused it?"

She looked truly astonished. "No! Why?"

Cador had no time or inclination to explain. "Name?" He held the warm leather reins loosely and patted his mount.

"I'm—"

"The *horse*."

She flushed. "We called her Melwyn since her coat looked like fresh honey when she was born. It's darker now as you see, and she eats so much we started calling her Dybri for the special hay she loved devouring. And—"

He'd already wheeled Melwyn—make that Dybri—and spurred her into a run. As the hot winds rose and the distant smoke came nearer, Cador kept his head low, searching for Jem and calling his name until he was hoarse.

AS HE NEARED the stable on the outskirts of the Holy Place, Cador should have been ready for a mug of ale and a proper meal of something other than byghan and the cured boar they'd brought for the voyage. Yet he felt sick with worry, the massive knot in his stomach only expanding.

Was Jem injured? Lost? Kidnapped? What if Cador had been right after all and he'd been grabbed? It might have been Western spies, that wicked King Perran plotting against them. The bastard controlled the sevels with an iron grip, and he hated Jem's mother. Tas had planned to use that to Ergh's advantage, but perhaps the West had beat him to it.

Cador reminded himself no one had known they were sailing to the mainland. They'd seen no other ships, but that was no guarantee they hadn't been spotted, was it? It was possible that—

"Shut up," he muttered to himself, dismounting with a groan.

Only a few horses grazed in the nearby field, the grass short and dry, but not burned. The smoke on the orange-tinged horizon lingered, but remained in the distance toward the east now. Perhaps the rain would come soon and put an end to it as the cleric had said. A rhythmic scraping echoed from the barn, setting his nerves even more on edge. Leading Dybri, he unsheathed his sword.

Inside the barn, a girl of about fifteen years swept a stall, the brittle straw high-pitched as it scratched across the stone. "You there!" Cador called.

She spun, the broom clattering to the stone floor. Her pale eyes were wide, dark red hair pulled back from a round, freckled face. Her trousers and tunic were dusty, but in good condition. "Me?"

Her squeak made him think of Jem on their wedding night, cowering at the prospect of fucking. The memory made him ache. "Is Jem here?" He had to protect him and keep him safe. "Prince Jowan, I mean."

His heart sank as she frowned. "No, sir. I haven't seen Prince Jowan."

Fuck. *Fuck, fuck, fuck.* The urge to shout remained, but he forced a breath. Unleashing his impotent fury on this girl would solve nothing. Manners. Mainlanders liked manners.

"Sorry to startle you. I'm Cador of Ergh."

She nodded seriously. "Oh, yes. I remember."

In the ensuing silence, he asked, "What's your name?"

"Tamsyn." Her eyes flicked between his face and something else.

Cador realized he was still holding his sword and quickly sheathed it. He petted Dybri and gave the girl a smile. "Did you see my friend Jory? His hair is like yours. Lighter and messier, though."

She smiled tentatively. "Yes. He and his horse rested before continuing. He said he was going to the castle in Neuvella. It's

41

where the queen and her family live."

That was one damn thing going to plan, at least. "Yes, he's bringing word of our unexpected arrival. Speaking of which, can you inform the clerics I'm here?"

"Well, the thing is… They're gone. Most of them, at least."

"Gone? Where the fuck did they go?" Whatshername on the trail hadn't mentioned it.

Eyebrows high, Tamsyn gasped softly. "I, I don't know."

Cursing silently this time, he asked, "Do they often travel?"

"Not often, sir. Our exalted chief cleric, Ysella, does journey to the corners of Onan from time to time to meet with royalty. She left suddenly—a few days ago. You'll remember her, of course. She performed your wedding ceremony."

Yes, he fucking remembered the stooped, wrinkled woman who wouldn't shut up. He traced the raised edges of the brand on his palm with his middle finger. "And she took other clerics with her?"

Tamsyn nodded. "Only a few have stayed behind. And—"

"Take care of Dybri." He spun on his heel and marched out of the stable. In the doorway, he remembered to add his thanks before continuing to the main compound. It was deserted, and Cador didn't like it. Not that he missed the clerics, but there had been so many people in the spring. He supposed it had also been a peace summit with many visitors, but the emptiness put him on edge.

When he entered a blissfully shaded courtyard, he discovered a gray-robed cleric seated on the side of a babbling fountain with his feet in the water. The fountain seemed a waste in the drought, although Cador had to admit it was tempting to dunk his head.

The cleric's eyes were closed, and he hadn't seemed to notice

Cador's arrival. He was fit, with tawny hair and skin, the gentle waves of his short hair brushing the tips of his ears. He was blandly pretty in that common mainland way. Was he praying? It looked more like napping. Cador cleared his throat impatiently.

The man didn't open his eyes. "Yes?"

"Where the fuck did all the other clerics go?"

Jolting, he opened his brown eyes and leapt up all at once. Now he was standing in the fountain staring at Cador. He quickly hopped out and slid on the leather sandals the clerics seemed to favor, the hem of his robe dripping. He gaped at Cador a bit more, his brow furrowing.

"I—*you*—you're here?"

Cador held his hands out to his sides. "Indeed! Here I am." He imagined Jem cringing at his rudeness and choked down his irritation. They were wasting time. He had to find Jem. "Cador, son of the chieftain." *The new heir, whether I like it or not.*

"Yes, I recall." The cleric peered beyond him. "Where is your husband?"

"I don't know. He—"

"What have you done to him?" The accusation rang out around the courtyard, several birds taking flight from the roof in a flap of wings.

Who the fuck did this daydreaming cleric think he was? Cador swelled with anger that was quickly consumed by guilt. His face heated.

The cleric narrowed his gaze. "Tell me what's become of him."

"I don't know. That's the point. We were separated on the way here from the coast."

"How?" The cleric still eyed him suspiciously.

"It doesn't fucking matter! You must know the area. Organize a search party."

The man seemed at a loss. "Er, yes." He shook his head. "Forgive me. I was lost in prayer and not expecting anyone. Let alone a hunter of Ergh."

"Where are the rest of your clerics? The girl didn't know." He nodded in the vague direction of the stable, although given the identical long, low buildings and snaking pathways, he might have been turned around.

"Some have gone to Neuvella and the rest are traveling over Onan to help calm the people. Unrest is simmering. This drought and the wildfires—fear is growing that we have angered the gods."

"Well, the gods are fickle bastards," Cador muttered. The cleric had probably heard worse in his time. "Now we have to find J—Prince Jowan."

The cleric nodded solemnly. "Indeed we must. Prince Jowan must not be harmed."

Wasting no time, Cador refilled his flask and fit the iron stopper tightly before returning to the stable. At least he could agree with a cleric about something.

Chapter Four

L AVENDER FILLED JEM'S nose. Hatchlings chirped in the aviary and water lapped gently at the shore, rippled by the afternoon breeze. With the sun high in the summer sky, even with his eyes shut, the world glowed with perfect, golden light. Luscious grass cushioned him as he dozed, tickling the soles of his bare feet. His swim-damp hair dried in the warmth.

Home.

Mmm. He wondered what the castle's wonderful chefs were creating for dinner. Likely succulent roasted meat of some kind with perfectly tender-crisp vegetables—oh, and fresh bread with creamy butter. Dessert promised to offer a variety of cakes and surely berry pies still warm from the ovens. Mother always made sure the kitchen made Jem's favorites.

Oh, oh—and the mead would be sweet and chilled deep in the castle's storerooms below the ground. He could almost taste it already, refreshing and heady, giving him a pleasant tingle…

Jem woke sweating on the hard-packed earth, hip and shoulder sore from curling in the same position too long. Dusty with ash and dirt, he pushed himself to sitting with a groan. He wiggled his bare toes, dreading pulling his thin-soled boots back on.

The cursed sun that he'd missed so much was lower in the sky at least. The tree had provided meager shade, but it'd been better than nothing. He peered around at the empty landscape of clumps of trees and dry grasses. The orange haze still hung on the horizon. Was that east or west?

Lost. He'd made it back to Onan—his homeland!—only to get hopelessly *lost*. Clearly it had been foolhardy to sneak away from Cador and the others in the night. He'd been filled with purpose and confidence, telling himself he had far more to fear from his traveling companions than venturing out alone.

Was Cador looking for him now? Perhaps he was even worried. Once, Jem had imagined he'd heard Cador call for him, an urgent, raspy shout. What nonsense. He'd sipped more water, afraid the heat was overtaking him.

"Doesn't matter," he muttered hoarsely. He'd filled his canteen earlier and allowed a mouthful now. What Cador thought or felt was no longer his concern. And hopefully Jem would make it to the Holy Place before the Ergh contingent and Cador would never know he'd gotten himself lost.

Humiliation prickled his sweaty skin. With only one road—which was being generous since it was more of a path or track—it should have been easy to find the Holy Place. Head south. The end. While crossing the sea, he'd glanced at Delen's map of the mainland and thought he'd known it well enough.

The wind had started blustering around noon. Hot, painfully dry gusts that made him anxious and strangely melancholy. Worst of all, the haze had become thick in every direction. It became like the fog that blanketed Neuvella during a particularly hard rain, but it burned his eyes, nose, and throat. Somehow the sun still penetrated to roast him as he plodded along.

He'd thought he was going in the right direction, yet doubt crept in. Soon enough, Jem had no idea which way was up, and he'd somehow left the path completely. He took shelter under the oak tree to rest rather than get himself even more lost.

Now, the haze had retreated, though the air still seemed singed with smoke. Though Gwels had some scrublands, he'd never known the area near the Holy Place to be this dry. But what did he truly know of it? He'd barely left Neuvella in all his years. Barely left the castle grounds, content to wile away his days as he pleased. The spring summit had been the first time he'd journeyed to the Holy Place since he was a boy on a tour with his parents.

At least he was certain the sun set beyond Ebrenn. Blinking, he shielded his eyes. Once the afternoon grew long enough, he'd know which way was west. That was something. He could do this. He *would* do this! He would find his way.

What would Morvoren do?

His throat tightened. Oh, how simple it had all seemed when Morvoren was the one being kidnapped and fighting battles. If ever she found herself in too big of a scrape, her merman lover invariably turned up to save the day and vice versa. They'd rescued each other countless times and celebrated with passionate fucking in thrilling positions.

Hugging his knees, he allowed himself to think of Cador.

If Jem was in need, Cador would come. Despite everything, he knew it to be true. It should have been wonderfully comforting, yet it left him desperately sad. For what if he was wrong again? What if Cador would happily abandon him to starve in the wild? Jem reminded himself that what he thought he knew to be true likely wasn't. He coughed and sipped more water.

What would Morvoren do?

Jem barked out a laugh. "She'd never have to deal with this because her lover would never betray her in a thousand years. Because such loyal perfection is possible when you live only in books." His voice was a terrible rasp, and he allowed another sip

He sipped more water, and soon they reached the stables, the thunder of other hooves approaching. In the darkness, a familiar figure leapt from his horse and barreled toward him. Jem resisted the urge to throw himself into Cador's arms— though in the end he had no choice in the matter.

And for a single beat of his wounded heart, Jem allowed the comfort of being held aloft in a mighty embrace, his arms locked around Cador's neck, face against his sweat-damp skin. Along with the musky tang, he swore he could smell moss on stone.

He kicked Cador's shin, shoving against his broad shoulders. "Put me down!"

Cador tightened his arms around Jem for a moment, then did as requested. Jem ached and his knees almost gave out as his boots touched the ground, but he was determined to stay on his feet.

"Why the fuck did you run off?" Cador demanded.

Jem was very aware of their audience and lifted his chin. "We'll discuss it later."

"Prince Jowan, please come this way." A servant holding a lantern ushered him toward the sprawling compound, night settled around them fully now. Jem thanked the other members of the search party, though he couldn't see them beyond the circle of yellow light.

He was surprised to hear most of the clerics were not in residence and that Delen and the others were now traveling the long way through Gwels to go south. It was a relief that Hedrok would see a healer quite soon, though.

"You must be famished," the servant said. "Both of you. Your husband didn't rest until he found you."

It shouldn't have delighted Jem. He crushed the unfurling

tendrils of joy, not glancing at Cador, who made no sound. The servant went on about cheese the clerics made themselves and bread freshly baked in anticipation of his return.

"Thank you," Jem said. "That sounds delicious and very welcome." He asked about Neuvella and the threat of the fires, but of course the servants only knew so much.

He found he truly was ravenous and told the servant he'd eat before bathing. Cador shadowed him silently, and Jem didn't want to make a scene. They sat in the courtyard at a small table under the dark hazy sky, only the faintest breeze offering any relief from the heat. A fountain burbled, a lamp burning. At least the sun had set.

The bread and cheese really were delicious, and Jem gulped them down with honeyed mead, nibbling from a tray of fresh fruit as well. A man approached from the shadows, and for a moment, Jem thought he was a cleric due to his garb.

He smiled broadly. "Jem, I'm so glad you're safe."

For a moment, Jem didn't recognize him. The context was all wrong—the plain robes, no crown of emeralds. His mind struggled to comprehend, but...yes. It was he. "Prince Treeve?"

"It's so good to see you again." Treeve smiled again—a brilliant flash of teeth, full lips curving.

Jem returned his smile. "Oh! It is." Treeve was little more than a stranger, and Jem's mother had forever been at odds with Treeve's father, but he was still something familiar from Jem's old life. It was oddly reassuring to see him. Jem reached out to clasp Treeve's arm.

In an instant, Treeve was lifted completely from the stone floor. "Fucking liar," Cador gritted out, one hand around Treeve's throat, the other fisted in his robe.

Gasping, Treeve clawed at Cador's hands. "Wait. I—" Choking, he wheezed. "I can explain."

"What are you *doing*? Stop!" Sputtering, Jem yanked at Cador's thick arm.

"You knew who I was. You had more than enough time to tell me who the fuck you were." Nostrils flaring, Cador gritted his teeth, giving Treeve no quarter.

Jem had seen that expression before, that particular surge of fury clouding Cador's eyes. He tugged at Cador's wrists. "Let him explain! If you kill him, your problem with Ebrenn will only get far worse. He's King Perran's only remaining child. I imagine his father is quite fond of him."

Jaw clenched so tightly it might snap, knuckles white, Cador lowered Treeve's feet to the floor, only loosening the grip on his throat an inch. He hissed to Jem, "What is this? You told me your mother hates his father. That they've been on the brink of war for years. Yet you act like you are old friends."

"We act *polite*." He pried Cador's fingers free. Cador allowed it, dropping his hands to his sides in fists. "I wouldn't expect *you* to understand," Jem snapped.

"I thought you hated them," Cador muttered.

"When did I say I hated Ebrenn or its people? I left the politics to my mother." He gave Treeve a smile. "Please accept my apologies."

Treeve glanced uneasily at Cador, who grumbled under his breath. Treeve's voice was rather wheezy. "Of course. It's forgotten."

Jem frowned. Part of him didn't even want to know, but he had to ask. "What *are* you doing here?" He had the sinking sensation that the journey home was about to get even more fraught.

Chapter Five

T HE WESTERN PRINCE? Pretending to be a cleric? Or at least he hadn't said otherwise. Cador hadn't spoken a word to him at the summit—had barely noticed him across crowded rooms. He hadn't paid attention, and clearly he should have.

Especially given the way this fucking mainlander smiled at Jem.

And how Jem had smiled back. It was a dagger in Cador's heart though he deserved it. To think of never being bestowed such a smile again—given so freely to this stranger like it was nothing—was unbearable.

What if Treeve was as treacherous as his father was purported to be? Tas had been dead set against asking King Perran for sevels and help.

And look at where Tas's plan got me. Maybe Tas's arrogant pride and suspicious mind doomed us all. I should never have agreed to it. To marry an innocent and allow him to be harmed in any way is the worst kind of treachery.

"Shall we sit?" Jem asked, motioning to the courtyard table.

Cador followed, sure to grab the chair closest to Jem's. He had no cause to believe a word from this Treeve. He would protect Jem whether Jem liked it or not. He would keep him safe from barbarians and pretty-faced, smooth-tongued princes alike.

That was at least one thing Cador could do. He might never

convince Jem to trust him again—might never earn that trust back. But he would protect his beloved from any further harm with his dying breath.

Jem said, "I don't recall you having any interest in joining the holy order."

Treeve smiled ruefully, voice still hoarse. "No. I arrived last night and wore the robe while they laundered my filthy clothes. I discovered it's quite comfortable." He motioned to their dusty clothing. "I'm sure you'll see for yourself soon." He began coughing.

Jem quickly refilled his cup with mead and gave it to Treeve, who drank gratefully. Jem asked, "Do you need water?"

Cador gritted his teeth at Jem's fussing. Fancy Prince Treeve was fine! Cador had only throttled him a little. Well, perhaps a bit more than a little, but hardly!

Treeve put down the cup, his annoyingly full bottom lip glistening as he said, "I never intended any deceit, but when your husband appeared without you, I was afraid you'd been hurt or worse."

"I'd never—" Cador bit back the lie in time. For it *was* a lie to say he'd never hurt Jem. He never would again though, not knowingly. But how would he ever convince Jem of that? Jem's stony silence said it all. Cador asked, "Why didn't the servants I encountered on the road mention you were here?"

Fine brow furrowed, Treeve held up his hands. "I don't know. I didn't divulge my purpose to any servants. Perhaps they didn't think it relevant. Jem, I—"

"That's Prince Jowan to you," Cador snapped.

Ignoring Cador, Jem said, "Treeve, tell us what's happened. Why are you here? Where is your father?"

Treeve swallowed more mead from Jem's cup and plucked a

grape from the platter of fruit on the table. His fingernails were unnaturally neat. "He should still be four or five days behind me, assuming the fires are still under control. He's stopping in every village to fan the flames of discontent." He grimaced. "Pardon the metaphor."

Cador wanted to shake him until answers tumbled out but resisted as Jem asked, "Why are you here without him?"

"I gave an excuse and rode ahead to warn the clerics only to find them gone aside from a few relics. I suppose Ysella's spies were a few steps ahead of me and she's already sprung into action. I've spoken privately with the old clerics still in residence about the threat my father poses, and they agree that blaming Ergh for these fires is not in Onan's best interests."

"Blaming *us*? What madness is that?" Cador clenched his fists. Where was his sword? He'd been distracted by Jem. Had he left it in the stable? Fool! "We have nothing to do with fires."

"I'm sure you don't," Treeve said. "These past months since the summit and your wedding, my father's grown more and more surly and suspicious. He's convinced Ergh wants to wage war with him."

"What?" Jem shook his head. "Nonsense."

Saying nothing, Cador was impressed with the ease of Jem's lie and grateful for it, though he hated that he'd put Jem in this position.

"Then the fires began. Most importantly, a blaze in the Valley of the Gods."

Jem went still. "The Valley of the Gods?"

"What's that?" Cador demanded.

"Part of the border between Neuvella and Ebrenn," Jem said. "It's been contested for years as to where precisely the divide lies in the valley. My mother and King Perran have argued about it incessantly the past year or two especially."

Cador asked Treeve—what a simpering name—"How did this fire begin?"

He shrugged. "It's hardly rained since the winter snow melted and spring was scorching. But there are rumors that Neuvella sparked it to punish Ebrenn."

Jem's hackles rose. "My mother would never do that! She wouldn't destroy the Valley of the Gods for spite!"

"I'm sure not. I hope she wouldn't. We've tried to contain the damage to the forests and the sevel fields, but—"

"The sevel fields?" Jem and Cador demanded in unison.

Treeve blinked. "Yes. My father believes the queen is trying to destroy the crops. Sevels are one of our chief exports."

Jem cleared his throat, his voice calm again. "True, I suppose they are. But my mother wouldn't do that. I know our parents don't see eye-to-eye, but—"

"It's worse than that. My father's now linked this strange drought to Ergh, saying the gods are punishing us for allowing Ergh's return. For allowing your marriage. That Ergh hasn't repented after being banished and now the mainland is suffering. At first, I didn't pay it much attention. My father has always had a doubting, unsettled mind. After my sister died and later my mother, it's been one conspiracy after another. The difference now is that the people of Ebrenn are starting to believe this one."

"Fuck," Cador muttered. While Tas had plotted to wage war for control of Ebrenn and the sevels, the idea was to use surprise to their advantage and force a quick surrender. If Perran was preparing for battle already, it could go very badly.

Managing to keep his voice steady, Cador asked, "Why didn't you tell me all this when I met you?"

"You were the last person I expected to see, and I wasn't sure I could trust you. I was afraid you'd done something to poor Jem. For all I knew you'd kill me the second you discovered my identity."

Treeve glanced behind, but they were still alone. "As I said, I came here to forewarn the clerics so they can talk him out of this madness. He's come to engage them in starting some holy war against Ergh. A war he'll surely use against Neuvella as well. My father has a hundred soldiers in his royal regiment, and they are duty bound. Not to mention he's been poisoning their minds against Ergh and exploiting their faith in the gods."

Jem said, "If we tried to speak reason to him—"

"He won't hear it from either of you. He was furious about your marriage. Ergh beat him to it."

Jem frowned. "What do you mean?"

"When he heard you were attending the spring summit for the first time, he concocted a scheme whereby I wooed and married you. Of course you'd have been nothing but a tool to manipulate your mother."

Cador tried to hide his wince, the well of shame and regret boring deeper.

Jem smiled grimly. "A familiar tale."

As he glanced between Jem and Cador with a raised eyebrow, Treeve said, "I refused, of course. I must say though that once I saw you, the notion of marriage was much more appealing." He gave Jem an easy, charming smile.

As Cador considered ripping out Treeve's spine, Jem scoffed. "You jest."

"Not at all." Still smiling, he added, "Alas, Cador's gain is my loss." He raised a brow again. "I'd thought given Cador's concern earlier you were a winning match. Was I mistaken?"

"No!" Cador blurted. While his actions had made losers of them both, he didn't want to discuss it with this man. Jem simply shrugged, and Cador was grateful he revealed nothing more.

A few of the elderly clerics who'd apparently been left behind because they were too frail to travel came to pray with them. One stooped old woman eyed Cador suspiciously and he glowered back.

Praying to false gods was the last thing they should be wasting their time with, but Jem stood, smiled, and bowed his head along with Treeve. Cador rose and held his tongue, which would have to be good enough.

But the prayers went on and on and *on*, and Jem wavered on his feet. Didn't these clerics care that he was clearly exhausted? Jem and Cador were both grimy and weary from their journey.

"That's enough," Cador declared. He could be rude on Jem's behalf. "We must clean up and rest. We have a long journey south tomorrow." He motioned Jem ahead of him toward the main building, and it was a sign that Jem truly was exhausted that he didn't argue. Treeve said goodnight and something else Cador didn't bother listening to.

Jem murmured, "I thought they'd never cease."

Cador grunted his agreement as they escaped down a lamp-lit corridor. He quickly realized he had no idea where they were to sleep. The girl from the stable appeared, jerking as she caught sight of them and shoving one hand behind her back.

Cador stiffened. "What do you have there? T…" Damn it, what was her name again? This day had been full of new people.

She swallowed hard. "Tamsyn. It's nothing, I swear!" She blinked at them, still not revealing what she was hiding.

Cador took a breath to demand the truth. Before he could,

Jem said softly, "It's all right, we won't tell on you."

Her eyes flicked between them, and she gave Jem a tentative smile before holding out a half-eaten sweet bun.

"Oh, that looks delicious," Jem said kindly.

"Do you want some?" she asked eagerly.

"Yes, please. Also, do you know where our chambers are? I presume the usual guest wings for the summits are unprepared."

Cador was ready to sleep in the stable with Dybri—and would surely get a warmer welcome considering Jem had asked about multiple rooms. Not that Cador blamed him.

Tamsyn bit her lip. "I'm sorry, I'm not sure. Most of those in charge here accompanied the clerics, so those of us left are pitching in all over. I think Prince Treeve is staying—oh! I know where to take you. Follow me!"

When they reached their destination after turning and twisting through the corridors, it took a moment for Cador to realize where she'd brought them. She lit the lamps with a flourish.

Jem stared at the large bed under a high stained glass window where they'd spent their first night of marriage, blushing prettily and refusing to even glance at Cador. Well, *Cador* had spent the night in the bed, and he recalled it was far too soft.

He remembered Jem cowering on the colored rug. So innocent and right to be afraid. For the thousandth time, Cador wished he could go back and change everything.

"It might be a bit dusty, but the sheets are clean." Tamsyn seemed eager for approval. "Most couples never have the chance to sleep in the wedding chamber again after the first night. But it'll be our secret."

Gaze on Tamsyn, Jem smiled stiffly. "Thank you. You've been too kind."

"It's my pleasure, Prince Jowan. Let me fetch you sweet

buns—oh, and soap and water. There's no tub, but I can find a basin. What else do you need?"

"That will be more than enough, thank you." Jem gave her another smile before she scurried out. She had barely gone before he hissed at Cador, "Don't say anything. Don't gloat or tease or, or…"

"I'm not!" Ugh, he sounded like a scolded child. He cleared his throat. "I won't. Take the bed. It was too soft anyway."

Tamsyn returned as promised, bringing spare cleric's robes and leather sandals and offering to take away their soiled clothing if they left it outside the door. Neither of them ate the buns, and after stripping, Cador pointedly turned away while Jem scrubbed himself clean as best he could with the cloth and basin of water.

Cador faced the corner, arms crossed as he examined the stone wall and tried not to imagine Jem's beautiful body wet and bare, the soft splashes of water and drag of the sponge not helping a bit.

Jem made a sputter of disgust. "Would you cover yourself? You're shameless!"

Puzzled, Cador peered at him over his shoulder. Jem rolled up the sleeves of a gray cleric robe that was too big for him, dragging on the rug around his feet.

"It makes no sense to put on the robe before I'm clean."

Again, Jem wouldn't look at him. "As if you don't enjoy parading in front of me, trying to—"

Cador bit back a swell of irritation as he faced the wall again. "I'm not *parading*. I'm standing here waiting for my turn."

"Fine," Jem grumbled.

"It's not as if you haven't seen my body before."

"That's not the point! But yes, as a matter of fact, it was here in this very room you were first naked and shameless in front of me."

After everything, *that* was what Jem was angry about? Cador was utterly fucking confused. "Then I'm sorry for that too."

"Don't! Just stop talking." Jem twisted the oil shut on the lamp by the bed, clambering under the covers. "And hurry up. Get dressed."

Well, at least Jem was still clearly affected by Cador's body. It was a paltry, hollow victory, yet he couldn't help but revel in it. If a part of Jem still wanted him—even if it was a base, animal instinct and connection that had grown between them as lovers—Cador would take it. He would treasure it. Perhaps nurture it to grow?

He washed quickly and dutifully yanked on the robe. Damn it that Treeve was right—the robes were surprisingly comfortable. He peeked at Jem before dousing the final lamp and stretching out on the rug.

When it was clear Jem wouldn't speak in the darkness, Cador did. "I know you're not sleeping."

No answer. Not a sound, but Jem was awake. He knew it.

"We must talk."

No answer.

"Even if you never forgive me—"

"*If?* there is no *if* about it."

The words twisted like spears through Cador's heart. Unbidden, he remembered Jem saving him and killing the boar, their frenzied coupling after in the mud and blood.

His voice was hoarse when he said, "Still, we must be a united front. Or else people will get between us and our mission for the children. That *Treeve* will slither his way in."

Jem scoffed. "Treeve can't marry me now anyway, even if he

wanted to."

"No, but…" He swallowed thickly, staring at the dark ceiling, only the faintest light coming in the high windows. "When we married, it was understood we would spend most of our time apart. I will return to Ergh as soon as I can. If you… If you stay, you'll be almost as free as you were before we met."

Jem was silent for so long that Cador thought perhaps he'd fallen asleep after all. Then he whispered, "Almost."

Cador pushed to his knees, wishing he could grasp Jem's hand in the darkness. "Even if—even though you'll never forgive me, I will do everything in my power to keep you safe. More than safe. Happy. I will see you happy again if it's the last thing I do. I swear it."

This time, Jem's silence went on so long that Cador gave up. He yielded and returned to his back on the rug, closing his eyes resolutely. He could at least sleep and gain energy for the fight still to come. He couldn't protect Jem otherwise.

Chapter Six

TRY AS HE might, Jem couldn't sleep. It should have been impossible given how weary he was, yet the night was still young as he crept from the wedding chamber—of all the rooms!—and wandered the compound.

He should have stayed in bed and hoped sleep would claim him eventually, but being in that room with Cador so near and tempting and infuriating and heartbreaking was too much. He'd burrowed under the blankets but immediately felt too hot, kicking at the coverings. Yet sleeping uncovered had felt far too vulnerable.

Jem's branded palm itched, then his scalp. How could he forgive Cador? How could he be *happy* again? Even if Cador returned to Ergh, far across the sea, the idea of finding another man, of being *happy* was unfathomable.

He rolled the hem of his robe and wandered until he found the courtyard, just enough stars poking through the clouds—or distant smoke?—to light the way to the fountain. He sat on the edge, trailing his fingers through the burbling water.

"Your grace!" Tamsyn appeared, looking sleep-tousled and hastily dressed. "Your husband is thundering around looking for you."

"Oh, for goodness sake! I'm fine."

Cador appeared, exhaling noisily as he spotted Jem. "I woke and you were gone. I thought—"

"What?" Jem demanded. "That Treeve kidnapped me under your nose?"

"Perhaps!" Cador hissed. He rubbed his face, his light beard scratching his palm audibly. "I'm sorry to wake you and the others, Tamsyn."

The smile she gave him was undeniably indulgent. "No need to apologize. You were concerned for your husband." Gods, the girl was mooning at Cador as though he was Morvoren's heroic merman come to life.

"Yes, well, we won't bother you again," Jem said.

She opened her mouth, then closed it. After glancing about, she whispered conspiratorially, "Would you like to soak in the healing waters? I'm told it's lovely and cool down there in summer. It's only for the clerics, but the ones left will be fast asleep. They'll never know. Besides, you're a prince! If ever there was reason for an exception, this is it."

Truly cool water? Jem almost moaned at the notion. He should have said no thank you, but he found the words, "Yes, please!" escaping. With the parched condition of the land, he was surprised to learn this spring was apparently unaffected.

"It's said that Glaw themselves blessed the spring!" she added with a beaming smile.

"My nephew is being brought to an elder who lives at the source of healing waters. Are these the same?" Cador asked.

"Yes! The source is in Gwels, and the waters travel underground, like a secret. I'm sure the gods will bless your nephew."

Cador made a noncommittal sound, and Jem wished that were true as he asked, "Should the water not be used to help with the droughts?" Though he had no idea how it would be transported.

Tamsyn seemed confused. "But these are holy, healing waters. Glaw will send rain when the time is right."

Cador seemed to want to scoff but instead said, "Let's bathe, then." To Tamsyn, he added, "I'm sure you want to rest."

As much as Jem wanted to argue that he hadn't invited Cador, it was better not to draw any unnecessary attention to their lack of accord, and arguing would only keep Tamsyn up longer.

They followed her down a slanting tunnel, Cador muttering about his borrowed sandals pinching between his toes. She lit lamps set into the sloping walls and went on about Glaw and blessings and how praying and making offerings to the gods while bathing in these pools could work miracles according to the clerics. Jem was too tired to do more than nod, and Cador said nothing.

Though it was damp in the cavern that housed the pools, the stone had been polished so finely that it felt luxurious under Jem's bare feet as he left his sandals neatly against the wall.

The spring seemed to have a gentle current, the pools stretching out down a long cavern. The smooth walls curved overhead, reflecting the peaceful water. Tamsyn left a small glass flask of water and two cups on a small table before retreating.

Jem's nerves jangled. He was overtired, and being alone with Cador was both familiar and unsettling. Part of him wanted to believe Cador's vow to keep him safe and see him happy. That soft, romantic portion of his soul that had grown up devouring Morvoren's tales wished this was a book where he knew all would be well eventually.

But his anger blotted out that softness the way the moon had eclipsed the sun one summer morning when he was a boy. There was too much darkness now. Cador could watch him with blue eyes brimming with sadness and regret all day, and Jem would not give in. For if he did...

If he allowed Cador a second chance—if he bestowed his trust on his husband again and was betrayed—his soul would shatter. Only that hard, sunless fury would be left.

Though he realized with a touch of surprise that Cador wasn't looking at him at all. Instead, he gazed around in wonder at the pools. Jem supposed it was fair enough given he bathed standing in a tub on Ergh.

Cador kicked off his sandals and strode to the edge of the pool to stick in his foot. "The water does feel good."

"Can you not leave your sandals right there for me to trip over?" Jem snapped.

Cador seemed about to protest, then lined up the sandals neatly by the wall. Jem was oddly disappointed that Cador didn't argue, which was petty and silly. Gods, he really did need sleep. He hoped a bath would relax him, even if Cador was there.

Even if Cador was naked, his robe tossed to land near the sandals.

Jem's fingers shook on the simple silver stopper of the flask. The green glass was familiar under his hands as he poured a small cup, similar to the flask he brought to his aviary at home. He gulped the cool water, careful not to waste any.

It wasn't only his persistent, aggravating desire for Cador's body. To be alone with him again reminded Jem of how vulnerable he was. Cador could snap his neck with his bare hands if he pleased.

Jem wanted to at least trust that he wouldn't, but memories invaded—pine needles sharp on his cheeks as he hid and listened to Cador and Delen discuss his kidnapping, riding with Austol thinking he was safe, the horrible bag over his head, Bryok screaming in rage with sword high, jumping into the blackness—

He rubbed his face, letting himself scratch his head just for a few seconds, the sting welcome as he closed his mind to all that had happened. When he opened his eyes, Cador was still bare in all his glory, up to his knees in water and frowning at him.

"What's wrong?"

"Would you like an itemized list? For gods' sake, get in the water."

"I am in the water."

"*Under* the water!"

For once, Cador did as he was told. He took a breath and lowered himself all the way under the surface, lying back with his nose plugged. Then he stood again, rivulets streaming down his taut muscles. The water only came to his hips even in the pool's center.

His chest hair was darker when it was wet, droplets clinging to his dusky nipples. His cock was just at the surface, ruddy against the thatch of wet hair. Jem was staring, yet he couldn't force his eyes away until Cador spoke softly.

"You still desire me." It wasn't a question.

"Shut up," Jem muttered, ears burning as he ripped his gaze away and fiddled with the rough fabric of the belt on his too-big robe.

"There's no shame in it. It's to be expected."

This gentle tone meant to soothe infuriated Jem. He did not need placating from Cador of all people. "I said shut up!"

Cador's voice hardened. "I'm only trying to—"

"Stop. I'm fine."

Everything was fine. This was *fine*. Jem stripped off his robe. He wouldn't be ashamed or *bashful*. He was an innocent virgin no more, and the pool was certainly big enough for them both.

hand to fondle his bollocks, his gaze locked on Jem. "I don't think it'll be the same. Not now that you've been fucked. Now that you've begged for my cock, and I've taken your sweet, tight hole and filled it with my seed. I think you still need me. In this if nothing else. I don't think your candle and your fantasies will be enough."

"I suppose I'll have to find a lover like you said. Treeve should suffice."

Cador's eyes flashed. He opened his mouth, then snapped it shut.

Jem forced a nonchalant shrug. "It's what we agreed upon when we married, after all."

For a long moment, they stared at each other. Then Cador dropped his head and let go of his shaft. All the teasing, arrogant defiance vanished.

When they married.

Here they were, after all. The temple to the gods was just outside, where they'd stood and pledged their fealty, where the old cleric had branded their palms. Jem clenched his fingers over the tusks.

Cador's voice was barely a whisper, his face tormented with grief. "Jem, I…"

The first thud, Jem hardly noticed. He couldn't tear his eyes from Cador's. It was the thud next and the next and the next, the distant sounds like…

Bolting to his feet, Cador stared upward and growled, "Who the fuck is that?"

It was undeniably distant footsteps overhead. Many footsteps for the vibrations to travel down to the pools. Jem hurried from the water and slung on the too-big robe. "Perhaps the clerics have returned?" In the middle of the night?

Beyond the faint thumping above, a single set of footsteps echoed down the tunnel, and Jem braced for whatever new problem approached at a run.

Chapter Seven

T REEVE SKIDDED TO a halt in the doorway, breathless and flushed, his gray robe hanging askew. "Hurry! You must—" He gaped at Cador.

Cador glanced down at his own bare body in confusion. "What the fuck is going on now?" Damn Treeve. Cador had been acting like a bastard, but he'd been desperate, grasping for the only connection with Jem he could.

"I—pardon the interruption. My father and his royal guards have arrived early! I'm afraid he'll take you captive or worse. We mustn't alert him to your presence. I instructed the servants, and they'll tell the old clerics not to say anything when they wake."

"Why will the servants and clerics follow your commands?" Jem asked.

Treeve grimaced. "Servants are rarely enthusiastic fans of my father, and they remember him and his demands painfully well from the spring summit." He glanced back the way he'd come. "You must hurry! My father will want to soak in the pools."

"I thought these pools were only supposed to be for the clerics," Cador said, tugging on his robe.

Treeve barked a laugh. "My father does as he likes."

Jem grabbed the flask of water, and they followed Treeve up the tunnel. The stone was dusty beneath Cador's damp feet, and he realized too late they'd forgotten their sandals. His had been stupidly tiny, but they were better than nothing.

The wall lamps cast an eerie glow amid the long shadows. Instead of returning to the main buildings, Treeve pointed down a smaller tunnel.

"I'm told this joins up with the tunnel between the temple and fields," he whispered. "Do you recall it from your wedding day?"

Jem nodded. "I do. He was probably far too drunk."

As much as Cador wanted to protest, Jem was right. He vaguely recalled a tunnel and...vomiting. Shame coiled through him. How disgraceful to greet his husband in that state.

A din of voices and movement traveled down the main tunnel, sounding suddenly closer. "Go now!" Treeve hissed, squinting down the smaller tunnel. "Piss and shit, I've no lantern or flint to light the lamps."

"Watch your step!" Tamsyn said too loudly. Too close.

Jem grabbed Cador's hand and yanked him into the blackness. They surged forward. With his right hand outstretched, fingers trailing along the dank wall, Cador staggered, the tunnel sloping down once more. Jem clung to his fingers. This tunnel was also laid with dusty stones, even more grit beneath Cador's bare feet since it apparently wasn't used as frequently.

Behind them, Treeve's voice echoed. "Father! I was just coming from the healing waters myself. Let me accompany you. I'm sure we've much to discuss."

The light was faint behind them, and as the tunnel curved into the black belly of the earth, the glow disappeared entirely. Cador jerked to a stop without meaning to, fumbling for the wall to keep oriented.

Gripping Jem's hand, chest tight, Cador continued with

tentative steps, sweeping his right arm across the tunnel before finding the wall beside him again.

When the voices had faded completely and there was only the sound of their shallow breathing and the odd drips of water in the dank stillness, Cador whispered, "Are you all right?"

"I'm fine!" Jem's voice was reed-thin. He yanked his hand free.

Frustration and fear swelled, Cador barely managing to keep his voice low. "What are you doing? Don't be stupid!" Keeping his right hand glued to the wall, he grasped for Jem with his left, catching the loose neck of Jem's robe.

"I'm not afraid!"

"I am! If we get lost we'll die down here in the blackness." He tugged Jem closer, and he'd throw him over his shoulder to keep him safe if he had to. "Stay with me. Please. The sooner we find our way out of here, the sooner you'll be rid of me."

Jem's breath was too quick, but he sounded more confident than Cador felt. "All right. It's fine. We'll be fine. We'll each keep a hand on the wall on our side."

Jem's fingers found Cador's on his shoulder. With their hands clasped once more between them, Cador reached out with his foot, tracing a seam of stone with his big toe.

It would take all night to be so cautious, so he started walking again, following the tunnel with his right hand on the dank wall, hoping there were no sudden steps or drops. He couldn't imagine why there would be in a tunnel, but his heart thumped as they moved along in the utter darkness.

It's just a tunnel. Same as it would be in the light.

The crash made him jump so violently he was sure his feet left the cool floor. For a panicked moment, he couldn't understand what had shattered.

As he realized, Jem whispered harshly, "I dropped it!"

He meant the flask of water, which instead of being fashioned from tusk or animal skin was glass because the mainlanders were ridiculous. Had they crept far enough down the tunnel, or would the noise give them away? They'd find out soon enough.

Yet with the next step, Jem gasped. "Glass," he muttered, the sound seeming to come through clenched teeth. "It's deep."

Twisting while trying to move his feet as little as possible, Cador bent and hoisted Jem into his arms. Jem was rigid, his breath loud in sharp pants that ghosted over Cador's face. Otherwise, they remained in silence. His fingers dug into Cador's neck painfully.

Reaching with his foot again and knocking away a large shard, Cador hoped he was going in the correct direction. He whispered, "Can you touch the wall with your toes?" Jem's dangling feet should have been near the right side of the tunnel.

"Yes." The whisper caressed Cador's cheek.

Cador took another step. And another, realizing how familiar Jem's lithe body had become. How comfortable it felt to have him safe in his arms. He'd had plenty of lovers, yet it had only been fucking and fun.

He'd rarely lain the night—or morning or afternoon—with them. He hadn't held them close while they slept and felt so unbearably tender toward them. Sometimes, it was hard to believe how deeply he'd allowed Jem to burrow under his flesh.

Yet Jem rippled with tension. Cador could hear the scratch of fingernails as if he was raking his own skin. Cador murmured, "It's all right. I don't think they heard."

After a few more careful steps, reaching out with his toe to push aside any shards of glass that had scattered across the tunnel, Cador walked faster. But without being able to reach out into the blackness, he stumbled and hesitated.

"Put me down. We must be past any broken glass now. I'll get this shard out."

Reluctantly, Cador bent and placed Jem on his feet. It was the most practical thing to do, even though he would have happily carried him for miles inhaling his sweet musk. Jem sucked in a pained breath.

"It's stuck in my foot."

"Here." Cador dropped to his knees, running his hands down Jem's slim hips and thighs, the robe bunching. "Which one?"

"My left."

Carefully, Cador slipped his hands past Jem's knees. Jem hopped, trying to balance on his other foot. "Hold on to me," Cador whispered. A shiver ran down his spine as Jem's hand brushed over his head before dropping to his shoulder.

On the Cliffs of Glaw, he'd knelt this way and declared his devotion, and Jem had caressed his hair before walking away from him.

In the blackness, it was still and silent but for their breathing. It felt strangely like they were floating—like nothing else existed. He spread his hands around Jem's calves, needing to ground himself, to feel flesh and bone and know he wasn't alone. Cador wanted to lean into Jem and rub his face against his stomach. Wrap his arms around his waist—

This isn't a dream. You have to keep moving. Get out of this fucking tunnel.

Concentrating, he lifted Jem's injured foot, skimming over the arch of it with his fingertips. Jem gasped, squirming and clutching Cador's shoulders.

"Tickles," he mumbled. "It's near my heel."

Ah yes, there it was. A small piece of glass—yet far too thick for Cador's liking—lodged in the flesh. Working blind, he struggled to get a grasp on the shard, knowing that as he poked and prodded as gently as he could with his big hands, he was causing Jem more pain. But it had to come out.

Finally, a whimper of relief escaped Jem, and Cador eased out the glass, barely able to grasp it with the tips of his fingers. He tossed it away, and it landed with a faint *plink*. "Try a step."

Jem relaxed his grasp on Cador's shoulders and did, hissing in pain. "It's out. Let's go."

"I should wrap it." He tested the hem of his robe. He could tear it, though it would take some effort.

"Later. We need to get out of here. It's too dark." He urged Cador up and took his left hand. "Go!"

The darkness did seem to press in suffocatingly around them, and Cador reminded himself that if they had a lamp this would merely be a tunnel. There was nothing to be frightened of. Well, aside from King Perran and his army. And the wildfires that apparently would keep burning until it rained. If the sevels were lost...

Sweeping his arm out and following along the wall, the stone of the tunnel feeling wetter as the path angled down again, he ordered himself to focus on one problem at a time. If he must fight the king's guard, he would battle with his head high and sword higher. Except he didn't have his sword because he was a piss-poor fighter.

Oh, for his spears. When would he have them again? He was a hunter, not a warrior. Tas and Bryok had seemed to think one was like the other, but Cador wasn't convinced. After all, here he was scurrying away like a rat from the enemy.

"Perhaps I should have faced the king," he said before he could silence himself.

Jem's fingers twitched, and he sounded confused. "What?" he whispered. He rhythmically tugged lightly on Cador's hand as they walked, giving away that he was limping. "You mean now?"

"Yes. The bastard's here. Apparently trying to turn the mainland against Ergh. I shouldn't be running away."

Jem scoffed. "Don't be ridiculous. Perhaps if the king was alone, but you heard Treeve. His father's lost his mind and blames Ergh. He's out for blood. Do you think you're going to battle his soldiers all by yourself? You'd just get yourself killed. Probably me as well. Or we'd be prisoners. There's no telling. Treeve clearly thought we were at risk."

He grunted. *Treeve.* "You never mentioned you knew him."

"Didn't we already go over this? I don't. Not really. We met as boys, but not again until the summit. We didn't even speak. I was too busy being forced to marry you."

Cador ignored that, for what could he say? "He seemed quite familiar with you."

"I don't think so? But we've always been friendly enough, I suppose. We owe him now. I hope he can keep his father in line." He inhaled loudly. "And if the sevel fields burn…"

"We can't allow it." As if they could control a fire on the other side of Onan from their dark tunnel. "Will Ebrenn have stockpiles?"

"I would think so, but I don't know for certain. I've never thought about it." He moaned plaintively. "Gods, how much farther?"

"The end must be soon. Unless—"

Jem clutched his hand. "What?"

"I've been feeling along the wall to our right. What if there was another tunnel branching off on the left while I carried you?"

They stopped in their tracks. Jem's breathing was louder again. "I've no idea which way is which. We're still going in the right direction, aren't we?"

Cold sweat prickled the back of Cador's neck. Were they? Yes, they had to be going the right way. He'd been careful when he picked up Jem. After he'd removed the glass, when he stood... Had it been the same wall he groped for?

"We have to get out of here." Jem sucked in little gasps. His palm grew damp in Cador's grasp. "It's too dark. I can't breathe."

Tamping down his own panic, Cador forced a deep inhalation and exhalation. "I think we're still going the right way. If not, we'll end up back where we started, and we'll simply turn around. They won't see us down this dark tunnel, and we'll spot the lamps. We're all right."

Jem exhaled loudly. "Yes. Treeve would have told us if there was another tunnel partway."

Unless he was lying. Unless this is a trap. Grudgingly, Cador thought, *unless he didn't know.* Giving Jem's hand a squeeze, he walked on, hoping they'd hear any danger in the distance. Neither of them spoke again until Cador blinked and squinted ahead.

"Is that...?" he murmured.

"It looks a shade lighter, I think?"

They crept forward now, Cador almost holding his breath. Had they gone back the wrong way? He'd settled into a rhythmic motion of touching the curved wall to the right and then sweeping his outstretched arm back and forth in front of them before dragging his fingers along the wall once more. It did seem to be a slightly less black darkness, and—

He jerked to a stop as his outstretched fingers hit stone. His heart hammered. A dead end? Fuck, they were trapped. Fuck, fuck—

"This way," Jem murmured, nudging Cador to the right. "It's a bit brighter."

With a flood of relief, he realized they'd entered another tunnel traveling left to right. "This must be the tunnel from the temple." Since they had no idea which way led to the field of flowers Cador barely remembered, going toward the steadily graying light seemed the best choice.

Before long, they crept to the mouth of the tunnel and peered out at the square temple bathed in ghostly moonlight beyond the white marble arch. The stone chairs on each of the four sides sat empty. The temple was deserted, and only the faint music of distant insects broke the silence. Any threat of King Perran and his soldiers seemed ages away.

Jem breathed deeply, eyes on the dark sky, clearly relieved to be out of the darkness. "I guess we chose the wrong direction," he finally said.

Cador stared at the altar where they'd wed. It was just a piece of polished stone—no more important than any other, despite what the clerics might say. Yet...

He was still holding Jem's right hand, their branded, sweaty palms pressed together. He was struck by the mad idea that he should repeat their vows—and this time he'd mean every word. If he could even remember the words given how much he'd had to drink that day. *Ugh.* He really had been a beast. Jem had deserved so much better, and now...

"Well, there's nothing for us here," Cador muttered.

Jem yanked his hand free. "Clearly not. Come on." He took a step and winced.

"Let me bandage that." Before Jem could object, he added, "You'll only slow us down."

Begrudgingly, Jem limped to the closest chair. Cador knelt at his feet once more and bent his head to examine the wound, cradling Jem's foot on his lap. The blood oozing from the cut was dark in the pale moonlight. It didn't gush, at least. He wished he had water to clean out the dirt, but it would have to wait.

"Must hurt," he murmured.

Jem's shrug was brittle. "It's my own fault for taking the flask."

"It wasn't wrong to think to bring water with us." The smattering of hair on Jem's shin tickled Cador's palm as he rubbed reassuringly. "It's not your fault."

"But—" Jem seemed to relax a fraction. "Come on, we have to go."

Cador took the hem of his robe to tear a strip, but Jem stopped him, reaching down to grab Cador's wrist. "My robe is too long anyway."

Ah. He was right, of course. Cador gripped the fabric and pulled. And pulled. Grunting, he cursed the clerics for making robes of such sturdy material. "An unnecessary amount of stitching," he muttered, his muscles tensed as he tried again.

A giggle burst out of Jem, and he clapped his hand over his mouth. It was such a glorious relief to hear even one little nervous laugh from him, and Cador found himself grinning.

He puffed up his chest. "I am a mighty hunter of Ergh. I will not be defeated by this robe." He yanked, muscles straining, and the fabric gave way with a *riiip*. He tore off a wide strip and wrapped it tightly around Jem's heel and foot and ankle, tucking the frayed end in and hoping it would hold for the time being. He glanced up at Jem, his heart skipping at the way Jem watched him so closely.

"Thank you," Jem murmured. His damp curls hung close to his eyes, and Cador reached up to brush them back and—

Jerking back, Jem stumbled to his feet, almost toppling onto his arse. Cador dropped his hand, digging his blunt nails into his palm. Was Jem truly frightened of him? He couldn't blame him given his own betrayal and Jem's near murder.

He wished fervently he could go back and tell Tas he wouldn't be part of the plot to hurt Jem so cruelly. So casually. If he thought the gods were real and listening, he'd pray for it day and night.

Jem stiffened, looking back down the tunnel. "Do you hear that?"

Drawing him to the side of the archway, Cador planted his feet. "Get behind me."

Jem hissed, "Yes, obviously I'm going to get behind you!"

They waited, the soft footsteps drawing near. Tentative. Then a golden glow emerged from the mouth of the tunnel. Closer, closer…

The girl gasped and leapt back, red hair flying, almost dropping her lantern. Cador relaxed his stance. "Tamsyn."

"Prince Treeve sent me to meet you. I thought I heard voices, so I came in case you were lost. This isn't the right way."

Cador grunted, then belatedly added, "Thank you. Lead on."

They were only a few steps when he heard Jem hiss in pain. Cador turned and lifted Jem into his arms without a word. There was no reason not to carry him.

Jem opened his mouth to say something, but apparently

realized there was no sense in arguing. His rigid body relaxed just enough that it was clear he wasn't going to fight. Cador rejoiced in the small surrender as he turned to Tamsyn, who watched them with a beaming smile.

He frowned. "What?"

"Nothing!" She hurried down the tunnel, and he strode after her.

It didn't take long to follow the tunnel out, and she led them to the field where Dybri waited, grazing on the brittle grass near the base of the hill that protected the temple. A small sack waited as well. Too small.

"My boots?" Cador asked. He wanted his sword too, but that could be replaced. His summer boots were broken in perfectly, and he hated all this running around in bare feet.

"Only food and water, I'm afraid," she said. "You know the way to Neuvella and your castle?" she asked Jem, who poked at Cador to put him down.

Now on his feet—or more accurately one foot as he balanced on the right, he said, "Yes, of course."

Cador frowned. "Didn't you get lost on your way here?"

Jem glared. "The smoke confused me."

"I didn't mean—" He held up his hands. "Forget it."

Tamsyn looked between them nervously. "Er, there should be road signs as you go south."

"Thank you," Jem said. "We won't forget your help."

Cador nodded his agreement and bent to take Jem's waist to lift him onto Dybri's broad back.

Jem batted at him and hissed, "Stop it! I can do it myself." Glancing at Tamsyn, he seemed embarrassed.

Ah, yes, all the lessons with that fucking liar Austol. Not that he was in much of a position to judge given his own lies, but

Chapter Eight

B ENDING LOW OVER the horse's neck, Jem clutched her mane and squinted in the dusty wind. His lungs barely seemed to work, and he reminded himself he could breathe and see, that there was no rough sack over his head, that he wasn't slung helplessly over a thundering horse bearing him away to the Cliffs of Glaw.

He could admit he was very glad of Cador's thick arm locked around his middle as they raced from the Holy Place. Though he didn't fear horses the way he once had, his heart still felt like it would burst through his chest. This gallop was a far cry from tentatively trotting around on sweet, gentle Nessa on Ergh.

Memories of bouncing painfully across a horse's back and that horrible sack suffocating him persisted. The ground seemed very far beneath them, a dark maw that reminded him of the plunge from the Cliffs of Glaw.

It's not the Askorn Sea. If I fall, it's only grass and dirt. It's not that far.

Still, he choked down a whimper and prayed to the fickle gods not to let him fall. Prayed that Cador's strong arm around him would not falter, allowing himself to be grateful Cador was there with him.

He had no idea if they were going the right way, but escaping the soldiers of King Perran's personal guard was certainly the priority. Even if he fervently wished they could slow down. The air was gritty on his tongue, that hint of distant smoke inflaming his throat.

When Cador steered them into the woods, Jem almost couldn't watch, convinced they were about to run headlong into one of the broad maples. Yet Cador guided their mount expertly, the horse weaving nimbly through the forest. Jem couldn't see back beyond Cador's bulk if Treeve had been able to follow, but he hoped so.

Gods, what a welcome home, and it was still at least two days' journey to the castle. Possibly three or even more. He had no idea what to expect at this point.

He wasn't sure how long they'd raced before he realized the thumping that filled his ears was his own heart, not pursuers. Cador eased up, a deep "Whoa," rumbling from him. He kept his left arm firm around Jem as he reined in their mount completely and turned her the way they'd come.

For a moment in the darkness, the trees blocking most of the moonlight, there was only the hoot of an owl and cicadas chorusing. Then hoof beats, but only a single rider by the sounds of it. Jem exhaled in a rush as the dark figure resolved into Treeve reining in his horse.

"Good thinking coming in here," Treeve said. "We lost them."

"What the fuck happened?" Cador demanded.

"Turns out one of the clerics *does* think this hot summer is the gods punishing us and that Ergh is to blame. The old bitch told my father you're here and that I came ahead to warn them about his delusions. He wasn't best pleased."

Jem blinked in shock at the language. The woman was still a cleric, after all. Some of his distaste must have shown on his face since Treeve winced.

"Forgive me. I'm sure the woman is genuine in her belief."

"Forget her," Cador snapped. "What of your father? And why should we trust you?"

Jem grasped Cador's wrist. "Please. If Treeve was doing his father's bidding, why would he have helped us escape?"

Cador muttered something that was probably profanity.

"I understand your suspicion," Treeve said. "If you want to go east to find your people and take the longer route south, I can escort Jem to the castle myself."

Arm tightening around Jem, Cador practically growled. "No. My sister will protect my people. I have faith in her. She will get them to Neuvella safely."

Treeve's mouth drew down as he sighed heavily. "I've never seen Father so furious. His moods are often black, but I fear he actually believes the gods are punishing us for welcoming Ergh into the fold. If that sentiment grows…"

If it spread, they'd have fires of a different kind to douse. The people of Ergh were safe for a moment, but what if the king took his battle to Ergh's shores? And they needed the sevels. They needed Onan.

Treeve glanced around. "I must get moving. I don't think my father's guard will venture any farther—he'll be left too unprotected. I'll wait until morning and his temper has cooled before I return to reason with him."

"Reason with him? He sent his guards after you."

Treeve laughed thinly. "Oh, my father has thrown me in the dungeon more than once in a fit of anger. I'm accustomed to it. So long as I'm his only heir, I'll be perfectly safe, I assure you. And for you, Jem, I wish safe travels to Neuvella." He nodded to the sack Jem clutched. "Should be enough food and water for a day or two."

Jem looked inside, glad to find bread and cheese and fruit. Even a few sevels, which felt more precious than ever. Also two large leather wine skins, which were certainly more practical than glass.

Jem flushed, still angry with himself for dropping the flask. His heel throbbed. "Uh, yes," he said, trying to focus. "Stay safe. Thank you again. Oh, er, do you know which way is south?"

Treeve pointed. "Please tell your mother we must come together for the good of Onan." With a final nod, he spurred his horse and disappeared.

With a loud exhale, Cador clucked his tongue and turned their horse to walk in the direction Treeve had pointed. Jem sat straight, not wanting to lean back against Cador. Still, he didn't object to Cador's arm around him, and his mind chewed over Treeve's ridiculous, puzzling words from the day before.

A winning match.

Jem certainly didn't feel like the victor.

Cador seemed content to let the horse walk for a time, though content in nothing else. He was like a wall of tension, his arm still iron around Jem's waist. He had to admit his relief that Cador was with him. If he'd had to navigate the forest alone—let alone that pitch-black tunnel...

Jem should be glad of the silence, but as it stretched out, his anxiety only grew. There was no reason for him to break it. What did he have to say to Cador? Nothing. They were stuck together for the moment, but there was no need to speak. In two days time, they'd finally reach the castle, and Cador would be locked away in the dungeon with Kenver. Delen would join them later.

That thought had been a bitter reassurance during the voyage across the Askorn Sea. Jem had never thought anything so resentful and sour could be a comfort. He hated that it was. But as he grasped now for the welcoming weight of it, he found tears pricking his eyes instead. He cursed himself. This was no time for sadness. He must stay angry.

"Do you trust him?"

Ah, there. Jem gratefully seized upon Cador's question. "Of course." It was an exaggeration, yet he couldn't resist.

On cue, Cador grunted. "Why? You said yourself you barely know him."

"I know enough. He helped us escape his father."

"I know he lied about who he was when I met him. Why the fuck should we believe a liar?"

Jem bit out, "You say that as if *you're* not a liar too."

No reply—only a warm huff of breath on the back of Jem's neck.

"What, no response? No plea of innocence? Come on."

When he spoke, Cador's voice was soft and calm. "What's the point? I'm not innocent. We'll only waste our breath. It's not my innocence I want you to believe."

Jem opened his mouth but found he had no reply. Cador spurred the horse into a trot, then a run, and Jem held on, wishing he had the faintest idea of what he should believe.

AN HOUR PAST dawn, Jem had to admit the heat was already oppressive. They'd found a trail through the forest, stopping only to rest the horse that Cador called Dybri. Jem was careful to only sip water from one of the wine skins.

Leaning past Jem, Cador rubbed Dybri's neck, murmuring

to her as he did every so often. "It's all right, girl. We'll stop soon." His breath tickled Jem's ear.

Jem almost argued that they had to keep going, but he was only being peevish and ridiculous. As wonderful as it would be to finally get home—oh, to dive into his lake—it was only sensible to rest during the day as the heat compounded.

At least he didn't see any unnaturally orange sky through the trees, and no ash or smoke drifted on what little breeze lifted the brown-tipped leaves.

"What villages lie this way?"

It took a moment for Jem to realize Cador wasn't speaking to the horse this time. "I don't know."

"Who will we encounter on this trail?"

"I have no idea."

"Shouldn't we have seen someone by now?"

He gritted his teeth. "I told you I don't know."

"Can't you guess?"

Jem made a show of gazing around at the forest. "Well, I suppose a marauding woodsman with his mighty ax might come along."

"I wasn't speaking of your boyish fantasies."

Spine stiffening, Jem squawked. "Nor was I!"

Dybri snorted and stamped, and Jem felt chastened. By the horse. He clamped his jaw shut as she stubbornly veered off the path despite Cador's attempts to stop her. Jem made sure to keep an eye out to make sure he knew which direction they were going in.

Dybri's destination was a pond at the base of a rocky out-cropping that was apparently shaded enough from the sun to still hold murky water. Jem swatted at flies. "Should she drink that?"

about at this point. But clearly he was thirsty, so he reached for the sack and yanked the stopper from one of the wine skins. He sipped the water, wanting to gulp, before wordlessly offering it to Cador.

With a nod, Cador drank, gulping deeply. Sweat glistened in the hollow of his throat. "What?"

Jem tore his eyes away, clasping his hands tightly in his lap. "Nothing."

Fingers grazing Jem's thighs, Cador tugged at the bottom of the robe. "How's this?"

The fraying threads tickled below his knees. "Much better. Thank you."

"You're welcome."

What was he doing thanking Cador for anything? Jem fidgeted, a rush of nervous tension gripping him. He plucked up one of the ribbons of torn fabric and tried to wrap his foot.

"It needs to be tighter. Let me do it."

"It's fine."

Before Cador could argue any more, he brushed at something on his arm—then leapt up, hopping in a skittish little dance. "What the fuck was that?"

Jem could only stare at him. "What?" He gazed around, but saw only dry leaves and dirt and tree roots amid brown, pathetic grass.

"It was crawling on me! Long and thin and dozens of legs!"

"Oh, a gwiader. They don't bite."

Cador rubbed at his arms and legs, spinning in a circle, clearly trying to find the insect on the ground. And Jem couldn't help himself, the burst of laughter shaking his shoulders. "The mighty hunter of Ergh fells boars but fears a tiny insect!"

"That was not tiny!" He glared—then his lips twitched, his

own laughter bubbling up. "Well, it wasn't! All those legs!" He lifted his bare feet over and over, shaking them and doing a little march on the spot. "At least if I had my boots," he muttered.

"Surely you have more insects than worms on Ergh."

"Yes, reasonably sized insects. Small. Unobtrusive. Not fond of crawling on people. When we go back, I'll—"

Their laughter died. Cador dropped his head and knelt to bandage Jem's foot. He finished the task with economical movements before striding back to the pond to tend Dybri. Jem forced down a piece of bread and a hunk of cheese before rolling a bruised sevel between his hands.

There was no sense in *not* eating it, yet guilt simmered as he bit into the sweet flesh that was too mealy. Sevels were best crisp and fresh—how he'd always had them. The guilt swelled, and he thought of Hedrok, hoping he was safe.

Pillowing his head on his arm, he curled on the ground. It was a far cry from the lush grasses that grew by his lake, but he was so tired he'd surely be able to rest.

Yet sleep remained stubbornly elusive, flies tickling his face, the dry earth under him like rock. He'd have been far more comfortable curled on a bed of pine needles in the forest near the cottage on Ergh. Neuvella was home, and everything was supposed to be better. Why did he feel even worse?

Because I've been traveling for weeks, and I've barely slept or eaten, and I'm trapped with the man who betrayed me. I'm thirsty and hot and in pain, and it won't be like this when I finally get home to the castle. I'll be safe there.

Able to breathe a little easier, Jem realized he was scratching his head. His nails had grown longer than usual, and he sank into the pleasure-pain as he raked his skull. His thoughts grew confusing as he drifted into the twilight before sleep…

Needles clawed his cheeks as he ducked under the boughs, pines growing so thick he could barely see. The chasing strangers were only a breath behind. He ignored the throbbing agony in his bare foot, limping forward, wishing more than ever that he could fly with his beloved birds.

He'd never known Ergh to be so sweltering. It must have finally been summer, though the distant sky was still that endless gray. Jem ran and ran, bursting from the forest to the cliffside, salty sea spray burning his eyes. It was dark now, and he realized with horror he was at the Cliffs of Glaw.

There was nowhere to run.

Spinning around, he faced his pursuers. It wasn't Bryok, Creeda, Hedra and the others. He didn't know these people. They didn't hesitate, cornering him, his feet on the very edge of the cliff now. Torchlight flared, and he recognized the man standing impassively nearby.

Cador watched, ignoring Jem's cries for help. He watched as one of the pursuers raised a sword. They imprisoned Jem in their vicious grasp, too many of them to fight as the sword came down on his wrist.

But it wasn't a clean cut. Over and over, the man hacked away at the bloody, ruined flesh, finally crunching through bone and tearing Jem's hand loose.

Orange flames flickering over the hard lines of his face, Cador loomed. He yanked the rough, horrible sack over Jem's head and cinched the knot around his throat as Jem screamed.

"Jem!"

Gasping, his throat dirt-dry, Jem saw Cador above him. He kicked and shoved, backing away with another hoarse scream. He blinked in a beam of blinding sunlight as he scrabbled in the dirt, flexing his fingers and fisting his hands over and over. He stared at his right hand, the branded tusks stark on his palm.

"It was a nightmare." Cador's voice was low and soothing.

Jem jerked his gaze to where Cador stood nearby, his hands out in placation, the dillywig brand dark on his pale skin. Though part of him wanted to hurl himself into Cador's arms, he commanded, "Stay back!"

"I won't hurt you."

Gods, how Jem wanted to believe it. His sweaty hair clung to his tingling scalp, and he backed up against the tree trunk, the shards of glaring sunlight all around indicating it was near noon. The dry rasp in his throat transformed to a hacking cough.

Crouching, Cador held out the water, clearly trying to keep his distance. "Drink." After a moment he added, "Please."

Jem took a gulp, grimacing at the warm liquid. It was better than the murky pond, at least. He tugged at the loose collar of his robe. He realized the hem was rucked up over his knees and tugged it down despite the heat. He scratched at his shins, stopping himself from threading his fingers through his hair since his scalp twinged from earlier.

Still crouching, Cador had backed up a few paces. He watched Jem with a furrowed brow, his blue gaze piercing. "Are you well enough to ride? We must get you home."

Of course, he had no idea that getting Jem home meant his own imprisonment in the dungeon. A fresh wave of acid flooded Jem as his mind eagerly revisited his litany of worries. What was the chieftain up to now?

Jem had to warn his mother about Kenver. Gods, for all he knew Cador's father had slit the queen's throat and taken control of the castle. Not a single thing had been as Jem expected since he'd reached the mainland.

He simply nodded and pushed to his feet, hand on the rough tree trunk as he fought for balance. He took a few limping steps, but Cador had already run to get Dybri. He eyed Jem warily and asked, "May I help you up?"

Jem nodded again, letting Cador lift him astride the horse. He tucked his shortened robe under his legs, keeping his back straight as Cador mounted behind him and they returned to the trail. Cador assured him he'd paid attention and they still headed south in the right direction.

Dybri walked at a steady pace—better than making her gallop in the heat. Cador didn't try to wrap an arm around Jem this time, his hands resting on his thick thighs bracketing Jem's.

"What kind of birds are these?"

Jem blinked. It took him a moment to understand Cador was asking about the trilling birdsong echoing through the forest. "What does it matter?"

"Only curious."

The silence stretched out, the afternoon windless and humid, a whine of cicadas joining the birds. "They're edhens. Sweet little things. They nest wherever byghans are found and seem to be friendly with them for some reason. I've seen them perched on the byghans' backs."

"Ah. What do they look like?"

He couldn't imagine why Cador cared but answered his questions as they plodded on. After a time, he realized he was breathing more easily and even leaning back against the wall of Cador's chest.

Yet when his eyes grew heavy and his thoughts took on the unreal quality of dreams, the nightmare memory of the hood over his head and his missing, savaged hand returned. Now with the vision of Cador watching it unfold with cold eyes.

He sat straighter, pinching the backs of his hands. He must stay awake lest he topple off the horse, and because he'd had quite enough of his nightmares. He focused his mind on happy memories of home and his sun-dappled aviary, laughing with Santo and reading his books with a gentle breeze rustling the pages. Warm, safe recollections that brought him peace.

A new vision intruded—Cador hopping around in a circle, flapping and frightened of a mere gwiader—and Jem allowed himself a smile.

"Yes. May I have some water? And if you can fetch the village guard. I need help returning to the castle, and—" Again, he hesitated. Cador would be gone on Dybri soon if he hadn't left already. Surely they could chase him down and take him into custody. This was the logical course for Jem to take. They were likely only a day's ride or less from the castle.

She sneered. "There's nothing for you here. Get out!"

"Please. As I told you, I'm Prince Jowan. We need water and—"

"Thief!" Her shout could have woken the dead, and apparently roused her husband, who tripped out of the cottage shirtless, tugging up his trousers. "Thief!" she repeated. A bell rang somewhere, a heavy *gong-gong-gong* of iron.

The guard would be coming, at least. Jem knew he had to look a state in his filthy, torn clerical robe and bare feet. He tried a smile. "There's no danger, I swear it. I'm Prince Jowan. I won't harm you."

The man now held an ax, his bushy eyebrows meeting. "Prince Jowan, is it? And I'm the queen herself."

"But I am. Really!" He took a step back, unease growing. His impetuous choice had perhaps been imprudent rather than brave.

Other sleepy, angry-looking villagers arrived. With more axes. Jem backed away. "I'm sorry. There's no need to—I understand I don't look myself at the moment." Of course, since he'd rarely left the comfort of the castle, they wouldn't know what he looked like at all.

Cursing himself, Morvoren, and the gods, he raised his hands beseechingly. "Please believe me."

The kerchiefed woman frowned. "What kind of marriage brand is that? You're no cleric if you're married. Not that I believe you're a cleric anyway."

"I'm not!" His heart leapt. "You see my brand! It's the boar tusks of Ergh! Because I was forced to marry the chieftain's son! Surely you heard about that!"

The angry expressions faltered slightly, the villagers clearly dubious. Was Cador still in the bushes? Was he listening? No, he'd undoubtedly fled, and Jem should send the guard after him.

"My mother the queen is in danger from Ergh's chieftain, Kenver. I must return to the castle. My traitorous husband is in these woods, and you must seize him."

There. It was done.

His pulse raced, gorge rising. This was what he'd promised himself he'd do, so why did he desperately wish he could snatch back the words? And why were the villagers still sneering at him and coming closer with their axes? He stumbled back.

"Oh, yes, *Prince Jowan*, we'll do your bidding!" a man said.

"Right away, your grace!"

Laughing, they surrounded him, rough hands grabbing and dragging Jem off his feet. Horrified, he kicked and wanted to scream, only pathetic little squeaks and cries escaping his raw throat. "Please!"

"It's an original tale, I'll give you that, boy."

"The prince won't be back until the Feast of the Blood Moon after harvest."

"No, I'm back early!" Jem struggled fruitlessly. "Stop!" He imagined any moment a sack would be thrust over his head and—

A low roar that might have been an angry, charging boar rumbled, and Jem crashed to the hard-packed earth on his back, the air knocking out of his lungs. There were shouts and movement all around, and he blinked in disbelief at Cador brawling with the villagers, his tattered robe flying up.

Why hadn't Cador fled when he'd had the chance? When he'd heard Jem's plea to seize him? Here he was, fighting them off. Should Jem be glad of it? Or frightened of Cador's growls? He could only watch, gasping shallowly.

There were too many villagers, and Cador finally raised his hands in surrender in the face of the ax blades. They shoved him down by Jem, and Jem pushed himself up so they knelt together.

He motioned to Cador. "He's the barbarian! My husband! Look at our brands. We've returned early. I assure you."

The people laughed. "Oh, he *assures* us!" a woman said. "In that case, let 'em go so they can steal from the next innocent village they come across."

"Let the queen's magistrate deal with these bandits. Bad enough to thieve, but pretending to be Prince Jowan? Or clerics? Shameless."

How could Jem blame these innocent people for thinking barefoot, bedraggled strangers in cleric robes—yet who were clearly not clerics—were up to no good. "Will you take us to the castle, then?" he asked, relieved that the answer was yes.

It was clearly meant to be a harsh punishment, but at least he'd be home soon. They'd certainly know him at the castle. Cador was stonily silent beside him, not even glancing at Jem.

When a harassed-looking woman arrived driving what was apparently an enclosed prison wagon pulled by several horses, Jem cringed at the thought of getting inside. Not that he had a vote at this point. At least the locals had fetched Dybri, and their jailer tied their horse to the wagon's rear before ordering them into what was little more than a box.

Jaw clenched so hard it looked like it would snap, Cador obeyed, stooping to get through the door at the back of the wagon. His shoulders barely fit through. Jem followed. There were two tiny, barred windows on either side of the wagon above hard benches. Wrist and leg irons waited, and his stomach lurched.

He hesitated in the small door. "A messenger went ahead. I'm Prince Jowan. The queen really is expecting us."

The woman snorted and shoved him inside. Jem caught himself on Cador's knees, strong hands steadying him. Sitting across from each other, they allowed the woman to shackle them.

Cador spread his long legs, his knees jammed into Jem's bench. Legs primly together in the space between Cador's, Jem concentrated on breathing as steadily as he could as he was confined. At least there was a short chain between their wrists and ankles that allowed for a bit of movement.

The woman dumped the sack Tamsyn had given them, which now only held their empty wine skins and a remaining crust of stale bread. Holding the empty sack, she turned to Jem.

"No! Please!" His plea was almost a cry, and he shrank back against the hard wall, already struggling to breathe at the thought of the rough fabric over his head suffocating him.

Cador and the jailer stared at him. She frowned, but said nothing as she leaned in and tugged Jem's shackles, then Cador's. She dropped the sack on the bench and slammed the door shut with a thud. A key scraped the lock.

Eyes on his own clenched fists, Jem could feel Cador watching him. *Probably thinking how weak and pitiful I am.*

Though Cador's calm question held only concern. "Are you well?"

"Of course! I'm fine." He rattled the chain between his wrists. "All things considered. At least poor Dybri won't have to carry us the rest of the way."

"Mmm."

Silence stretched out, Jem keeping his eyes on his clasped hands. He wanted to scratch his scalp but could only reach if he bent his head low, and Cador would surely find it odd. Not that he should care what Cador thought.

Still, he wanted to keep this strange habit hidden. His skin crawled, the wagon stiflingly hot. Barely any air came in the tiny windows as they lurched onto the road. Cador was still silent, and finally Jem had to look.

Cador watched him steadily, his expression too bland. Too impassive. Jem swallowed hard. Their jailer had at least let them drink water from their cupped hands before loading them into the wagon. His tongue still felt too thick. Cador's gaze had him fidgeting.

When he could take it no longer Jem asked, "What?"

"Why did you say your mother was in danger from Tas?"

Because she is. "I wanted them to help me. They are loyal to their queen."

"Mmm. And you would have them capture me? You'd have me alone in this box while you rode in one of your fancy carriages?"

"Why shouldn't I?" He'd intended the words harshly. Accusingly. Yet they sounded more like a plea. He cringed, fixing his gaze on the wagon's thick door.

After a silence, Cador spoke. "When Bryok…"

Jem winced, looking anywhere else but at Cador as the wagon jounced over a rut. "I'm fine," he mumbled.

"What did they do?"

Squirming, Jem wished he could be anywhere else but discussing *this.* Well, almost anywhere. He only realized he'd reached up to scratch at his scalp when the shackles dug into his wrists with a jolt. He whipped his hands back to his lap.

"Jem…"

"I said I'm fine!" He stared at the dusty, stained floorboards and tried not to think overmuch about the origin of said stains.

"What did they do?"

It was somehow worse that Cador asked gently, not demanding an answer. They had hours to go until they reached the castle. If Cador wouldn't drop it, then *fine*. It was nothing.

"They put a sack over my head. I could barely breathe. I couldn't see. I… I don't wish to repeat the experience."

"Who?" Cador demanded through gritted teeth.

"I'm not sure. Whoever met Austol after he convinced me to go with him instead of Jory. I should have known better. But I didn't trust Jory." He snapped his jaw shut. He was prattling, trying not to remember the suffocating cloth knotted so very tightly around his neck.

"I'll find out who hurt you."

"*You* hurt me." As the cart jostled them violently from side-to-side, Jem thwacked the back of his head. He tried again to reach up, iron biting his wrists. A burst of panic erupted, and he tamped it down.

"I know. I'm sorry. I deserve your scorn."

"You do. We can agree on that."

As much as Jem was dying to get home, there would be so much to tell his mother. He'd have to deal with Cador and his father, and now he'd recklessly let Cador hear him tell the villagers the chieftain was a threat. He'd told them to seize Cador himself. Would he suspect now that Jem planned to have them thrown in the dungeon? He wasn't a stupid man.

Yet he'd stayed and tried to help Jem when he could have

For someone who didn't read much, Cador also seemed to enjoy stretching his imagination. Perhaps that was Jem's influence? It shouldn't please him, yet it did.

Jem nodded. "A marauding woodsman. Dastardly and fierce."

"But Kitto will surprise him. He'll turn the tables."

"Oh, yes."

They both grunted as the wagon hit another hole. It swayed and bumped constantly now, the road apparently in desperate need of repair. At least his heart beat normally again, his breath calm. Yet now Cador winced, his face flushing, sweat damp on his face. They rocked, and he groaned under his breath.

"Are—" Jem was about to say "you," but paused. "Is the marauding woodsman unwell?"

Cador seemed about to deny it, but pressed his fingers to his wrist. "It's like being at sea."

He couldn't deny it pleased him that Cador used the treatment Jem had taught him. "Shouldn't the woodsman be used to motion like this from riding? Surely he rides through the forest on his trusty steed as he…*marauds*."

"Yes, but riding a horse isn't like this." He inhaled sharply as they swayed violently. "It's his one weakness."

Jem thought about giving the woodsman a name, but somehow it fit that he was anonymous and mysterious. "Perhaps he just wants Kitto's sympathy."

"Ah, perhaps." Cador raised an eyebrow. "He's dastardly, after all. And Kitto is so kindhearted."

As the wagon jerked and bounced, they slid around, knees bumping. "Where does the woodsman come from? Presumably nowhere near the sea."

Cador grimaced. "Definitely not. He's from the deepest,

darkest forest of Rew." He kept his fingers to his wrist, closing his eyes and breathing deeply.

"Too bad he's not a merman. I don't think they ever get ill."

"Not ever?"

"Well, there was one time. It was a poison, and Morvoren was beside herself with worry." He recounted the story, enjoying the retelling himself perhaps as much as Cador relished the distraction.

Eventually the road smoothed out, and Cador's nausea seemed to abate. They dozed in silence but for the wagon's rumble and the horses' hoofbeats and whinnies. Soon, Jem would finally be home. There was still so much to worry about—to say the least—but he clung to that comfort and his lone certainty.

He was never leaving Neuvella again.

Chapter Ten

A T FIRST, CADOR thought he had something in his eye. Straining his neck, he peered through the barred window behind him, grateful for the disgustingly hot air that brushed his face. He lifted a hand to shield the sun, the irons thwarting him. He squinted.

No, the structure was real, and as they crested the rise, he could only stare as the castle came into sight. Atop high ground across the valley, it towered over the lush spread of forest. There were no signs of fire or drought here, although the heat was unbearable.

Beyond a stone wall and gates, the castle perched on a hill with a spiral path looped around it. The palace rose to incredible heights in rounded towers of unnaturally colored stone that gleamed blue, red, green, and purple.

A lake shimmered in the valley, sunlight glinting off its peaceful surface. Cador would have given almost anything to be able to dive into the clear blue depths. The awful nausea had subsided, but he was sure he was going to sweat to death in the unbearable heat.

Jem's home was a wonder, though. "This must be your lake."

"I can't see." Jem tugged on his chains, unable to lift himself off the bench high enough to peer through the barred window on his side. Sweat stained his ruined robe. "Is the castle in sight?"

"Yes. And there's a beautiful lake in the valley below."

Chains clanged as Jem jolted. "We're truly here? You can see it?" His face creased in a beaming smile that made Cador want to smile in return. "That's my lake! Can you see my aviary by the shore? I'm sure we're too far still."

"So much color. Even the castle itself."

Jem's smile faltered. "Yes. It's very different from Ergh. We enjoy pretty things. Foolish, I know."

"It wasn't an insult."

Jem didn't answer, and Cador mourned that fleeting smile. Jem squirmed, his chains rattling. If only Cador could hold him close and calm him. It would be a comfort to them both.

He cursed Bryok again, anger and guilt returning. To see Jem's desperate terror in his nightmares—both waking and asleep—was hideous. Cador could only imagine the horror of being kidnapped the way he was, and the question of who had put that sack over Jem's head and stolen him away plagued him.

Could it have been Ruan? Cador's trusted mentor and friend? He'd known every person at the Cliffs of Glaw that night. Even if they'd acted in the interests of the sick children, how could they be so cruel to Jem? Ruan had called him *expendable*, and it boiled Cador's blood to think of it. Yet he'd thought the same when they'd married. Kidnap him, cut off his hand—he hadn't cared.

This was why he couldn't be surprised to hear Jem tell the villagers that Tas was a danger to the queen. To instruct them to capture Cador. He'd surely do the same. No, he'd felt no surprise, but it had hurt all the same. He worried about what exactly Jem was going to tell his mother.

Was Cador heading into a trap? Not that he had any choice

at the moment. Jem had given his word that Cador and Delen could speak to Tas before unpleasant truths were revealed. Yet Cador could hardly blame him if he'd lied.

Worry for Delen returned, and he wondered pointlessly where she and the others were on their journey and if Hedrok was all right. He cursed himself for arguing with Delen before they'd parted. Hopefully, they'd arrive within a day or two. It would be a relief to see Jory and Tas soon, no matter what kind of welcome awaited.

He'd considered running when he'd hidden in the bushes watching Jem's ill-fated encounter with the villagers, but it was impossible. It was his solemn vow to keep Jem safe and happy at any cost, and he would, damn it.

Once the villagers dared put their hands on Jem, Cador had longed for his spear or sword. It was just as well he'd been vastly outnumbered, particularly since some of them wielded axes. They were only protecting their home and their people.

Once they were down in the valley of thick, leafy trees, the journey went quickly, a chorus of birdsong echoing around them. *Jem's friends welcoming him home.* Cador scoffed at himself for the sentimental thought.

He glimpsed a glimmer of the lake through rustling leaves and dreamed again of diving in. Iron dug into his flesh. Crammed in the roasting wagon, slamming over any ruts in the road, he was desperate to get out. Their jailer had given them water a few times on the journey, but not nearly enough. His tongue felt swollen with thirst.

The road up to the base of the castle was steep. It was no wonder Jem was so fit if he'd spent his days going up and down to the lake and his sanctuary. Distant voices and activity drifted from above like bees buzzing, and when Cador craned his neck, the castle seemed to soar all the way to the fluffy clouds.

How had they constructed such a building? The Holy Place had been largely austere and simple but for the vaulted murals above the great hall. Still, Cador could see how men had built it. This? This had to be the work of the gods. Cador could see why so many in Onan believed, if this was the kind of magic they witnessed.

They'd passed villages where he'd spotted homes of two or even three levels, but the tallest towers of the Neuvellan castle had to be ten. *How?* Who lived here? It couldn't only be Jem's family and the servants. Surely the whole population of Cador's bustling home village of Rusk could move in quite comfortably.

Colorful banners fluttered atop the wood and iron gate—a gate the wagon rumbled straight by without so much as a pause before heading down once more. All Cador could see now was the stone wall.

"Where are we going?" Jem strained to see. "We need to go up! To the castle!"

Their jailer ignored his cries, naturally. The wagon banged over a hole, the impact jarring all the way up Cador's spine. For the time being, he didn't care where the fuck they were going as long as he got out of this cursed wagon.

Unsurprisingly, their destination was a prison. Carved into the rock, at least this dungeon would perhaps be cool. The castle loomed high, high above. The guards wore plain cotton uniforms and bored expressions as Jem pleaded their case.

"I'm Prince Jowan!"

The woman who'd driven them rolled her eyes, and the guards didn't even bother responding. As someone led Dybri away, Cador assessed whether he could overpower the guards. Aside from the odd ale-fueled arm wrestle after feasting on fresh

Kenver, the chieftain. Our parents are expecting us. Have you not heard that a rider brought the news of our return?"

The woman yawned widely. "Anyone heard that there's been news of the prince?"

Along with a chorus of denials, one guard said, "He won't be back until the Feast of the Blood Moon. If he ever makes it back. Those barbarians probably roasted him for dinner."

Cador ignored the insult, worry suddenly gnawing with sharp teeth. "Perhaps word of the rider didn't reach you."

They laughed, and a young man grinned. "Oh, we hear of most things. We may not get to swan around the castle, but whispers are like shit. Rolls downhill."

Cador looked to Jem, who clearly shared his concern. Jem said, "His name is Jory. He has wild ginger hair and rode a gray horse. He'd have created a stir, I imagine."

She pointed with a vicious-looking club. "Get moving."

Jem and Cador had no choice but to shuffle into a dim tunnel. The stone floor was unpleasantly damp, and he wished for the hundredth time for his boots. Jem limped beside him.

What had happened to Jory if he truly hadn't arrived? Perhaps he'd only been delayed for some reason. Or lost. Cador told himself not to worry, but his empty stomach twisted.

The nausea wasn't helped by the acrid stench of vomit that greeted them in the dungeon. They were shoved into a dark, empty cell only slightly bigger than the wagon. Cador couldn't see any mess on the dank stone floor, at least. He grimaced at the bucket in the corner, not wanting to even see what might be inside.

The woman locked them in with an ominous clang and screech of metal. Jem called to her, "When will we see the magistrate?"

She was barely visible in the weak light of an oil lamp on the tunnel wall. She shrugged and was gone.

Not wanting to sit after all day in the wagon, Cador slumped against the wall, which at least was cool, if rather slimy. "I guess you never dropped by the dungeon when you brought flowers to the old villagers."

Jem rubbed his face. "Can't say I did. I suppose I knew this was down here, but I never gave it even a passing thought."

"Will this magistrate recognize you?"

"I hope so." He whimpered. "I'm so close. My mother and Santo and everyone are *right there*. Cool water and food! Beds! Yet they're so far out of reach we might as well still be crossing the sea."

"Don't remind me. That damn wagon was nearly as bad." His stomach was still uneasy, and the stench in the cell didn't help. "At least it's cooler down here. Like summer on Ergh. I hate to miss it. The snow will return before we know it."

The *we* had slipped out, and now he thought of Jem with snowflakes caught in his curls, the two of them hiding away in the cottage as the wind raged and the land was blanketed in white. The fire crackling, fresh bread baking on the hearth. Keeping Jem warm with kisses in their bed…

Pacing the stone floor, Cador reminded himself he shouldn't imagine such lovely things. He must keep his mind sharp. Surely their true identities would be discovered soon. Then he'd see Tas and…

And he dreaded it.

If he could just see his parent and drink ale with him and talk of the hunt and laugh about nothing in particular, it would be perfect. But he must tell Tas his son was dead. Not only that, but how he died. Why. Surely Tas would understand that Delen had no choice, but… Bryok was still his child.

The first Tas and Father had adopted. The first they taught to walk and talk and be a future leader. Would Tas expect this failure? No question he'd grieve, but would he be angry with Delen and Cador?

Now Cador would be the next chieftain. *Unless I die too. Delen will do a much better job anyway.* She truly would. She'd surely get Hedrok, Creeda, and the rest of the group to the castle soon. She wouldn't let them get captured. She was too clever for that. He should have told her how clever she was before they parted.

"What?"

He blinked at Jem's question. "What?"

Jem exhaled loudly from where he stood by the iron door. Apparently he didn't want to sit yet either. "You keep sighing, and you're making me nervous pacing like that. It's annoying."

"A thousand apologies," Cador muttered.

"I just—well, what's the matter? Aside from the obvious."

"What concern is it of yours?" As soon as the words were out, he regretted them. Before Jem could snap at him, he added, "I wonder how Delen and the others fare. We argued before parting. I was a prick. I'm sure you're shocked."

A tiny smile tugged Jem's pretty mouth. "Stunned."

"I suppose none of us are perfect. Jory always says—" Worry surged. "Do you think the guards down here truly would have heard if he'd arrived?"

"I don't know. It does make sense. About gossip reaching them." He rubbed his head, wincing. "I'm sure Jory simply got lost or delayed. I hope he isn't in a situation like ours."

They fell into silence, Cador wishing he could tear off the damn robe that felt sweat-crusted to his body. There was nothing stopping him, though Jem would surely object. He chuckled to himself.

"What?"

"Just thinking of how you'd react if I stripped off this robe." He tugged at the open collar. "It's disgusting."

"Don't you dare."

"If I were the marauding woodsman, I'd tear it off without a second thought. Then what would innocent Prince Kitto do?"

"Ignore you."

He laughed. "He wouldn't gasp and avert his eyes as you did on our wedding night?" His laughter died. Cador would give anything to go back. To do it differently.

Jem didn't answer, his arms crossed tightly as he turned to lean his other shoulder against the stone wall. There was a strange sound—low, like a moan. Jem wheeled about. "What are you doing? If you—" His jaw clenched.

"It wasn't me." Cador raised his hands. Listening carefully, he heard it again. "Must be another prisoner."

Standing still, they waited. The next moan was louder and higher, followed by the unmistakable sound of retching. Jem grimaced, edging away from the door. The stench and sticky, humid air made Cador's skin crawl. He dropped the talk of Kitto and the woodsman. Neither of them seemed in the mood for stories.

Sometime later—minutes or hours—Cador couldn't bite back a pained groan of his own as he stretched his arms overhead where he sat. He curved his spine and reached a hand behind him, but he couldn't quite get the cramped muscle.

"What is it?" Sitting by the door with his arms around his knees, Jem watched him with a gaze either concerned or suspicious. Perhaps both. The lamplight from the tunnel flickered, illuminating his honey eyes.

"Nothing." He twisted his arm, but his fingers only grazed the spot.

Jem huffed. "Doesn't seem like nothing."

"If you must know, I was injured. Years ago now. I—" He flushed, glad for the dark.

"What?"

"I was trampled. It's nothing."

"Trampled? By a boar? Gods, with those hooves it wouldn't be nothing. Or a horse?"

He could lie, of course. *Oh yes, it was a beast of an animal! Merciless and mighty! A miracle I survived.* Yet Cador found he didn't want to tell Jem another lie, even one as meaningless. "Goats," he muttered.

"Pardon?"

"I said it was goats. Yes. Goats. Just one, actually. She was flighty and easily frightened. I tripped in the pen and startled her."

Lips pressed tightly, Jem made a choked noise suspiciously like laughter.

"Go on, mock me. Everyone else did at the time. There I was, sprawled out on my stomach, and she ran over me. Kicked me a few times for good measure. There's a spot just beside my shoulder blade. It still cramps at times, especially with too much damn sitting."

His shoulder protested as he bent his arm back. "At home, I can get to it with the handle on the cold storage on the barn floor. I'm sure I look ridiculous, but I can work out the cramp." He gazed around the cell, wincing. "Sadly nothing here can help."

Jem was silent for a few moments. "The marauding woodsman would have told a much more dramatic story."

"Undoubtedly. He'd tell Prince Kitto of an angry boar that took its revenge after the woodsman speared its mate. No, he wouldn't have a spear. Chopped off its head with his ax."

"The unfortunate boar."

"No sympathy for the woodsman? It was kill or be killed. He roasted both boars and fed dozens of hungry children."

"How noble."

"Indeed." Cador grunted, bending his arm back.

Jem sighed. "Oh, here. I—Prince Kitto will never sleep with the fuss you're making."

In the shadows, Cador could barely see him crawling across the cell. His heart skipped as Jem's outstretched fingertips grazed his shoulder. Cador shuffled a bit so Jem could kneel behind him.

He bent forward. "Just to the left. Of my right shoulder, I mean. To the right of my spine." He sounded breathy and nervous and snapped his jaw shut.

Tentatively, Jem poked Cador's back. "Here?"

"Left. There, yes!" He grunted.

Jem massaged the tender spot with his fingers. It was a cruel tease, the cramping muscle needing far more pressure. "Better?"

He should just say yes, but that wouldn't be the truth, would it? "Can you use the heel of your hand? I need more." He inhaled as Jem dug in. "That's it."

In the silence, Cador's breathing sounded too loud. But it really was a relief, like a deep itch finally being scratched. "Harder."

Hearing himself say the word had his bollocks tingling. What had become of him? How did Jem's other hand curling around his ribs for purchase as he leaned in, his thumb digging into the tender spot perfectly, make Cador's head spin? He clearly needed more water.

Jem's breath tickled the back of his neck. They were both reeking and filthy in the piss stink of a dungeon, yet Cador wanted to turn his head and catch Jem's mouth in a kiss so badly he shuddered.

He looked behind, and Jem was *right there*, eyes big in the sliver of distant lamplight. Jem's lips were parted, his hands seizing on Cador as they leaned toward each other—

The shout made them both jump, Cador scrambling to his feet and hauling Jem behind him. His fingers grasped uselessly for his spear or sword as he blinked in the darkness. The sound echoed again, pained and terrible, and he realized it was coming from the other prisoner.

"Shut up!" a guard shouted distantly.

Yet the person—it sounded like a man?—did not shut up.

Nearing footsteps echoed. Cador and Jem shared a glance as the female guard who'd locked them in the cell reappeared with a pail she dropped in front of the iron door, water sloshing over the sides, a ladle poking out. The ladle seemed just small enough to get through the gap in the bars. Cador resisted dropping to his knees and slurping the water desperately.

The other prisoner moaned. "I said shut up!" she barked.

"Who is that?" Cador demanded. It didn't sound like Jory, but... Was it possible?

Elbowing Cador aside and stepping in front of him, Jem said, "They clearly need the healer. Tregereth lives in the castle. I'm sure if you—"

"I don't take fucking orders from the likes of you."

Jem gripped the bars. "When will we see the magistrate?" At the guard's careless shrug, Jem's fingers visibly tightened. "You don't understand. We've been delayed already. King Perran could be marshaling forces to declare war. I demand to see the magistrate at once!"

"Oh, in that case," she muttered. "Don't know what game you're playing, but you're shit out of luck." She disappeared down the dim tunnel.

Cador knew one thing was certain—she wasn't wrong about their luck.

Chapter Eleven

J EM RAN FROM Bryok along the cliff top, the sword's blade gleaming in brilliant moonlight despite Ergh's constant clouds. He was so thirsty. He'd been running for so long. Creeda was there with her bundle of precious sevel twigs, praying to the gods while her boy wailed. Austol watched, saying something Jem couldn't understand.

Just before the sack closed over his head, he realized his right hand was gone. He cradled the bloody, ragged stump, curling into a ball as powerful hands took hold—

"Jem! Wake up."

It was pitch dark, but he knew that voice. He knew that warm touch.

Relief flowed through him like sweet summer mead as he slumped against Cador, allowing himself to be eased up until he sat sideways in Cador's lap. He'd permit the comfort just for a minute. His hip and shoulder ached from where he'd curled on the stone cell floor, and he gasped for breath as the nightmare receded.

Cador rubbed his back rhythmically. "You're safe."

Jem's ragged breath caught. How he longed to believe that was true. Hard to believe when he was locked in his own dungeons with the man who'd originally conspired to have him maimed. He wrung his hands together, feeling the solid bones of his fingers. He raked his nails briefly over his scalp.

Though he should have, Jem couldn't bear to shove his way out of Cador's embrace. He allowed himself to rest.

"As safe as possible locked in a dark dungeon, that is," Cador added, clearly trying for humor.

Jem found himself smiling. "It's a relative thing these days." His voice sounded scraped raw. "Was I screaming?"

"No, that was our neighbor. You need water though."

Jem was about to protest, not wanting to move an inch from Cador's lap, but apparently they were close enough to the barred door that Cador could grab the ladle, mumbling to himself as he did.

"Here."

They fumbled a bit, fingers touching as they felt in the darkness, Jem finally grasping the ladle. Cador held a hand to the back of his head, his thumb stroking the tip of Jem's spine as Jem gulped the tepid water, spilling half on his face. It dribbled down his throat, but he didn't mind. Cador refilled the ladle, and Jem drank again.

He jumped, spilling more water as the other prisoner cried out. "It's all right," Jem called. "I'll get you out of here soon. You'll see Tregereth, the healer."

His words seemed to soothe them for the moment. Jem squinted, but could see only blackness. "Strange that the guards let the oil in the lamp burn out."

"Mmm."

"How long did I sleep? What time is it?"

"No more than a few hours. I'm not sure. It must be midnight by now. But underground, it could be noon and we'd be none the wiser."

Jem shivered. He didn't like that thought for some reason. Cador stroked his back again gently.

Cador said, "Now we just need a merman to come to our rescue."

"Yes."

"Unless Prince Kitto has a brilliant idea."

"Surely the woodsman does. He's battled boar, after all. And goats."

A tremor rolled through Cador as he laughed softly. Jem breathed normally now, and it was time to get off Cador's lap and recover some dignity. Yet he was so comfortable for the first time in ages.

"How did the woodsman become a marauder?"

"Hmm. It's quite a tale."

And Jem let him tell it, curled on Cador's lap, comforted by the familiar rumble of his voice. He let himself remember two words he'd heard atop the Cliffs of Glaw—words he'd done his best to forget.

My love.

No matter how wonderful it would be to believe those two small, simple words were spoken truly, Jem couldn't let himself be a fool again. No matter how tenderly Cador held him now in the darkness, spinning a disjointed tale that made little sense for no other reason than to comfort.

"Then the woodsman... Well, he was angry, of course. So he..."

Jem was about to make a suggestion when a sharp *rap-rap-rap* sounded in the distance, quickly growing louder. Nearer. Jem scrambled up, Cador fumbling in the darkness to loom in front of him.

"Stay behind me," he whispered.

"Yes, obviously!"

He blinked at an orange glow, peeking around Cador's bulk

as a swaying lantern came into view held by a frantic-looking guard. The sharp footsteps rang out, Jem's mother emerging from the shadows.

"Mother!" Jem's knees almost buckled in relief as he stepped around Cador.

Dark hair curling loose down her back, clad only in her nightgown with a flowing robe cinched tightly around her slim waist, she strode to the cell door, her metal-heeled slippers ringing on the dank stone. Mouth agape and eyes wide, she stared, shaking her head as if she couldn't believe what she was seeing.

She didn't wear her golden crown, and her brown skin so much like Jem's own glistened at her hairline with a faint sheen of sweat as though she'd exerted herself.

The young male guard was already struggling with the key, bumbling and dropping it with a *clang* as she hissed, "Open this door at once!"

The female guard from earlier appeared with another lantern. She elbowed him out of the way and used her key to open the cell in the swaying light. Jem hurtled into his mother's arms. Lavender filled his nose, tears prickling his eyes. *Please let this be real and not a dream.*

"Oh, my darling. My poor boy." She clung to him. "Are you hurt?"

Yes! He wanted to scream it. He'd never been hurt so much in his life. But he shook his head against her shoulder before forcing himself to step back and stand up straight.

"Only tired and hungry. We—" He looked behind at Cador still inside the cell. Cador watched him with a flat expression. Waiting.

Jem couldn't breathe. Here was his chance. Slam the door

and twist the key. Lock Cador in the dungeon and haul his tas down. Make them pay for plotting to hurt him, for their lies. Yet now that the moment had arrived, now that he stood before his mother again...

She looked from him to Cador and back again, concern pinching her bare face, her eyes and lips not painted with her usual makeup. Jem couldn't remember the last time he'd seen her so unguarded, the lack of makeup somehow making her seem younger rather than older. He thought of how marrying Cador was the first princely duty she'd entrusted him with.

He couldn't disappoint her. He couldn't fail. And to help Ergh's children, he must put aside his own needs.

Jem said, "We told them who we were, but they wouldn't believe us." He extended his hand to Cador, who stepped from the cell and grasped it tightly, his palm clammy.

What are you doing? Tell her!

She would believe him—of course she would. Indeed, she eyed Cador suspiciously. But Jem couldn't make himself say it. It made no sense, but he felt like he'd failed somehow, though he'd done nothing wrong.

Most of all, he couldn't leave Cador in the stinking darkness.

Perhaps he truly was weak, and this was precisely why the chieftain had considered him nothing but a pawn. Yet Jem took Cador's hand as he had in the black tunnel beneath the Holy Place. He couldn't abandon him to the dungeon. Not now at least.

If not now, when?

The guards fell all over themselves apologizing, and the queen silenced them with an impatient flick of her hand. "Enough! You're lucky my maid woke me with gossip, knowing how concerned I've been since we learned my son had returned early from Ergh."

"Oh!" Jem sighed in relief. "Jory did arrive to tell you?" The dungeon guards weren't as well informed as they thought. "He is well?"

Mother brushed back Jem's hair from his forehead. "Yes, albeit exhausted. Still, he insisted on accompanying the chieftain north."

"Tas isn't here?" Cador exhaled sharply. "But…"

She sighed. "I'm afraid he's gone to find you. When we received word, he was beside himself with worry. I tried to convince him to stay, but…" She smiled softly, pressing a kiss to Jem's head. "I can understand a parent's desire to see their children safe and sound with their own eyes. I sent my son Locryn with them in my stead."

Jem rubbed his face. "Gods, nothing has gone to plan. We'll all have run pell-mell over Onan by the time we're reunited."

"I'll send riders immediately to fetch your brother and the chieftain back," Mother said. "My darling, don't fret. I think bathing and rest is an immediate necessity, yes?"

She glanced at the guards. "Send word to have Prince Jowan's bath readied." She frowned at Jem. "We have no appropriate marital chamber prepared, and it's the middle of the night."

After another moment of debate, Jem said, "We'll be fine in my room." He smiled. "I've missed it." That much was certainly true.

"Of course, my dearest. Now let's leave this place."

A groan echoed, and Jem said, "You must send the healer to see the other prisoner. They have been quite unwell."

Mother nodded to the female guard. "See to it."

Jem realized he was still holding Cador's hand as they made

their way through the dungeon's tunnel. He hadn't imagined touching Cador could ever feel so natural again. He tugged his hand free. It was unwise to let himself get too comfortable.

By the time they were outside in the fresh night air, Jem limped, his cut heel throbbing once more. Mother narrowed her gaze. "You said you were unhurt."

"Oh, it's just a cut."

She looked between him and Cador. "Mmm." To another harried-looking guard, she snapped, "Tell the healer to see to Prince Jowan as well."

An open carriage awaited them, and Jem had to admit he was glad not to have to trudge all the way up to the castle. He sat wedged beside Cador's bulk, his mother on the seat across watching them with a mild expression Jem knew hid a whirlwind of thoughts.

"What have you heard of King Perran?" Jem asked.

Her face soured. "I suspect he means to attack us, and we are preparing accordingly. We'll discuss it once you've recovered from your journey."

Jem couldn't deny his relief at postponing that discussion. He was so very tired, and his mother likely already knew more than he did thanks to her spies.

"You haven't had fires here?" Cador asked.

"No, praise the gods," she said. "It has been certainly drier than usual, but we've been extremely fortunate. Summer is almost over, so we're hoping the rains will come any day now."

Another tense silence descended, broken only by the clatter of hooves and creak of the carriage as it bore them up the steep, winding slope. Jem gazed up at the castle, joy fizzing through him.

So many times he'd run up this hill after a day with his

hatchlings by the lake. Stars blanketed the sky, and he breathed the sweet, clean air deeply.

Home.

At the castle, the old housekeeper—who'd clearly been roused from her bed—greeted him fondly, and Mother bade her to show Cador to Jem's chamber, holding Jem back with a firm hand on his arm.

As ridiculous as he felt standing in the castle's grand foyer in his ratty, torn, and stained cleric robe with his feet dirty and bare, at least he and his mother were soon alone. In the day, the foyer was staffed and bustling, and it was strange to be there in the wee hours.

Mother squeezed Jem's hands, meeting his gaze intensely. "My darling. I've been so worried about you. Tell me the truth. Did that beast hurt you?"

He opened and closed his mouth, then shook his head. "I'm fine."

Her nostrils flared. "*Jem.*"

Without warning, resentment surged through the desire to make her proud. "You were the one who forced me to marry him!" His words rang off the grand entrance's tile mosaic. "Where was all this concern when you shipped me off to Ergh alone?"

He waited for her to speak of his princely duties, but she only watched him silently before asking, "Has he hurt you? Did he force you to return to Onan? For what purpose? You're safe from him now. Shall I call the guard? There's room in the dungeon."

The tug of war inside him raged, now the desire to punish Cador and then to protect and defend him pulling Jem this way and that. "No. Things were not as we were led to believe in

Ergh, but I'm all right."

"I don't think I believe you." She gripped his hands.

"I've struggled. It's been very difficult. But I've prevailed, and now Cador and I have a shared goal in returning early. I'm not in danger from him."

After a moment, she nodded. "If you insist, I'll leave it for now."

"Yes. There are more important things we must deal with. I hardly know where to start."

Face softening, she pulled him into a welcome, warm embrace. "It can wait until you've rested." She leaned back, nose wrinkling. "Once you're not so...bedraggled."

"I'm amazed you're willing to hug me in this revolting state."

Smiling, she took his face in her hands. "My darling, I'd jump into the pig pen if it meant holding you again. Actually, you look a bit as you did that time you traipsed through the mud to rescue that dillywig with a broken wing. Do you remember?"

He laughed, and it was *wonderful.* "How could I forget? Father was furious since the clerics were visiting and I was late to the feast."

"You still had dirt under your fingernails and smudged on your chin even once I banished you to get clean."

"Is everyone well? I can't wait to see them." Especially Santo, but he didn't say that aloud.

"Yes, Pasco's and Locryn's wives and children are safe down at the summer house on the shore. Santo and Arthek are well, but worried about you, of course. Pasco as well, but I let them all sleep. I didn't want to raise hopes unnecessarily, and with your father you know it would take an army to wake him, so it was easy for me to slip away."

Jem was dubious his brother Pasco would worry overmuch about him, but didn't argue. The mention of armies returned his thoughts to King Perran, then Ergh and Hedrok and the terrible suffering. Had the healing waters helped? Were Delen and the others far from the castle? Oh, and the clerics!

"Most of the clerics had left the Holy Place before we arrived."

"Ysella is here, yes. We are coordinating." She paused. "Are you sure Cador is not a threat?"

He hesitated. "I'm sure. For the moment, at least."

Her frown didn't dissipate, but she nodded. "You're home now, my darling. Everything will be all right. Rest and stop worrying."

Nose full of lavender, Jem hugged his mother and prayed it was true.

incredible tapestry of a seascape covering another wall.

He was likely to break anything he touched. It all looked so delicate. Of course, that's what he'd first thought of Jem, and now he knew Jem's strength and resilience.

What is he telling his mother?

Cador couldn't let himself worry about it. Jem could have left him to rot in the dungeon and didn't, and for the moment, he should simply be grateful. His gaze found the bed—not that he could have overlooked it given the massive size. It even had its own roof of fancy purple fabric.

The four posters were carved of the same cherry wood as the table in a swirling pattern, the pink sheets and pillows a silk that looked impossibly soft. He resisted running a dirty hand over the material and shut down thoughts of Jem between those sheets pleasuring himself with his candle…

He whirled back to face the door, forcing control. The fireplace loomed on the right, and to the left was a sitting area of padded chairs and tasseled footrests, the wall dominated by shelfs of books, and books, and even more books.

Guilt thundered back as he remembered how carelessly— how callously—he'd tossed Jem's beloved books to the dirt before they left for Ergh.

To his shock, the men returned with *another* tub of steaming water, and soon the metal bath was full and the servants departed. He waited for Jem, trying not to worry about what he was discussing with the queen. Trying not to worry about Tas and Jory. Delen, Hedrok, Kensa, Creeda—so many of his people were still at large on the mainland.

White bubbles of frothy soap covered the water, a scented oil that was fresh and sweet swirling on top. Such decadence, and in the dead of night! He was torn between scorn—*this* sort of thing was why the mainlanders were so soft and useless—and the urge to sink into this bit of heaven. After all, it would be wrong for it to go to waste after the servants' efforts.

He supposed this luxury was commonplace for royalty. Jem had grown up here, pampered and spoiled. Cador remembered his horror at pissing outdoors and could understand it now. Though it seemed so long ago, and not at all like the Jem he knew now. His Jem was—

Not mine.

"Go on," Jem said from the doorway.

"It's your bath. I'll use it after. With all these fine soaps I'll be cleaner than I ever have been."

Jem hesitated. "Let's just—there's plenty of room." He motioned to the tub. "I don't want to disturb the poor servants again when they should be sleeping, and the healer will be here soon to bandage my foot. And we must sleep, so let's just get this over with. We need to bathe."

Cador couldn't argue with that. He yanked off the robe, which was fit to be burned. From the corner of his eye, he could see Jem very decidedly *not* watching him undress, arms crossed and gaze on the ceiling.

As wonderful as the cool waters of the Holy Place had felt, this steamy, soapy bath had Cador groaning in pleasure as he lowered himself into the tub. He sank down, arching his back to wet his hair in the suds.

The flared end of the tub was high enough for him to rest his head against, the metal warm. The earlier ache in his back eased even more in the delicious heat. He rolled his shoulders with satisfaction.

"Are you going to tease me?" Jem asked tightly. "Because I'm tired, and I want to get clean."

After a moment of confusion, Cador realized his groans sounded like the kind he made when fucking. Remembering how he'd taunted Jem at the Holy Place, he flushed with guilt. "No. I swear it."

Jem met his gaze for a moment, and Cador expected him to ask why he should believe a single vow he made now. But Jem only nodded tensely. He'd seemed so relaxed and relieved to see his mother again, and Cador hated that it was his presence that put the hunch back in Jem's shoulders.

He bent his legs, knees poking out of the suds. "There's plenty of room, as you said. I'll behave."

Slim fingers on the ruined hem of the cleric robe, Jem paused. Cador almost laughed at this bashfulness given the things they'd done. How he'd seen Jem naked dozens of times now, most recently in the baths at the Holy Place.

Yet his mind filled with images of the first time—how he'd watched Jem laid utterly bare with need, licking Cador's seed from the cottage floor…

The laughter died in his throat, and he had to close his eyes against the wave of forlorn regret. "Go on," he said, his voice too loud. He cleared his throat. "I won't look."

He listened to the rustle of fabric. He felt the ripple of water as Jem stepped one foot in with a soft *slosh*. Gripped the sides of the tub when a faint moan of pleasure escaped Jem as he sank fully, the warm suds surging over Cador's nipples all the way to his armpits.

Jem's toes brushed his, and Cador opened his eyes. Jem sat against the other end of the tub, clutching his knees to his chest, watching Cador as though he was a sarf that would bite. Only an hour or two ago, he'd been curled on Cador's lap, safe in his arms…

As enormous as the tub was, they had to be smart about it if Jem didn't want to even brush against him. Cador moved his feet to the edges and let his knees fall open to rest against the sides of the tub, which flared out from the bottom.

Jem's throat bobbed. Tentatively, he stretched out his legs. If he put them in Cador's lap, he could straighten them. Still, there was enough room for Jem to scoot low and duck his head back, plugging his nose as he submerged completely.

Wiping his face, Jem rested back against his end of the tub, bubbles clinging to his smooth chin, bent knees poking out. Cador was certain the tips of Jem's toes were unbearably close to his bollocks. That if Jem only moved an inch, he could rub at Cador's tender flesh…

He wouldn't, though. This was as close as Cador could hope to get. He tamped down his lust, his foolish cock eager to be buried inside Jem's perfect body. His prick would have to get used to disappointment.

He scoffed at himself, acting like his cock had a mind of its own. He really did need sleep. Still, his stubborn, unruly prick nagged, reminding him how easy it would be to lift Jem over his lap and—

Squeezing his eyes shut, Cador regained control. He'd promised Jem not to taunt him, and even if the bubbles hid his erection, it wasn't allowed. He breathed the sweet fragrance of the water deeply and asked, "Is this a flower?"

After a few moments, Jem answered, "Roses."

"Mmm." It was familiar, though Cador was sure he'd never seen a rose.

It should have been strange to share a bath together, but as the water cooled, it was oddly peaceful to listen to the rhythm of Jem's steady breathing. He told himself to stay awake and appreciate it, for one day he'd be alone again on Ergh. Alone in his cottage, with only the howling winter wind. For now that Jem was home in such comfort, how could Cador hope to win him over?

"Feels wrong to be resting," Cador blurted. He waved a hand at the colorful room. "To be in a place like this while my family is out there. While Hedrok suffers. I should get dressed and go find them."

"Then they'll arrive hours after you leave, and you'll have missed them on the road somehow, and we'll all keep spinning in circles."

He grunted. Jem had a point. And he was so, so tired. The last time he'd felt that weary, he'd caught a terrible fever one winter and had been trapped by a blizzard for a week, shivering yet burning with barely the strength to drink water. Merely drawing the bucket from the well had exhausted him so much he'd slept for a whole day. Yet he wasn't ill now, and after a good night's sleep, he should be ready to mount up.

"Besides, what would you wear? That filthy old cleric's robe?"

He grimaced. "Those rags need to be burned."

"No arguments here. But really, I think it's best to stay put, at least for a few days while we figure out what to do."

We. Cador silently reveled in the word.

Jem added, "Though I'm sorry Jory and your father aren't here."

"I'm not." Had he just said that aloud? He rubbed a damp hand over his face. "What I mean is—" He should stop talking and quit while he was ahead. Not that he was.

"What?" Jem asked softly.

"I…" He shouldn't confess such a shameful thought, yet the

words spilled out under Jem's kind gaze. "If Tas and Delen find each other before reaching the castle, she'll have to tell him about Bryok. It would be done, and I wouldn't have to bear it." He shook his head. "Fucking cowardly, I know."

"Understandable, though."

He didn't deserve Jem's understanding but greedily embraced it. "Delen is just so much better at saying the right thing. She'd make a far better chieftain than I ever will. What kind of leader am I? I abandoned her and my people to chase after you."

Jem blinked. He watched Cador in the yellow lamplight, droplets of water clinging to his thick lashes. It seemed he would say something, but then the moment passed, and he closed his eyes, leaning back against the tub once more. Cador watched him, his own eyes growing heavy.

When he woke, the water was cold and Jem was gone. Only one lamp still flickered, the others burned out. A thick towel sat folded on a stool, along with a silky nightshirt like the kind Jem preferred.

Though this one was far too big for Jem, the ends barely grazed Cador's knees. It was all he had, though he'd have preferred greatly to go naked. But Jem wouldn't have left it for him if he didn't want him to wear it.

Creeping into the bedchamber, Cador held his breath. Jem's curls still appeared damp on his pillow, his lips parted. The satin sheets tucked around him were the palest pink. The bed was huge under its ridiculous canopy, Jem small and defenseless in sleep.

This is where he belongs.

Though he was clean and wearing a fancy Southern nightshirt, Cador felt again like an intruder. An impostor with no place in Jem's bed, even if it was so big they could easily sleep without coming near each other. Even if there was another pillow beside Jem's, surely it wasn't an invitation.

The rug was so thick Cador didn't need a pillow. He stretched out on his back and ordered himself to sleep. Yet his mind galloped. How far away were Tas and Jory? How did Hedrok fare? Could he be saved? What would Tas think of...everything?

Jem murmured in his sleep, the sheets rustling. Cador couldn't see him, but imagined Jem rolling over, pillowing his head on his hands. If they shared the bed, he'd draw Jem against his side and feel the tickle of his breath across his chest.

Just be glad you're not in the fucking dungeon.

Morning would come not soon enough and all too quickly.

Chapter Thirteen

T HE PURPLE CANOPY almost shimmered in the sunlight. Jem blinked up at the fine silk atop his bed as he had countless other mornings. He typically woke long before the sun was this high in the sky, heating his room.

He'd kicked off the sheets, and now he starfished on the soft mattress, stretching his aching limbs. He could almost believe he'd overexerted himself swimming, and this was just another easy, lazy day at the castle.

Almost, but not quite with his husband snoring softly on the rug to Jem's left.

Still, it was the first time in too long that he'd actually slept without slipping into nightmares of rough hands and suffocating with a sack over his head, his hand hacked away in a rush of endless blood. Stretched out on his familiar, wonderful bed, it could almost seem like a ghastly dream.

Almost.

He'd longed to wake in his own bed again too many times to count, but the relaxation quickly dissipated as his mind helpfully cataloged the many items he had to worry about. In great detail. He wasn't sure how long he'd been scratching his scalp before he dug in too deeply, wincing. He fisted his hands, then rolled to the edge of the bed and tucked them under his cheek.

He peeked down at Cador on the cream and purple swirling-patterned rug, sleeping on his back with one arm over his head and legs parted. Jem was surprised Cador had deigned to wear the nightshirt one of the servants had fetched—not that it did much to hide his body.

Especially not when it was rucked up to one hip, the shadow of coarse hair and his cock stark through the thin white silk. His heavy bollocks peeked out below the crooked hem.

What would happen if Jem knelt between his legs and bent his head to lick and suck that meaty flesh? His mouth practically watered at the thought, his morning erection surging. How wonderful it would be to slake his desire and find release. To not have to think and only feel pleasure. To rut like animals with no place for the litany of worries circling his mind.

A rapid-fire knock was the only warning before Santo thrust open the chamber door and burst inside. They were wearing skirts today, and the delicate layers swished around their shins, gauzy in the brilliant sunlight streaming in. Jem shoved himself up to sitting, realizing he'd clearly forgotten to bolt the door.

Santo's breathless smile froze, then vanished as they looked between Jem on the bed and Cador now sitting bolt upright on the floor, his right hand grasping the air as if seeking a weapon.

Crestfallen, Santo dropped their gaze. "Forgive me. Too eager to see my baby brother. I forgot myself." Their long dark curls were up in a simple ponytail and bronze bracelets shone on their brown skin, clinking as they clasped their hands.

Cador blinked around the room in apparent confusion. He pushed to his feet, fiddling with the neck of the pale nightshirt before crossing his arms. Jem couldn't recall ever seeing him look so unsure.

Santo flashed Jem a smile. "My Arthek discovered a dillywig with a broken wing last week. She's recovering safely in the aviary. Shall we stroll down to check on her after your breakfast? Ah, here it is."

As Jem beamed at the thought of visiting the aviary—such an enticingly normal activity—two servants entered with trays of steaming tea, fresh juices, grilled meat, warm bread, and all Jem's favorite pastries. They brought the trays to Jem's little breakfast table by the window, bowing to him as they passed. Cador shifted from foot to foot, arms still crossed.

"I'll come back to fetch you at the hour," Santo said. "This time, I'll wait for permission to enter." They turned their smile to Cador. "I apologize again."

"It's fine," he said gruffly.

"Your marital chamber will be ready soon. I've raided the guest rooms and given the decorating instructions."

"Oh! Thank you," Jem said. "Already?"

"I needed something to occupy me while you slept the morning away. It'll be a bit of a hodgepodge, and of course you can change everything once you settle in. I corralled the chamber next door since I know you love the sunshine. I'm surprised you stayed abed as long as you did, but obviously you were exhausted." Their face pinched. "Oh, Jem. How I missed you."

Jem launched off the bed, past Cador and into Santo's familiar embrace. They smelled faintly of the spicy cinnamon perfume their husband loved. "You've no idea."

Santo squeezed him, tucking Jem's head against their shoulder. They ran a hand over Jem's unruly curls, and Jem jerked back guiltily, his scalp sensitive. Santo's sculpted brows met, but they forced a smile and a light tone.

"Cador, our mother is planning a welcome feast tonight. It's a shame your father ran off to find you. We'll just have to have another feast when he returns!"

Jem blinked in surprise. There were so many vital issues to discuss—the disease, the sevels, the wildfires, the clerics, mad King Perran—where to begin? It surely didn't seem the time for a feast. He'd already slept ridiculously late. Not that he didn't appreciate the welcome rest, but… Well, half the day was gone.

Cador glanced at Jem, then nodded to Santo, who exited with the servants after kissing Jem's cheek. "Decorating and feasting," Cador muttered.

Jem's spine stiffened despite his own reservations. "It's only natural to welcome us."

"So frivolous." He pushed up the thin sleeves of his night-shirt. "I need real clothes."

Jem's immediate urge was to again take offense, but he fought it, remembering how out of sorts he'd felt when he first arrived on Ergh. "I'll make sure they bring you a wide selection." He sat at the table, inhaling the salty aroma of sizzling meat. He was suddenly starving. "Come and eat unless you're truly that offended by the idea of feasting." He speared a sausage and groaned at the fatty deliciousness.

"We have more important things to worry about than food."

Jem's spike of irritation gave way to laughter as Cador's stomach growled so loudly it could likely be heard throughout the castle. "Are you truly going to stand there like a stubborn oaf watching me eat?"

Face flushing pink, Cador recrossed his arms. "I don't need to eat."

Through a mouthful of warm, buttered bread, Jem said, "Right, fierce hunters of Ergh are too tough for mere hunger. More for me!" If Cador was going to be ridiculous, Jem would eat every last bite even if it made him ill. Which he realized was also ridiculous.

Pretending he wasn't watching Cador from the corner of his eye, he dipped his sausage in honey, moaning at the sweet, salty flavor. He licked a sticky drop from the corner of his mouth. It had been months since he'd eaten such rich food, and he forced himself to take a breath and sip the hot, sweet tea. Cador had rounded the bed toward the bathroom, but still lingered in the door.

Sighing, Jem turned to him, but any words died in his throat. The sunlight streaming in through the bathroom's tall windows behind Cador outlined his muscular body in the thin nightshirt, making the white fabric all but invisible.

He spun back and shoved a roasted potato in his mouth. Between the rich flavors and the burst of lust, sitting on a plush chair with blue skies through the wide expanse of windows, his body hummed with too much pleasure.

When Cador returned from the bathroom and still didn't join him at the table, Jem sighed again. "If you don't help me eat this, I fear I'll devour it all." Cador really did need to eat, and Jem was starting to feel uncomfortably full.

Cador pulled out the other chair and sat on it hesitantly as though he thought he might break the curved, gleaming wood or burst the pale green cushioned seat. And his bulk was rather incongruous.

How strange it was for Jem to finally wake in his chamber again and sit at his familiar table with its view of distant verdant hills across the valley, yet to have Cador there.

His gaze returned to what he could see of his bookshelf beyond the bed's canopy. There were hundreds of books there, though he'd searched last night and his favorites Cador had dumped on the road had not been miraculously returned. He could replace them with new copies, but he still mourned those particular worn and well-read pages.

Reaching for a sausage, Cador stopped and picked up a fork. He still seemed grudging as he took a bite, but his eyes practically rolled up as he swallowed. Any stubborn hesitation vanished, and he gnawed off a bite of warm bread, licking the hot butter from his fingers. Jem's inappropriate arousal throbbed between his legs. It was all he could do not to climb over the table onto Cador's lap.

He ate a flaky, fruity pastry instead. It had been so long since his body had found release. It made sense that the rich food was overwhelming him. Confusing him. He'd have to find some time alone to pleasure himself so he didn't do anything reckless.

Besides, there were too many important matters to face. He had to tell his mother everything. And with that thought, his breakfast threatened to curdle in his stomach. He poured a glass of cool water and sipped.

"What?" Cador asked, swallowing a bite. "Are you really making yourself sick?"

An odd pulse of guilt made Jem's head tingle. He hadn't scratched very hard that morning. Now that he was home, of course he would stop the strange habit. He just had to tell his mother everything, and she'd take control. He wouldn't have to worry anymore.

"I confess it is strange to be talking of feasting and decorating. We must tell my mother what Treeve said. And of course tell her of the sevels and the disease. I shouldn't be wasting time going to the aviary with Santo."

"And what will you tell her of my tas's scheming? His lies?"

Jem toyed with his spoon, the cool metal perfectly smooth under his fingertips. "I gave my word that you and Delen could tell Kenver about Bryok before you face my mother." Naturally, he didn't add that he'd fully intended to ignore that promise. He'd fully intended to have them locked in the dungeon but here Cador sat at his breakfast table.

It wasn't too late. He could call for the guards and have Cador hauled away. But he wasn't going to, and it was time to stop feigning it was even a possibility. No matter how much Cador had hurt him, Jem couldn't bear to see him locked up. He shuddered to think of the dark, reeking dungeon. He couldn't do it.

"Are you planning to continue pretending that we're..." Cador motioned vaguely between them. "Wed?"

"We are, aren't we?" He flexed his right hand and displayed the brand. "Until we die is how the vows went, if I recall." He formed a fist. "Does it still count if the brand is gone?"

"*Yes.*" The word was low. Urgent. Cador leaned closer across the table. "Jem..."

"Don't. We've said it all before." He shoved too many grapes into his mouth and tried not to think of the ragged stump that remained of his arm in his nightmares.

"Then why pretend? You could have told your mother last night to give me another room. Any would do."

It was a fair question. He swallowed the grapes, truly too full now. "I don't want to talk about it. There's so much else already. I'll have my hands full with Santo's questions. And..." It really was laughable, but he couldn't shake the feeling. "This was the first true duty my mother gave me. I don't want to admit failure."

Cador's throat bobbed. Jem had the sudden urge to touch his growing beard. "You aren't the one who failed."

Picking up the spoon again, Jem squeezed it. "Still. It will be

glared at Pasco.

Pasco shrugged his broad shoulders. He wore the typical breeches, tall boots, and silk shirt, this one in an emerald green that complemented his brown skin. The whole family was fond of jewel tones, and thus it was the fashion for most in Neuvella. Jem had forgotten how wonderful it was to see so much color as opposed to Ergh's monotones.

And as much as he enjoyed the splendor, he frowned as he asked his mother, "Is a feast really appropriate? We have very serious matters to discuss."

"And we will, my darling." She cupped his cheek and kissed his forehead before lowering her voice. "But we must assure everyone here at the castle and the surrounding villages that all is well. That you were simply homesick and nothing is amiss. The word will spread through Neuvella as it always does eventually. There is too much risk of panic, and that won't help a bit."

As if on cue, a pair of courtiers in long, colorful dresses approached. "Prince Jowan, how lovely to see you!"

Jem painted on a smile and greeted them, exchanging pleasantries. He honestly had never given any thought to the other people who lived in the castle and nearby. There had just always been a flurry of activity and people around—courtiers and advisers, the servants and varied staff. He'd accepted it all without question.

The courtiers moved along, whispering with heads close, and Jem's mother gave him another kiss. "We mustn't worry anyone unnecessarily. And after your terrible journey, you deserve a day of rest."

He tugged her farther away into a nearby alcove, aware of Father, Pasco, and Santo watching closely, though they gave Jem and Mother space. "I must tell you…"

She brushed back one of his curls. "Yes, my dearest?"

Now here was the moment he'd waited for, yet Jem's mind stuttered like a wagon wheel hitting a rut. "It's, well…" He rubbed his face. "I don't know where to begin."

"Shh. It's all right. You don't need to worry. You're home and safe, and I'll take care of everything."

Oh, these sweet words he'd longed to hear! But no. He wasn't a pampered child anymore. As much as he'd assured himself that once he was home he could hand off all responsibility to his mother, he couldn't. More than that—he didn't want to.

Clearing his throat, he started with the most pressing problem. "King Perran is sowing seeds of discord in his people that could spread through Onan. Blaming Ergh for the fires. We found out when we arrived at the Holy Place and found Prince Treeve already there. He thinks his father has lost his mind. King Perran arrived shortly after, and Prince Treeve helped us flee thinking his father might kill us. The man is unstable."

She flattened her lips. "We've heard reports of this. Tell me more."

Jem relayed all Treeve had revealed, adding, "He seemed truthful." *Though I've been fooled before.*

"How asinine of Perran to believe I'd start wildfires in the Valley of the Gods. Or that I'd put crops at risk?" She grunted in disgust. "That damn man. He's infuriating. I've offered relief for the displaced victims of the fires, and he hasn't bothered to respond."

"Infuriating indeed. And regarding the sevel crop, there's even more to discuss."

"Your majesty, the holy ones await you." The queen's loyal

assistant murmured from where she'd suddenly appeared by his mother's elbow.

Jem's mother sighed. "I promised Ysella your father and I would attend a special prayer and offering to the gods at the temple in the village."

Jem couldn't bite back a groan. "That sounds torturous. But I should accompany you. Then we can discuss everything I learned on Ergh."

"Darling, there's no need for you to suffer through all that now. It's already afternoon, and we must prepare for the feast. Everything else will have to wait. We'll have plenty of time tomorrow to discuss what you learned on Ergh, and I'll dispatch another regiment north to monitor Perran in the meantime."

"Mother, forget the prayers and feasting. It's all for show anyway."

She laughed humorlessly. "The 'show' is half of what leadership is all about. More than half. You relax, my dearest. Spend time with Santo and catch your breath. We must keep our people assured that there's no need to worry."

Jem supposed that as long as she knew Perran could be on the move, the truth about Cador's father and the sevels and disease could wait a day. Hedrok was being examined by the healer in Gwels, and it would be tomorrow at the earliest before Delen and the others arrived.

What was the harm in taking a breath as Mother said? There was so much to think about, and… And he didn't *want* to think. He was so tired. He didn't want to remember the kidnapping and talk about the plans for his dismemberment and again feel the pain of Cador's betrayal.

Mother kissed him tenderly. "Leave it to me, my sweet boy."

Stepping forward, Santo smiled brightly. "All right, we'll see you all soon enough at the feast. Let's go to the aviary!"

Pasco slapped Jem on the back. "Go on. There's a little surprise waiting for you. You'll thank me later. Profusely."

Before Jem could hope to guess what Pasco was talking about—though it was surely some prank—Santo took his hand and tugged him along.

He reveled in the sun on his face as he and Santo practically skipped down the curving path from the castle. The healer had applied salve to the cut on his heel and bandaged it tightly, and he was able to ignore any lingering ache. He realized belatedly that Cador wouldn't know his way from Jem's chamber once he had some clothing, but surely he would ask for help.

He snorted in his mind. Or, Cador would roam the corridors, pretending he knew the way and stubbornly refusing to show any uncertainty. Or he'd stay holed up in Jem's chamber all alone—which shouldn't make Jem feel guilty. It was far better than the dungeon.

Once he and Santo reached the ground, it wasn't long before they disappeared from view beneath the arching branches and sun-dappled leaves of the lush forest. It was so different from Ergh's dense, forbidding evergreens, airier and livelier, birds singing in a chorus with cicadas and frogs, leaves rustling in the warm breeze. He inhaled the sweet, humid air gratefully.

Santo glanced around and squeezed Jem's fingers. "All right. Tell me."

The momentary peace disintegrated into dust. "There's so much. And some of it I cannot tell you. Not yet."

"Hmm. To do with why you've suddenly returned?"

"Yes."

"All right. But you *will* tell me about that husband of yours. Has he hurt you?"

Yes. So much. Yet he felt strangely protective of Cador. He didn't want Santo to think badly of him. "It's...not so simple."

Santo jerked to a stop, twigs snapping under their ankle boots. "He has! I knew it. What did he do?" Their eyes roamed over Jem as they inspected him, hands seeking injuries. "Does he beat you? Tell me!"

"No, no. Nothing like that, I swear. It's not what you're thinking."

"I'll find out if you're not being truthful." Santo narrowed their gaze. "I'll have him killed and make it look like an accident. Well, Arthek will arrange it."

Jem had to laugh. "I have no doubt." Though he had only known stoic, stalwart Arthek to be calm and measured, there was no end to what he'd do for Santo. "But truly—he hasn't beat me or done anything of the sort."

"And in bed?" they asked sternly. "Does he always sleep on the floor? Have you lain with him?"

Squirming with discomfort, he nodded, focusing on the blue petals of orchids blooming in the shafts of sunlight.

"Which?"

"The second one. Truly, we don't need to discuss this!"

"Is he too rough with you?"

Jem's face flamed as memories whirled through his mind of begging to be taken hard. "No," he whispered.

"Ah. Just rough enough?"

Tugging Santo's hand, he walked on silently.

"It's good between you? In bed at least?"

"Uh-huh."

"Really?" They glared. "Tell me truthfully. You know I'll persist."

Jem had to laugh with affection. "That much I do know.

Truly, we are…very well matched in that regard." *Were* well matched in that regard, he reminded himself swiftly.

Santo's face lit up. "He's good at fucking? I bet he is. How big is his cock? Proportionately matching to his bulk? Did you remember what I said about using your mouth? I have a few tricks that Arthy *loves*."

Jem groaned. "I beg you to stop talking. All you need to know is that I'm far from the virgin I was when leaving Onan."

Santo clapped in delight. "That is welcome news at least. I'm so glad you're back. I really didn't stop to think before going into your chamber. So strange to find a burly man in there— though I'm saddened he wasn't in your bed. Especially if you've lain with him before. Why—"

"May we see the birds now?" Jem walked faster. Was he lying to Santo? What he'd said was true, but it had been an age now since he'd allowed Cador to touch him at all.

That wasn't quite true, was it? He thought of their hands clasped in that black tunnel fleeing the Holy Place. Bodies pressed close while riding south. Cradled on Cador's lap in the dungeon after his nightmare. Would it be so bad to give in and let Cador bed him? His body needed release…

No! Stand fast.

Resolutely, he looked down at the branded hand he would have lost. No, he wasn't ready to relent. He couldn't.

"Is he disappointing? Men often are."

Jem had to chuckle wryly. "He has disappointed me, yes." It was far too mild a word, but it would do.

"How? Has he been unfaithful?"

"I don't think so." He remembered his jealousy over Jory, who would return at any time. Perhaps he should tell Cador to fuck his friend again and find a lover of his own as he'd said he would. He could ask Santo now for suggestions—surely there were some suitable men at the castle or the nearby village.

Yet Jem didn't ask. He pushed aside all thoughts as he spotted the aviary, rushing forward to see the dillywigs. The place was just as he'd left it, a large rectangular wood and metal cage nestled in the shade of wide tew trees in the grass at the lakeside—though the water was much lower than he remembered, reeds lining the marshy shore.

Tears pricked his eyes to hear the familiar creak of the aviary door as he opened it and dropped to his knees by the bandaged dillywig.

Did Derwa survive on Ergh? Had she returned to the cottage to find it abandoned? Surely not, yet irrational guilt seized him. A pessimistic voice again said she'd probably been eaten by a hawk or met some other doom in that shadowy forest, but he silenced it. He wanted to choose hope.

He *would* choose hope.

Santo mercifully changed the topic and regaled Jem with castle gossip. He didn't mention the Ergh chieftain, and Jem probably should ask. But it was all so blissfully normal to be back in his aviary as his beloved Santo talked and talked.

Only for today, he could let himself have this. The injured dillywig cried, and he fed her, deciding to name her Doryty, who was Derwa's sister in the books.

Arthek approached with his usual measured steps. Tall and lean, his white shirt was spotless, the sleeves roomy and closing around his wrists. He wore his brown hair neatly parted and short, and his wheat-colored skin was sun-kissed. He greeted Jem with a nod and partial bow before dropping a fond peck to the crown of Santo's head, his narrow eyes crinkling as he smiled. His trousers hugged slim thighs, knee-high boots gleaming.

They left Doryty to rest, going to sit on the grass in the sun-dappled shade. Jem thanked Arthek for rescuing the dillywig in his stead, and Arthek asked a few questions on caring for them.

"The beast is excellent at fucking!" Santo blurted. "As we suspected." They exhaled as though they'd been holding their breath for minutes.

Jem sputtered, and Arthek merely nodded and said, "I'm glad."

After tugging off their low boots to spread their toes in the grass, Santo waved a dismissive hand at Jem. "You know I tell him everything."

Jem sighed. This was precisely why he couldn't confide in Santo about the kidnapping plan or the sevels and the children or the possible war.

"And there's something quite serious afoot, but Jem can't tell us yet." Santo curled on their side, head pillowed on Arthek's thigh. Arthek began braiding Santo's hair.

"It's not that I don't trust you both!" He did, very much. But the best course of action was to hold his tongue for the time being.

"We know." Santo smiled. "But you can tell us all about Ergh, can't you?"

Oh. He supposed he could. "It's freezing. It *snowed*."

Santo gaped. "Actual snow? Like on the tops of the mountains in Ebrenn?"

"Yep. I touched it. My breath clouded the air it was so cold."

"Hmm." Arthek tilted his head. "I can't imagine."

Sitting by the lake with a warm honeysuckle breeze ruffling his hair, Jem could almost believe it had all been a dream. That he was telling Santo and Arthek a tale from one of Morvoren's adventures. "It was nice and warm by the fire, at least. Life is much simpler there. No castles. Nothing even close."

"And Cador hunts boar?" Arthek asked. "With a spear?"

"Yes." It was silly, but Jem puffed up with pride. "I actually speared one myself."

Santo and Arthek jolted and asked in perfect unison, "Really?"

"I'm sure I only got lucky, but yes. It would have gored Cador, so I had no choice."

Bolting up to sitting, Santo held up their palms. One was branded with a paintbrush, its answering brand on Arthek's hand a coiled braid representing Santo's hair. They clapped delightedly. "You saved him? Tell us everything!"

Jem most definitely didn't tell them about stripping naked in the mud afterward, still sprayed with warm boar blood as Cador took him roughly. He banished those memories, tamping down the tingle in his traitorous body.

"I'm glad to know I *can* do it, even if I'm not eager to repeat the experience. I can't imagine being out in those woods in the dead of winter. Of course they all grew up that way. It's cloudy and gray all the time. I missed the sun so much. Though I didn't expect a drought."

Santo grimaced. "The gods love toying with us. Did you hear there were fires in Ebrenn and even to the north in Neuvella? They say some in Gwels too."

"I saw the orange light from Ebrenn myself when we returned. Tasted the ash and smoke on the wind."

Santo and Arthek shared a worried glance. Jem swore it was like they were reading each other's minds, and jealousy surged, along with a pang he realized was him missing Cador. Wishing his husband was here sitting with them. Wishing...so much.

"Do you think it could spread here?" Santo asked.

"I hope not. I noticed the water in the lake is lower, but other than that, it seems the same." He spread his fingers in the lush grass.

"Mmm." Arthek seemed to ponder it. "We've had less rain here, but it's been far worse elsewhere. There's talk that the gods still favor us."

Jem scowled. "King Perran thinks Ergh is to blame and the gods are angry at Onan for welcoming them back."

Another shared glance with Arthek before Santo asked carefully, "What do you know of King Perran?"

"Not much aside from he seems to be a madman." They were treading into dangerous territory, and the urge to return to Cador nagged, so Jem stood. "Do you think our marriage chamber will be ready?"

"Oh! Let's find out." Santo grinned.

In the castle, Arthek returned to his studio, where he sketched and painted and likely composed odes of love to Santo. As they climbed several flights of the winding stone staircase, Santo said, "I know you like the early morning sunshine, so I thought your marriage chamber should be in the same wing as your childhood chamber. Did I tell you that already?"

"You did, but I appreciate the thoughtfulness just as much now."

Santo paused at the top of the stairs to pull Jem into a hug. "I've missed you so much."

"You too." His throat was thick. "You've no idea."

Concern pinched Santo's face. "Oh, Jem. Tell me what troubles you."

"I will. But for today, I need to breathe. Regain my strength."

"All right. You know I will pester you mercilessly if you don't." They held Jem again, squeezing tight. "Whatever it is, all will be well eventually."

Jem wanted to believe that so very, very much. He nodded against Santo's shoulder.

With another cheery smile, Santo released him. "Right, no more doom and gloom. Come!"

It was strange how foreign the castle seemed as he walked with Santo. At once entirely familiar yet at a remove. The vivid colors of the tapestries seemed too bright, the tile inlay in the corridor sparkling at such a high polish under their feet that Jem almost asked if it was new.

The castle was entirely unlike any building Jem had seen on Ergh. Did it fill Cador with scorn at the frippery, or perhaps… Did he like it a little?

Why should I care if he likes it?

He shouldn't. He didn't! Cador's thoughts on Jem's home were irrelevant.

Home.

It should have filled him with joy and comfort. Yet he felt somehow like a visitor as Santo chattered away, pointing out a beautiful seaside painting Arthek had recently completed.

They reached Jem's chamber, and he was struck with the urge to escape inside and curl up under the covers. He couldn't, of course, especially since Cador paced by the windows.

Sunlight glinted off his short golden hair, a red silk shirt stretched over his chest. Fawn breeches appeared painted on his tree-trunk legs over tall boots. He'd shaved and looked every inch the fine Neuvellan gentleman. Albeit a very large one.

Cador grumbled. "I look ridiculous, I know."

He looked aggravatingly beautiful, but Jem realized belatedly that he'd frowned. "No. Just different."

"They promised to have some plainer clothes made for me but insisted I wear this for the feast."

"You look delightful," Santo said. "You'll have everyone jealous of our Jem."

"Let's look at the new chamber." Jem gave Santo a nudge before they could say anything else.

As promised, the marital chamber was right next door in a former guest room. Santo whirled dramatically at the door, their colorful skirts fanning around their shins.

"I hope it will be to your liking." To Cador, they said, "I guessed that you prefer a firmer mattress like your father." They motioned to the absolutely massive bed. "The right side has been fitted with more support both in the frame and the mattress itself. Of course any adjustments can be made. A couple's bed is their most important compromise. Can't have you sleeping on the floor." They winked.

Cador muttered, "Thank you."

Santo's gaze flicked to Jem, and Jem forced a smile. "It's perfect." The large windows gleamed in the sunshine, a long, cushioned seat with pillows beneath as in his chamber. There was color everywhere aside from a sedate leather armchair and footrest by the blue-tiled fireplace that shone with no hint of ash. Fires were only required during the odd winter rainy spell, and even then not usually since the weather was largely the same all year.

Santo ran a hand over the rich, brown leather of the chair. "I wasn't sure of your favorite colors, Cador. But I thought something dark."

Jem couldn't imagine Cador had once thought about a topic as frivolous as his favorite color, especially given Ergh was all shades of gray, black, brown, white, and dark green.

"And Jem, there's a little something special for you." They motioned to the windows.

His breath caught as he rounded the bed to see what it was. "Oh!" Jem rushed forward, dropping to his knees on the plush purple rug. A small bookshelf lined the bottom of the window seat, and—oh! Yes! There were his dog-eared favorites that he'd thought lost forever. "Santo! How did you find them? Thank you!"

"Our dear brother Pasco discovered them, as I'm sure he'll remind you constantly until the end of your days."

Jem reverently pulled out the first volume of Morvoren's tales, running his fingers over the familiar embossed letters on the cover. After all that had happened, collections of paper shouldn't mean so much, but they did.

Hugging the book to his chest, he allowed himself a moment of pure joy. His eyes burned and he squeezed them shut, breathing evenly. He would not cry.

He looked up at Cador's bleak, guilty expression. He could forgive him for the books, he truly could. But now there was so much more, and he didn't know what to think. Or how to feel—other than torn. Torn deep within, the pieces ragged and confusing.

Santo glanced back and forth between Cador and Jem before blurting, "What? What's going on?" Fists clenched, they narrowed their gaze at Cador. "What did you do?"

Jem wanted to assure Santo. He wanted to protect Cador. He wanted so very, very badly to insist, *"He didn't hurt me."* He couldn't.

Instead, he carefully returned his beloved book to its new shelf and took Santo's hand. "It's all right. Much has happened and there's much to discuss. But I'm fine." Or it would be, he hoped. "Thank you for preparing this beautiful room for us."

Cador cleared his throat. "Yes. Thank you."

Santo nodded warily. "Of course it's only temporary. If you decide to stay permanently, you'll have a proper suite of rooms." They narrowed their gaze at Cador. "Provided I don't have you eliminated for breaking my brother's heart."

Jem forced a laugh. "Trust me, there are far more important things to worry about than my heart."

"Mmm." Santo nodded grudgingly before kissing Jem's cheek. "We'll worry about your heart in due time if you insist. First, we feast."

with a flick of her hand.

"Have you seen the portrait gallery?" she asked.

"Uh, no." Cador realized he was still fidgeting with his cuffs when she glanced down with a frown. He dropped his hands to his sides, then clasped them behind his back, digging his blunt nails into his knuckles.

She began walking, and after a moment of uncertainty, Cador assumed he was meant to follow. He overtook her with two strides and almost tripped over his own feet, the thin-soled boots skidding on the tiles as he tried to match her snail's pace.

She seemed completely content to amble while Cador felt like he dragged his feet through thawing mud. If he had somewhere to go, he preferred to just get there and do his business. It didn't help that the borrowed boots crushed his toes.

"I hope Pasco wasn't being rude, though I imagine he was."

He wasn't sure what the right thing to say was, so Cador shrugged. On Ergh, he would have agreed that Pasco was a prick.

"How does your brother Bryok fare?"

Cador's breath seized, and he realized he hadn't thought about it for some hours. Somehow, he'd *forgotten* Bryok was dead. "Why?" he asked too sharply, heart thudding.

Jem had said he'd filled in the queen on Treeve's claims about the threat from King Perran, but there hadn't been time to discuss Tas and the plot and Bryok's treachery. *Cador's* treachery. The lies of them all.

Should he confess the truth to her now that she was asking of Bryok? He could blurt it all out—the disease, the sevels, the fear of losing everything to the mainland if they didn't scheme for control.

She frowned at him. "I was just thinking of how siblings can tease and bicker. Pasco has always needled Jem, but of course he loves his brother."

"Of course." His voice was too raw, and he coughed to cover it, trying to banish the memories of Bryok charging forward with sword raised, determined to take Jem's head.

He said nothing else, for Jem had been clear he wished to tell her himself. The last thing Cador wanted to do was go behind his back. He'd give anything to earn back Jem's trust, so he'd bite his tongue no matter how fucking bizarre it felt to be strolling in fancy clothes making small talk like nothing was wrong.

As they climbed another twisting staircase, the queen told him about the women who'd weaved the massive tapestry hugging the curved stone wall. She lifted the hem of her dress with one jeweled hand, her voice lilting and calm as she detailed the invention of some special kind of yarn or something.

How would she have reacted to receiving Jem's head? Cador remembered her commanding presence in the dungeon and had no doubt steel lurked beneath her gracious, patient smile. Bryok's murderous cry echoed, and Cador slammed the lid on those memories.

He hesitated by a wide doorway, reaching out to touch the deep red stone. It felt like any other.

"Each brick was soaked for days in vermilion and dried for weeks before construction," the queen said, answering his unspoken question.

"How frivolous." He couldn't imagine such a waste of time on Ergh. He realized too late his rudeness. "Uh, it is striking though."

She smiled as though he'd said nothing wrong. "Isn't it?"

They entered a round room, sunlight streaming through a

windowed ceiling high above. They couldn't be atop the castle, so it must have been one of the cylinders that clung to the castle's side. Jem's mother motioned up.

"With light coming through the turret's roof, the paintings are protected from direct sun that would fade the canvases."

Indeed, the pieces hung under a thick ledge. He'd never seen such detailed drawings of people. The paintings seemed so lifelike and colorful that he could believe blood had been used to depict the royal ancestors. Until he spotted the painting of what had to be Jem's family.

"Is that supposed to be Jem on the left?" He pointed.

"Yes."

Cador snorted. "Ridiculous. He looks like a solider."

"My son is as strong as any solider." She clenched her jaw.

"Of course! But he's nowhere near that tall."

The queen's lips quirked into a rueful smile. "No, but my husband insisted the artist…embellish. It's always bothered him that Jem is so small."

Cador hadn't given Jem's father much thought one way or the other since Jem didn't seem to. He decided the man was a dunderhead. "His size has nothing to do with his strength. He is braver than a hundred soldiers." Not that Cador himself hadn't judged Jem harshly when they met. If he could go back and do it all differently…

He examined the false Jem in the portrait, standing stiffly, almost the same height as his siblings. No smile lifted his pretty mouth, and his honey eyes were dull. "There's no spark in his gaze. And is that a sword on his belt? There should be a bird on his shoulder and a book in his hand."

Silence stretched out, and he turned his head to find the queen watching him intently. He shifted uncomfortably, tugging at the collar of his borrowed shirt.

Finally, he gave in and demanded, "What?" before remembering he needed to keep her on Ergh's side. "I mean..." What was the polite mainland way to ask, *Why the fuck are you looking at me like that?* He imagined she was peering straight into his soul.

Finally, she tilted her head, dangling jeweled earrings tinkling. "It seems you *have* gotten to know my son during these months."

"Well... He is my husband."

"That he is. The time had come for him to do his duty as a prince. Though I confess I didn't understand how very much I'd miss him. It's a relief to have him back. Now that he's visited Ergh and met the people, I see no reason for him to return." Her face smoothed into a smile, her tone sweet. "I'm sure that will suit you both in the future."

She led the way from the gallery, late afternoon sun streaming down and illuminating her crown as if the gold were aflame. Cador had no choice but to follow, the thought of a future on Ergh without Jem haunting every heavy step.

THE TERRACE WAS at the rear of the castle, a raised balcony so large you could get lost in the trees and flowering vines. Yet Cador's gaze found Jem immediately—leaning close to a tall, slim man in the shade of a tree with gnarled limbs and yellow flowers. As Jem laughed, Cador estimated the strides it would take to cross the busy terrace and shove this man over the railing.

The queen was still talking, so he nodded, jealous fury rushing through him. Jem's father and other people had joined them by a useless fountain that sprayed precious water in arcs.

He knew it was foolish to be so upset by the idea of Jem staying in Neuvella. Jem had said himself he was going home for good. Why should he ever want to return to Ergh with a husband who betrayed him? Where people he'd grown to trust had conspired to use him as a pawn?

Now here he was with all the summer mead he could drink, people playing songs that sounded like birds on stringed pieces of wood, and trays of fancy food made into the shapes of animals. And whoever the fuck was making him *laugh*.

Sweat trickled down Cador's spine, the sun lower in the sky and beaming straight at his face. He gulped mead, choking down a belch at the last second. Jem's father was talking about Glaw and the drought and how blessed they were in Neuvella's royal district and praise the gods.

"We must pray to the gods that the rest of Onan returns to their favor." This husky, slightly hoarse droning voice was familiar.

Cador had to look down to find the speaker—the head cleric who'd married him to Jem. How long had the old bitch been standing there? What was her name again? Ysella. And why was Jem still talking to that man?

"The sooner we can build a proper temple on Ergh, the more blessings the gods will bestow," Ysella said.

Despite the heat, an icy shiver rippled through Cador. There it was, Tas's prediction come true. Jem's parents and the other people crowding around nodded and spoke their agreement while he bit his tongue so he didn't bellow that it would happen over his rotting corpse.

Sweat stung his eyes, and his face was surely scarlet. How

did everyone else seem so at ease? His shirt clung to his lower back, and he stood there nodding every so often, not listening as the old cleric went on and on about the gods. He should have paid attention so he could report it all to Tas, but blood rushed in his ears. His skin itched with too many curious gazes.

And Jem laughed again!

Muttering a half apology that was more of a grunt, he strode past the fountain, grateful for the spray of cool mist on his flushed skin. The borrowed boots felt flimsy compared to his own, the breeches too tight. He longed for his trousers and tunic and a spear in his grasp, cursing the sun and holding up a hand to block it.

He almost marched right into Jem and the slender man, blinded for a moment in the tree's thick shade after the glare. Jem's smile froze, then vanished as Cador barked at the man, "Fuck off."

Immediately squeezing between them, Jem glared up at Cador. "What is the matter with you?"

"Me? You're the one getting cozy with this, this—" He sneered at the man, who watched with a placid expression. His mind whirled trying to find the best insult.

Jem poked him in the belly. Hard. "*This* is Arthek, Santo's husband."

Oh. "Oh." Cador clenched and re-clenched his hands, the fury smothered by embarrassment. "Oh."

Jem smiled too brightly. "And now everyone is watching and gossiping, and you are making a spectacle of yourself. And me. So now *you* will laugh, and we'll pretend you aren't a complete jackass." He laughed himself despite the ice in his tone, shoulders shaking. "You see? Like that."

Arthek chuckled and smiled, and Jem shot him a grateful

glance that Cador coveted for himself. He imagined the old cleric's face if he belched during her sermon. His laugh boomed as though they'd shared a hilarious jest. But it had been too loud, and now all eyes were most definitely on them.

Santo appeared, speaking through their smile. "And what's going on here?" They'd changed into different skirts paired with a tight leather vest that Cador would have loved to wear himself if not for the blasted sun.

Arthek drew Santo into a kiss. "Merely a misunderstanding." He extended his hand to Cador. "It's a pleasure to meet you."

Cador had to shake the man's hand or make himself out to be an even bigger prick. Ugh, what a child he was being. It was shameful. He didn't deserve Arthek's understanding. He clasped his hand, then gratefully took another cup of mead from a passing tray.

Jem wouldn't meet his gaze, instead murmuring to Arthek, "I'm sorry. I have no idea what got into him."

Cador bristled despite his intentions, gripping his cup. "*He* was only…" There was no good way to finish the sentence, so he swallowed more mead.

Santo frowned. "What?"

"A bit jealous, perhaps," Arthek said with annoying kindness.

Laughing genuinely, Santo almost snorted. "I assure you, there's nothing to fear from my Arthy. He's all mine and I'm his." The two of them shared a look so affectionate Cador felt sick with a different jealousy.

Someone announced that the feast would begin, so they slowly made their way inside. Cador was grateful for the coolness, at least. He felt like they were crawling as he kept pace with Jem, who stared straight ahead.

"I'm sorry," Cador murmured. "I have no right to jealousy."

Jem glanced at him, frowning. He seemed ready to say something but only nodded curtly.

As at the Holy Place, this feast was held in a hall with vast murals, though there were even more fancy statues and strange objects everywhere Cador looked. And the food! He'd thought the wedding feast was extravagant, but somehow they managed to top it with the amount of roasted meats and countless dishes Cador couldn't even recognize.

Sitting with Jem to his right at the end of the royal table, he whispered, "How did the cook make all of this in a day?" Though people spoke and tinkly music played, it seemed so quiet compared to a feast at home. If he didn't whisper, he was sure everyone would hear his stupid questions.

"Feverish work and a large staff, I imagine. Though we usually eat well." He twirled his fork in a bowl of long strands that looked something like worms. "I never even thought about it before leaving."

Cador missed the simple freedom of eating with his hands. He tried to twirl his fork in the strange dish and splashed bright red sauce onto Jem's silk sleeve. Reaching to blot it, he knocked a mug of mead, which tipped, spreading dark wine over the oak table. "Fuck!"

Everyone heard that judging by the stares and whispers. Biting back more curses, he blotted uselessly at the spill with his hand until servants appeared out of nowhere and cleaned it all with quick, efficient movements. Cador sucked mead from one of his fingers before realizing what he was doing. Giggles skittered through the grand hall.

Beside him, Jem ate like nothing had happened, though

Cador spotted the flush on his cheeks. Cador was humiliating him, and all at once he wanted to shove back his chair and shout that nothing here was real. Fuck politeness and fluffy bread baked in the shape of fish. Children were dying, and he was sitting here pretending...what?

That he wasn't a barbarian like they thought? Why did he fucking care what these pampered mainlanders believed? If only Tas and Delen and the others were with him. He'd sat through the feast after his wedding without feeling like he wanted to climb out of his own skin.

But everything had been different then. He hadn't given a fuck what the mainlanders thought of him. Least of all Jem. He'd been doing his duty to Ergh. What was he doing now?

He shoved back his chair.

Jem's small hand gripped his wrist. The buttons of Cador's silk shirt dug into the thin layer of flesh over bone. Eyes forward, Jem spoke so softly Cador had to lean down.

"Please."

With that one word, Cador's confused anger drained away. He inched his chair back toward the table and bit the head off a bread fish. It was light and crumbly and delicious, and he ordered himself to enjoy it.

Jem let go of his wrist, and immediately Cador missed the pressure. He sat with legs wide under the table, and if he leaned his knee toward Jem to touch his thigh, would Jem allow it?

Awkwardly, he used his fork and knife to cut off a piece of roasted chicken. He was acting like a boy with his first crush, not a grown man with a husband. Still, that husband might as well have been on the other side of Onan. Cador wasn't allowed to touch.

By the time the old cleric, Ysella, stood—her shoulders so

stooped she could have still been sitting—during the dessert course and started sermonizing, Cador was ready to run down to the stables and ride away on Dybri. His skin crawled with the weight of hundreds of eyes on him, though when he glanced around, most people were paying attention to the cleric.

"Heard enough from this woman to last a lifetime," he muttered under his breath.

"Mm." Jem barely moved his mouth, his gaze on the cleric. He fidgeted, running a hand through his hair though it looked perfectly neat.

There were dozens of other clerics at a table near the royals, and they appeared mesmerized by Ysella. For her wrinkled, tiny appearance, her voice filled the vast space.

"We thank the generous and all-knowing gods for blessing us with this feast. We pray for the droughts elsewhere in Onan to end swiftly and for Glaw to bestow us with the autumn rains. Here, the queen has clearly pleased the gods in service of her people. In service of Onan." There was a murmur of agreement, and Jem's mother smiled and inclined her head.

If the clerics visited King Perran in the West, would Ysella be praising him just as much? Was anything she said true? Cador fiddled with a delicate pastry butterfly, and the treat crumbled into a pile on his plate. As at the wedding, there were piles of fruit, though fewer sevels. Had the fields burned?

"There are some who will say Ergh is to blame for angering the gods." Ysella's voice rang out.

Naturally, all eyes swiveled to Cador. He forced himself to remain motionless and his gaze distant.

"But how can we blame our lost children who wish to return to the fold? How can we not do everything we can to welcome them as part of Onan? It is our duty to the gods, and we will be rewarded for it."

Children? Resentment vibrated through Cador, his nostrils flaring. He wanted to leap to his feet and bellow that they didn't need the mainland's fucking charity, but they did. If Ysella decided to turn the people against Ergh, it was hopeless. They needed the people's sympathy. Their pity. And he hated it so much.

He hated also that his face was surely bright red, his cheeks flaming hot with humiliation and useless anger. All eyes were still on him, and he realized that many people watched him eagerly as though waiting for something. Waiting for him to explode. Waiting for him to act the barbarian.

So he sat, flattening his palms on his thighs and counting his breaths, tuning out the rest of Ysella's sermon and imagining he was home. Imagining he was on the hunt, riding Massen with cold wind reddening his cheeks. Returning to the cottage to find Jem in the little aviary with new hatchlings, jumping up into Cador's arms to kiss him…

He should have smothered such fantasies, but he allowed himself the distraction until the feast was mercifully over and he could escape. He followed Jem upstairs, only realizing at the last moment that Jem would be staying alone in his old chamber.

Cador had followed blindly, jolting to a stop in the doorway as Jem's palm met his chest, his arm outstretched. That touch through silk had Cador's heart galloping foolishly. Could Jem feel how he affected him?

Fuck, even if Jem couldn't sense the thud of his heart, the bulge of Cador's desire in the stupidly tight breeches was impossible to miss.

Jem's eyes flicked down and widened. His lips parted, pink tongue visible. Cador burned to bend and finally kiss him again.

To taste his sweet mouth and hold him close, protect him from the world that seemed to lurch out of control.

Their eyes locked, and Cador's mouth went dry at the raw hunger in Jem's honey gaze, the—

A thud from the corridor made them both jump, and before Cador knew it, Jem had shut the door in his face. Someone—a servant?—approached, and Cador ducked into the chamber Santo had prepared for them.

He tugged off the thin boots and wriggled his sore toes. Simmering with tension and frustration and longing, he tore off the Neuvellan clothing, relieved to find a pile of plainer garments in a neat pile on the end of the massive bed.

They were still finer than anything he'd ever worn on Ergh, but the material was more practical and the colors dark. He pulled on black trousers that were so tight they were practically breeches and looked around for the proper boots he'd asked for.

Apparently they weren't finished yet since he found nothing. He only wanted to go for a walk and clear his head, but he had to put on the ridiculous high boots again.

Fuck, he ached for his spear and horse and home and the comfort of his damn boots. He ached for the comfort of the man he loved more than anything. Jem was painfully close and still lost to him.

He paced restlessly on the soft carpet. When would Tas and Jory return? What of Delen and Kensa and the others? Poor suffering Hedrok. Would he die before Cador could see him again? He'd wasted so much time when he could have been a comfort to his nephew.

Jem's mother had insisted pretending all was well at the feast was necessary to soothe the people. But wasn't it past time to lay all the lies bare? If she threw Cador in the dungeon for his betrayal of her favorite child, so be it.

Before he could think twice, he was throwing open the door to Jem's chamber clad only in the black trousers, ready to insist they rouse the queen and get the fuck on with it.

Yet those words turned to dust as his throat went dry. He stared at Jem on the bed. Leaning back against a pile of pillows, wearing only his thin white nightshirt, the hem up around his hips. His slim prick in hand, one of his books open beside him.

A waiting candle resting on the pink sheets.

Chapter Fifteen

C ADOR WAS JEALOUS of a *candle.*

In the flickering light of a small oil lamp beside the bed, Jem stared at him in the doorway, one hand at his throat. They stared at each other across the plush rug. Cador wanted to snatch up the candle and snap it in two.

It should have been his cock Jem wanted inside him. They should have been sharing a bed, warm and safe together under a mountain of furs in their cottage. He hated himself for destroying the precious bond between them.

He'd vowed to keep Jem safe and make him happy—and now Jem was clearly in need of pleasure. Beside the candle, a green glass vial rested on the pink silk. Jem's chest rose and fell rapidly as he swallowed with a *gulp.* In that moment, he looked so much like an innocent that Cador was flooded with tenderness.

Heart in his throat, he asked, "Who do we have here? A virgin prince all alone."

Jem's brows met before understanding rippled over him, his breath hitching, fingers clutching at the gaping neck of his nightshirt. Cador could see the war within playing out, ending in another *gulp.*

He held his breath. Would Jem deny him? The seconds stretched out, and dread rose. Then came a whisper.

"Yes. I'm…Kitto."

the whisper-thin material ripping. Jem gasped, a damp gust against Cador's palm. "What shall I do with you?" Cador murmured.

Jem tried to reply, and Cador lifted his hand so Jem could say, "You'll have to gag me." His eyes glittered with excitement.

"I suppose I must." Cador twisted the silk nightshirt and shoved it between Jem's lips, knotting the gag behind his head.

Sitting back on his heels, Cador said, "That's better."

Breathing hard, Jem sat naked, his prick rigid. Waiting. His hands were free. He could have reached up and removed the gag, but he only stared at Cador.

He trusts me.

Cador shouldn't have been thinking of him as Jem at all—he should have called him Kitto in his head as well, but his mind refused. This trust was a precious gift, and he was grateful this connection between them hadn't died.

He ached to mount Jem and take him fiercely, mercilessly, until they both cried out for surrender. In his mind, he could hear how their flesh would slap as they grunted, Jem taking every inch of him. So willing and eager and strong despite his small size.

Yet in the next breath, he longed to press Jem back into the pillows and kiss him slowly, deeply, tasting him again for the first time in what felt like forever. He could have kissed him all night, swallowing his little gasps and moans, rubbing against him, both of them hard but stretching out the moment of sweet release.

The wild woodsman would do no such thing, sadly.

Jem still waited, breathing shallowly, the tip of his slender shaft glistening. As eager as Cador was to plunge into Jem and play his role, it had been too long for rushing. He refused to hurt him, even if the woodsman would have no such concern for Kitto.

He freed his prick, biting back a moan as he stroked himself. He was about to strip off the trousers, but the woodsman surely would not.

He commanded in a growl, "Turn over."

Jem obeyed perfectly, stretching out on his belly, gripping one of the bright pillows in his hands. His legs were locked together. He cried out—muffled through the gag—as Cador grabbed his ankles and forced them wide, careful not to disturb the bandage on Jem's foot.

He spread his hand over one cheek of that beautiful arse, his own skin pinkly pale on the lovely dusky brown. With his thumb, he caressed Jem's crease, the puckered flesh quivering.

"Can't have you running away, can I?" Cador murmured. "Not before I fuck your virgin hole. Not before I fill you with my cum." He leaned over so his lips were at Jem's ear. "I have to bind you, don't I, Kitto? Or else you'll try to escape with your innocence."

Jem's answer was a moan and vigorous nod. Such generous trust, and Cador was hungry for it—greedy and undeserving, but helpless to resist. He'd work to deserve it for the rest of his life. He'd be worthy.

"Don't move. Or you'll regret it."

In Jem's closet of ridiculously fine, soft, and bright clothes, Cador discovered enough sashes to do the trick. It was beyond him how one man could have a need for more than one silk sash, but he was glad of them as he went to work restraining Jem to the bedposts.

He straddled Jem's waist, leaning over him. As he shifted, his knee pressed onto the open book, and he picked it up.

Jem inhaled sharply, going rigid beneath him. "Don't!" The plea was clear even through the gag.

Did he truly think Cador would rip the pages? The pulse of hurt was foolish yet undeniable. The spine was loose and edges worn, and he certainly could have torn the book apart easily.

He carefully closed the cover and laid Morvoren's adventures on the small round table. Cador grasped one of Jem's arms out to bind him to the post, and Jem hummed contentedly.

Up close, Cador could see that the cherry wood of the posts was carved not with meaningless swirls, but the curving wings of birds. He ran a fingertip over the design, smiling at how perfect it was.

His heart swelled as he stood back and looked at his Jem, arms outstretched to the corners of the bed, his wrists bound to the posts. His stomach rested on pillows, arse up in the air and knees beneath him.

Mine.

Jem pressed a cheek to the mattress, whimpering when Cador spread his arse wide, exposing him completely. Cador couldn't resist burying his face in that tender flesh, licking and kissing, Jem pushing back against him. Again, the urge to abandon his plans and plunge inside burned. He resisted.

First, he surrendered to the need to run his hands all over Jem's back and legs and arse, his face following. He inhaled his scent, rubbing his face against Jem's skin. He'd missed having him close more than he'd even known, a strange relief surging just to smell him freely before going further.

Oiling the candle took but a few moments. Cador pressed it to Jem's hole. "Is this what you crave?"

Jem craned his neck to see, his brows knit. As Cador worked it inside, Jem moaned. His fingers grasped the air above the secure bindings on his wrists.

"It's your favorite toy. Though this candle seems unused. Is it harder than your other one?"

Jem nodded, moaning as Cador twisted the wax.

"You're not in control this time, Prince Kitto. I could do anything to you. But you like that, don't you?"

Jem shuddered. Oh yes, it excited him. Perhaps it was being here in his old, familiar chamber that allowed him to safely surrender to his fantasies. To give up control and escape just for a little while.

Cador's arousal surged with his desire to give Jem what he needed. "You're helpless. There's nothing you can do to stop me." Of course that wasn't true—Cador would never force him.

Yet aside from being half his size, Jem was gagged and bound. What if he *did* want to stop? There was a stray blue sash left on the bed, and Cador leaned over to put it in Jem's right hand, the blue fabric sliding over the branded tusks.

"Hold on to this. If you drop it, I'll know to stop whatever I'm doing." At Jem's nod, he returned to kneel behind him and play the woodsman.

He'd left the candle inside Jem and toyed with it idly now. "Do you want to know a secret? This isn't the first time I've been in your chamber. I hid in the wardrobe. You thought you were alone."

Jem groaned, wriggling his arse, begging for more. Cador gave him only another tiny bit of the hard wax.

"Yes, I've watched you. Watched you fuck yourself like the whore you really are." He drove the wax deeper.

Although he'd filled Jem with his prick before, there was something different and intense about fucking him with the candle. He watched the yellow wax disappearing into Jem's body, Jem's breathy moans music to his ears.

He could manipulate the candle more deftly, twisting it and using leverage to stretch his passage and find just the right spot that made him cry out through the gag.

"Do you want to come like this? The way you have so many times before." He reached under Jem's lifted hips and teased his rigid cock. The pillows were damp. "You're close already, aren't you? Such a pretty little slut."

Jem nodded, still clutching the blue silk.

Cador couldn't resist stroking his back, soothing Jem's quivering flanks. "But you don't have to be fucked by a candle anymore. Now you can spread your legs for flesh. You're born to take my cock."

Moaning, Jem shoved his arse back.

"Begging like a whore," Cador murmured, yanking out the candle without warning.

Jem seized up, tugging at the restraints but still holding the blue silk.

Cador sat back on his heels, dropping his hands. "What if I left you like this? Empty and begging. Helpless."

Groaning pitifully, Jem shook his head.

"You need my cock, don't you? Only mine." He gripped Jem's hips hard enough to bruise.

Moaning and whimpering around the gag, Jem still gripped the blue sash.

Lust fired through Cador like he was galloping hard on Massen's back, his quarry in sight. They both shouted as he thrust inside Jem to the hilt in one brutal motion. He pounded Jem's lithe body, grunting and taking him without mercy. He'd opened him with the oiled candle, but Jem was still wonderfully tight.

"That's it. Take me." Cador grunted. Jem was bent and bound and so small beneath him, and he marveled at how his little prince could fire his blood hotter than the fiercest mighty hunter of Ergh. Tangling his fingers in Jem's hair, he leaned forward, pinning him down completely, slamming into his delicious arse.

"Can't get enough," he gritted out, though Cador wasn't sure if he meant Jem or himself. Both. "You love my cock, don't you? I love your arse. Love fucking you. Love—"

He bit off the words as his bollocks tightened. He was an invading woodsman. There could be no talk of love. Only fucking. Only his prick filling Jem's slim body.

"You're going to take my cum until it—" He grunted, their slapping flesh loud in the stillness of the chamber. "'Til it drips out. I'm going to fill you and leave you leaking my seed. Tied up and powerless until a servant finds you. Should I leave you hard and unsatisfied as well?"

Jem cried out through the gag, clearly pleading for release, still clutching the blue silk.

Sweat slicked Cador's skin. He knew Jem could feel that he was still dressed where his open trousers met the fevered flesh of Jem's arse and thighs. He pulled almost all the way out, then slammed back into his grasping hole. "Perhaps I'll stay to watch you straining and helpless. I'll wait long enough that I can fuck you again."

His bollocks tightened, and he gripped the base of his shaft, pulling out to breathe and find control. Jem wriggled his arse, and Cador ran a finger over his oiled hole. "So greedy for it. What if I carried you off deep into the forest and kept you?" He pushed his thumb inside, rubbing. "You'd never escape. You'd be mine forever."

Chapter Sixteen

E VEN AT A distance, Jem recognized the cry as Hedrok's. After the endless voyage across the Askorn Sea, he'd know that doomed scream until the end of his days. He bolted up in bed as the door swung open. Spent cock still exposed, Cador strode back in.

"That's Hedrok!"

Jem said, "Yes. They must be in the entrance hall. We'll go down right away." He was about to throw back the sheets, but paused. "I'll meet you in the hallway."

"Now you're bashful?"

"No!" He had no idea why he was arguing. "But you need to make yourself presentable." He flung back the sheets—he wasn't bashful!—and rolled to his feet, wincing as he crossed to his wardrobe.

"What's wrong?"

"Why are you still here?" Jem shooed him with his hand. "I'm fine! Go!" Truthfully, his arse throbbed with each step, and he was uncomfortably aware of Cador's seed inside him.

He hurried into the bathing room to clean before tugging on breeches and a shirt, which he tucked in before yanking on his boots.

Cador had thankfully dressed and put away his prick. His silk shirt hung loose over the black trousers, and he winced in the tall boots as they raced down the circular staircase, another cry echoing.

As a boy, Jem had loved making himself dizzy by racing his siblings up and down the castle's stairs. Now, he shook off the lightness in his head impatiently as they reached the bottom to find Delen, Creeda, Kensa, and a few others just inside the castle's mighty wooden doors. They were filthy and looked positively wild.

Hedrok writhed on his bed of blankets in the back of the small wagon, which they'd pulled inside. The dirt-crusted wheels left marks on the colored tile. They must have hauled it all the way up the hill.

Delen held out her sword, keeping two disheveled guards at bay. Had there been a scuffle? Was that blood dripping from one guard's nose? Onto the ancient, colored tiles of the castle's entry?

Too many people were shouting at once, and Hedrok was screaming, and Jem wanted to clap his hands over his ears and run back to bed. It wasn't supposed to be like this! Where was his mother?

Thunder rumbled outside, and it took Jem a few pounding heartbeats to realize it was more guards. "No! Wait!"

But his cry was ignored, the guards streaming inside like floodwaters. Creeda kicked and punched, sending a guard staggering away from the wagon. Jem watched, his feet rooted to the fine tiles as Cador seemed to leap the entire distance to Hedrok, hauling the boy into his arms. The clang of metal blades clashing rang out over shouts and confusion.

"Stop! I said stop!" Yet no one heeded Jem's shouts. He climbed up a few steps so he was taller, yet it made no difference as his commands were drowned out.

The Erghians were vastly outnumbered, and it was inevitable they'd be overrun even though they resisted fiercely. With Hedrok in his arms, Cador shielded him, running in the only direction open—toward the east side of the grand entrance.

He'd never make it to the corridor that eventually led to the feasting hall. Jem was in the perfect position to spot the three guards in their fine red uniforms charging toward Cador.

Jem was the one flying now, not wasting his breath with more shouting through the cacophony. He came at the closest guard from the right side, hurling himself into the woman at a run, sending her crashing into the others, one catching Cador's leg. Cador stumbled, but kicked off the man, Hedrok shrieking in his arms.

The woman raised the butt of her sword to smash it into Jem's face. He scrambled back, slipping on the smooth tile, raising his hands in defense. The woman froze, her eyes widening as she gasped, "Prince Jowan!"

Cador spun around, and Jem pushed to his feet, holding his arms out to his sides with Cador and Hedrok behind him. "I command you to stop fighting! These are honored guests!"

The guards blinked at him disbelievingly. Beyond, Delen and the others had been overwhelmed, their swords and spears confiscated. They still struggled, and Jem was relieved they were alive. And even more relieved to hear his mother's voice boom.

"Cease this skirmish at once!"

Unlike when she'd found them in the dungeon, she descended the stairs fully dressed, her hair swept up, though in a simple series of knots he imagined she'd swiftly tied herself.

At Jem's back, Hedrok wheezed, his breathing terribly labored. "Mother! We need the healer!"

Her gaze swung to him, and he stepped aside so she could see Hedrok. In Cador's arms, Hedrok's bare, ruined legs dangled. Jem's mother sucked in a breath, emotions flitting over her face—horror giving way to determination. She nodded sharply to her retinue, then commanded the guards to stand down.

A wizened man Jem didn't recognize in a dusty brown robe stepped forward from the open doorway. "Yes, get Tregereth. I've done all I can. This is far beyond what the healing waters can cure."

Delen and the others staggered to their feet. Head high even as she listed, Delen nodded to Jem's mother. Limping to her son, blood stained Creeda's temple. She grimaced, blood coating her teeth ghoulishly.

She clutched the bundle of sevel twigs, which hung around her neck on a thin, fraying rope. Shuddering in revulsion, Jem had to stop himself from fleeing her approach.

She's not Bryok. I'm safe. I'm not there. I'm home.

Yet he could see flashes of firelight from that night on the Cliffs of Glaw, stark memories invading his mind. He did stumble then, stepping aside, Cador glancing to him with brow furrowed, still carrying Hedrok.

Before his mother could notice, Jem breathed deeply, mastering his weakness and clearing his mind. He allowed himself one rake of his nails over his scalp, craving the familiar burn in a way he didn't even understand. He'd felt such peace giving Cador control, trusting him again at least in that. Now he was right back in the thick of chaos.

"Not the welcome we expected," Delen growled.

One of the guards squawked in outrage. "If you'd have stopped for a minute while we could confirm your identity—"

"There's no time to stop!" Delen's shout echoed off the tile before it was drowned out by Hedrok screaming.

"Enough!" Jem's mother issued instructions, one after the other, *zip, zip, zip.*

Jem was finally able to inhale deeply. He stopped listening, letting himself be carried along in the reassuring current of his mother's guidance. He followed as Cador carried Hedrok up the winding stairs with Creeda and the healer from Gwels. Mother came to Jem's side, her arm snug around his shoulders.

They reached a guest chamber where breathless servants scurried in ahead with steaming water and towels and other supplies. They stole wide-eyed peeks at Hedrok squirming in Cador's arms, red-faced and panting.

Cador was speaking to the boy, surely words of comfort as Creeda's fingers worked the worn twigs, prayers undoubtedly on her lips. Jem's head buzzed, and he felt at a distance from them all, in the doorway watching.

He retreated with his mother a few steps down the moonlit corridor past tall windows where he could spot the stars. How wonderful it was to see the constellations again after the cloudy nights on Ergh.

"Jem." His name sounded like it was coming from underwater, and he thought of Morvoren's beloved merman.

Fingernails dug into his arms through the thin silk of his shirt, and he blinked at his mother. "Yes." He tried to dispel the strange fog from his mind. Had he been thinking of the stars?

She ran her hands over him. "Where are you hurt?" She prodded his sides and stomach, and he realized there was a splash of blood on the silk, though it wasn't his.

"I'm not." He shook his head, more sounds returning, footsteps down the hall along with Hedrok's cries and voices sharp with concern, just far enough that he couldn't pick out the words. He and his mother were in a tiled alcove that in daylight shone a glorious orange and yellow.

Forehead creased, she reached to inspect his head. With a bolt of alarm that banished the last cobwebs, he batted her hand away and cleared his throat. "I'm not hurt. Is Tregereth coming for Hedrok?"

"I've sent a servant to fetch them, but I'm sure they heard the commotion, even from their perch in the west tower."

Tregereth's salves had done wonders for Jem's cut heel, which only twinged faintly now even after all the running he'd done. But Hedrok needed far more than salves and a bandage. His mind drifted back to Austol's sister Eseld, and the sensation of her shrunken legs like dry husks, the horrible timber of her agonized cries...

"Where is Hedrok's father?"

He blinked at his mother in the silver moonlight. "His father?"

"He is Bryok's son, is he not? Where is Bryok?"

"The bottom of the Askorn Sea." At her narrowed gaze, he added, "I don't mean cursed to the bottom of the sea. He's really there. Dead. Speared straight through and tumbled off a cliff into the sea."

She blinked. "You're certain?"

"Yes. Bryok is dead."

"Who killed him?" she demanded.

Jem hesitated, but his mother would have to know the truth eventually. He'd promised Delen and Cador could tell their father first, but since the chieftain hadn't returned yet...

It was one thing not to volunteer the information, but another to lie directly to his mother. And why should he value that promise he'd made on the ship since he'd fully intended to break it?

"Delen killed him."

His mother went very still. "Why?"

"She was protecting me and Cador." Gods, he hated thinking of that night. But clearly it was time to confess it all. "Bryok, he…"

"He what?" she demanded. "Did he hurt you?"

"Yes," he said simply. There was much to tell, but that certainly was the simple truth.

She relaxed her grip on his arms before smoothing her palms up over his shoulders and embracing him. "You're safe now."

He allowed himself to relax, inhaling her faint lavender scent gratefully.

"I'm sorry, my darling. I shouldn't have snapped at you." She eased back, looking down at him tenderly. "You don't need to worry."

"But there's so much more to sort out."

At a fresh wail from Hedrok, Mother cringed. "If there's one thing I've learned in my years as queen, there will always be unpleasant waters to navigate."

Tregereth appeared carrying their ornately carved square box holding potions and salves and supplies, an assistant on their heels with more. Plump and older, Tregereth had short dark hair, light brown skin, and dressed in plain robes not unlike the clerics', though a rich scarlet and orange instead of pious gray.

Jem and his mother joined Tregereth at the threshold to the guest chamber. Inside, Hedrok writhed on the canopied bed, long tunic tangled at his hips as Cador and Creeda tried to soothe him. Tregereth paused before their shoulders slumped.

They glanced at Jem's mother, leaning close. "All the sevels in Onan won't save this one." They nodded to their helper and marched into the chamber, saying, "Right, let's get this pain under control. I'll take care of you."

"What's happening?" Santo asked from behind. They held hands with Arthek, both wearing slippers and long silk robes knotted over their sleep shirts.

"Come, let's leave this poor child in peace." Mother shepherded them all down the corridor.

Jem had to admit he was relieved when they entered another wing and Hedrok's faint cries faded away entirely, though he wished he could bring Cador with him.

In his mother's favorite receiving room, airy and filled with plants and colorful chairs, Jem's father and Pasco sat with Delen, Kensa, and the other Ergh hunters, who looked very much like barbarians who'd come straight from battle to perch on the plush chairs. Which he supposed they had, dirty and blood-splattered.

Delen jumped to her feet, knocking the chair back behind her. It hit the rug with a thud, and the other hunters leapt up as well, fists clenched. Their swords and spears had apparently been confiscated, which was surely for the best, at least for the moment.

"How is he?" Delen demanded.

"He doesn't seem well at all," the queen answered. "Our finest healer is seeing to him now."

Delen looked to Jem, and he nodded and said, "If anyone can help, it's Tregereth."

"Thank you." Delen righted the toppled chair. Her tunic was stained with sweat and drying blood, and she shifted from boot to boot in the silence. "I'm told my tas isn't here?"

"Please, let us all sit." Jem's mother motioned to the half

circle of chairs. "And I'm sure you're thirsty and hungry." She nodded to a servant.

How strange it was to be in his mother's sitting room past midnight, many oil lamps brightening the space, the windows dark beyond the glow. Even stranger to be there sharing a small couch with Santo and Arthek as they watched the Erghians eat and drink eagerly.

There was so much to say, and so many questions to ask, yet they all seemed mired in this strange game of politeness. Though Jem imagined most of his mother's guests ate the plates of slender sandwiches with far less gusto.

Wiping her mouth with the back of her hand, Delen asked, "Shouldn't our tas and Jory be back soon?"

"I expect so. My son Locryn has gone after them, and he'll find them soon, I'm sure. Perhaps they became lost."

Delen nodded. "Perhaps. Thank you for your help."

In her boots, Jem would have a million questions, but this was politics, and Delen seemed to be playing the game. In fact, when Ysella arrived with platitudes from the gods, Delen greeted her with surprising warmth.

Perhaps only surprising in comparison to Cador, who could barely refrain from rolling his eyes at the mere mention of the gods.

How is he? It's awful seeing Hedrok suffer. Is he—

Jem gave himself a mental shake. Why was he worrying about Cador? Cador would take care of himself.

Before Ysella could launch into a prayer, Jem asked Delen, "Any signs of fire?"

Tension rippled through her. "Yes. It seems to be worsening in Gwels, though several days ride from here."

"Let us pray for the gods' blessing upon us." Ysella stood, so small that she wasn't much taller when she did.

Jem wanted to protest that they still had too much to discuss, but his mother was nodding, deferring to Ysella in a way that made the back of his neck prickle. Beside him, Santo and Arthek dutifully bowed their heads. Pasco and their father followed suit.

Jem shared a glance with Delen, who gave him a wry little smile and minute shrug of her shoulders before she piously clasped her hands on her lap. The other Erghians awkwardly mimicked her.

Perhaps Cador was right and Delen would make a better chieftain. They needed to get along with the clerics and play their game. Jem fidgeted, remembering how bored he'd been at the peace summit on the hard stone chair.

He was glad at least for the plush couch under his tender backside, his face heating as he thought of the game he and Cador had played just, when? An hour before? It seemed like a dream.

The skin of his belly was tight with a smear of seed he'd missed when quickly cleaning himself. He squeezed his arse, the throbbing ache delicious. What a relief it had been to surrender. To be touched by those strong, familiar hands, speared with that cock. He'd let himself be Prince Kitto, fucked by the marauding woodsman, but of course he knew it was more than that.

As Ysella droned about Glaw and the other gods, Jem followed an emerald circle on the rug with the toe of his boot. He'd clasped his hands obediently, and now he traced the tusks branded into his right palm with his other thumb.

Even if he could trust Cador with his body, his heart was far, far too fragile. How wonderful it had been to feel Cador's touch once more, to not have to *think*, to come so hard his bollocks he'd changed his mind about using Jem for leverage.

He scratched at his scalp, gulping in the warm, dewy morning air, breathing through the memories. Stumbling on a root, he stopped beneath a low-hanging kalx tree, leaning against the smooth trunk until he could focus again.

If Cador's tas had changed his mind, the kidnapping plot would need to be scuttled. They'd have sent an envoy to Ergh to call it off. Maybe they had? Everyone seemed to be getting hopelessly lost these days. Locryn should be back any minute with Jory and the chieftain.

Could Jem's mother think she was protecting him from the painful truth of the kidnapping plot? It seemed reasonable. Didn't it? She would protect him at all costs, and if she knew the truth about Ergh's desperate need for sevels, she had good reason.

She *had* to. For weeks and weeks he'd comforted himself with the belief that she would set everything right. His certainty wavered, and he wished he could cast a magic spell like the sorcerer cousin Morvoren visited in her third book. He'd thought returning home would make everything clear, yet it was only murkier than ever.

It took a moment as he approached the aviary to realize someone was inside. His heart shouldn't have leapt joyfully upon recognizing Cador's bulk bent over the hatchling, but it did all the same. Especially when he realized Cador's fingers were muddy and he was chewing worms to feed Doryty just as he had Derwa.

There shouldn't have been anything attractive about the messy, dirty task, yet desire flitted through Jem. He flushed with memories of what they'd shared only hours ago. Though he'd cleaned himself properly upon returning to his chamber, his rear still twinged, excitement tightening his gut.

Worst of all, a wave of tenderness and affection washed through Jem as he watched Cador murmur to the tiny bird. He crept closer, straining to hear.

When Cador was alerted by the rustle of leaves under Jem's boots, he shot to his feet, fingers grasping for an invisible spear. "Why aren't you asleep?" he asked too loudly, clearly startled.

He wore the Neuvellan clothing, fawn breeches painted on his muscular thighs over tall boots, a blue silk shirt tight across his broad chest. Funny that Jem should prefer him in his plain Erghian garb.

Jem's spine stiffened as he grasped for the safety of irritation. "Why aren't you? Who said you could come here? And were you reading my book?" He pointed accusingly at the worn copy of Morvoren's first book of adventures, though he was the one who'd left it tucked in a little nook created specially for a tome or two to be kept.

Cador leaned out the aviary door and spit a bit of worm onto the grass. He gargled with his flask and spit a few more times before drinking. He bent to close the book and carefully slid it back into the nook. Then he said in a calmer tone, "Couldn't sleep. Santo told me yesterday which path to take here."

Naturally. Jem's instant defensiveness dissipated. "I couldn't sleep either. How is Hedrok?"

"Dying. But your healer drugged him enough to finally put him under. Creeda is with him. I couldn't take any more of her praying."

Jem shuddered, thinking of the bundle of twigs and the sack over his head. "I'm glad he is resting for the moment."

"We must speak with your mother today about the sevels.

scoffed even as his heart swelled at the earnest expression on Cador's stubbly face. "I'm sure you've had many lovers more skilled," Jem said.

"I don't mean lying with you. That's only part of it."

He hesitated, traitorous heart thumping. Waiting.

"Baking bread with you. Listening to your favorite tales from your books. Watching you tend to your hatchlings. Laughing with you."

It had seemed so long since they'd laughed. "About what?"

"I don't know." Cador lifted his hands and let them drop. "Nothing. Everything. I long to see your smile." His gaze dropped down over Jem's body. "I long to taste you. Kiss every part of you and bring you pleasure."

Groin tightening, Jem grasped for a defense. "You just said it wasn't about lying with me."

"I said it was part of it. Of course I want to lie with you. I know you want me too. There is no sin in craving it. Admit that much, at least."

Jem couldn't. Wouldn't. He shook his head.

Cador's jaw tightened as he sighed. He raised his hands. "All right."

"We must get some rest. There is much to…" Jem left the rest unsaid since he wasn't sure exactly how to go about it.

Cador nodded and turned toward the path that disappeared into the green foliage. After a few steps, he stopped, back still to Jem. "If I were a marauder in these woods… If I were a villain who stumbled upon you and had to have you. Well, it would be beyond your control."

The breath punched out of Jem, lust and *relief*, tremors seizing him. For if it were again a game, if they were not themselves… His exhale was a soft moan.

Turning slowly, Cador's lips parted, his icy eyes going dark with lust. "On your knees, boy."

As Jem dropped to the earth gratefully, of course he knew he shouldn't. But he couldn't sleep, could hardly eat—with everything that was happening, he was strung so tightly with worry that he would shatter without some kind of release.

Cador's nostrils flared as he neared. He rubbed himself through his breeches, his cock hardening under Jem's eyes. "You want this?" he asked, his voice going hoarse. He cleared his throat. "Poor innocent little prince lost in the forest. You've found more than you bargained for, hmm?"

Jem nodded. His fingers twitched at his sides. He wanted to yank out Cador's prick and swallow it whole. His own shaft swelled, trapped by soft fabric. He thrummed with desire and even better—anticipation.

Cador dropped his hands to his sides and ordered, "Take out my prick."

Eagerly, Jem released it, loving how big the flushed head looked in his hands. He should have waited for more commands but sucked it into his mouth, moaning and swallowing a bitter drop of fluid. Reveling in the fact that Cador was hard for him so quickly.

No, a marauding woodsman who'd captured him. It was a game. It was safe.

"What a pretty little whore you are," Cador murmured. "No idea what you're in for."

A thrill spiraled through him. He sucked harder and deeper, his lips stretching over the hard cock in his mouth. Try as he might, he couldn't think of Cador by another anonymous name and surrendered to it.

"So eager for me." Without warning, Cador gripped Jem's

hair and thrust.

Choking, Jem coughed and sputtered, swallowing and trying to breathe. He moaned again, rubbing himself as Cador fucked his mouth. His scalp burned, but the flare of pain when Cador pulled his hair only added to the pleasure.

"Mmm. You're no innocent. You love it, don't you?"

Eyes watering, Jem nodded, spit dribbling from the corners of his mouth. Cador pulled out and rubbed his wet tip over Jem's swollen lips. "Should I come down your throat? Or should I rip down your breeches and fuck your arse? Fuck you until you're so full of my cum—"

With a groan, Jem spun to his hands and knees in the fallen leaves and dirt, yanking at his buttons and pleading. "*Please*."

Cador was on him in an instant, teeth on his neck, a chuckle in his ear. "Since you asked so politely..." He tugged Jem's breeches to his knees. "Spread your legs for me."

He did, as much as he could with the material binding him. He gasped as Cador roughly grabbed his arse cheeks apart and spit on his entrance. "It doesn't matter," Jem muttered. "Do it."

It was easier with oil, but Jem bore down, desperate to be filled and find peace. He was shameless, letting Cador fuck him out in the open. He thought of the last time they'd done this outdoors, when he'd felled the boar and he'd felt so powerful and loved.

A sob welled in him, and he ruthlessly choked it down. This couldn't be about love. He couldn't allow it. This was only pleasure and release, a game. This wasn't them. This was what he needed. To be taken. Consumed.

He dug his fingers into the soft leaves and earth, little whimpers and moans escaping as he was fucked, Cador's big hands wonderfully rough on him, one fisted in his hair, the other bruising his hip.

"So good," Cador mumbled. "I want to fuck you forever."

Jem's heart constricted, then soared. *Yes, forever.* He shouldn't want it, but surrendering was too good to resist. "Yes, yes." His cock was like iron. He needed to come, but if he moved a hand to touch himself, he'd end up on his face in the dirt. "I need…" he begged.

Cador thrust powerfully. "I know what you need. I'll give it to you. No one else. You're mine."

Jem couldn't hope to speak now, all cries and moans and sweat-slick body straining. As Cador moved back, he wanted to sob once more and beg him to stay inside. But Cador did, sitting on his heels and hauling Jem with him over his lap.

With a loud rip, Cador tore Jem's breeches and undergarments right in half, and they groaned in concert as Jem sank down fully, his back against Cador's chest, their silk shirts damp and sticking. Jem was splayed wide, knees not reaching the ground, the legs of his ruined breeches dangling.

He was incredibly full. He could only gasp for breath, feeling like Cador was inside him so deeply he would rend him in two. But no, Jem was whole, and it was perfect, pain and a soul-deep pleasure combining. Resting his head back on Cador's shoulder, he moaned.

Cador slid his hands beneath Jem's shirt to twist his nipples, sending shocks straight to his bollocks. "Tell me what you need." His whisper shivered over Jem's ear.

And these words were no game, no command or arrogant demand. This was a plea. With Cador filling him completely, his hands spread over Jem's chest, not teasing now, but merely holding, it was all too real.

Shuddering, Jem's eyes burned. He needed Cador so badly.

To be able to trust him again. To forgive. He clutched at Cador's hips. He was going to break. He wasn't ready. If he asked Cador to stop right now, he knew Cador would.

But Jem couldn't do it. He would become hollow. He'd surely shatter into a million pieces. There was no going back. Only forward. He swallowed, his throat bone dry. It didn't hurt anymore where Cador's cock was buried inside him. He squeezed around that iron flesh.

"I need you. Only you."

With short, sharp thrusts, Cador fucked him, stroking Jem's leaking shaft, the fire blazing through Jem erupting into an inferno. His cries echoed through the trees as he came, Cador grunting, their skin slapping where his groin met Jem's arse.

As Cador found his release, he buried his face against Jem's neck, his lips soft and breath hot, stubble perfectly rough. Jem would barely have to turn his head to find Cador's mouth and kiss him once more. It had been so long, and it was such a simple pleasure. Could he forgive his husband and allow this?

Had he already?

Just as he leaned closer, seeking that sweet kiss, their lips a whisper apart, Cador went rigid. Jem blinked at him in confusion, following his horrified gaze. Cador stared down at his own hand, the wings of the dillywig branded on his palm speckled with blood.

"How?" Cador stared at his hand, then Jem. "I hurt you!" Horror creased his face. No, more than that—self-loathing. "How?" he repeated.

Jem hadn't even realized. He touched his scalp, his fingertips coming away with a faint smear of red. Heart thudding, panic took over. He shook his head violently. "It's nothing! You didn't hurt me!"

Cador caught Jem's hand, peering at the incriminating blood. His brow furrowed. "I didn't think I pulled your hair that hard." He sounded absolutely wretched with guilt. "I'm sorry. Gods. I hurt you." He reached for Jem's head.

Jem lunged off Cador's lap and softening prick, then scuttled back like a crab. "Don't!"

Dropping his head, Cador fisted his hands. "Forgive me. I didn't mean to, I swear it."

"You didn't. It's—I'm fine! Don't—" he broke off. What was that sound? Snapping twigs, leaves rustling—footsteps. "My breeches!" He scrambled, praying the material would somehow hold and cover him, but it was no use.

Someone was coming, and he was half naked, arse and cock completely exposed. The remnants of his breeches hung from each leg, his light undergarments on the ground.

On his feet, Cador yanked up his breeches and spun around, searching the clearing as if somehow a new pair of trousers or at the very least something to cover Jem would magically appear. Then they whirled together to face the intruder, Cador pushing Jem behind him.

Pasco appeared, and Jem cursed the gods to eternity and back.

There was a faint smear of blood at his hairline, and Cador tasted bile again, barely resisting the urge to grasp Jem's head and examine whatever these wounds were.

The more he considered it, the more certain Cador was that Jem was right. Yes, their fucking had been intense and rough, but he hadn't gouged wounds into Jem's scalp. He checked his fingernails again to be sure.

Who had hurt Jem?

Cador's breath came short as he imagined all the ways he could shock and overpower the bastard. Make them pay. Make them suffer. No one spilled a drop of Jem's blood and got away with it. Whatever had happened, he'd find out.

He shrugged out of the shirt, and Jem wrapped it around his slim waist before leading the way deeper into the trees. Cador ducked under low-hanging branches, the foliage dense and close around them. Birds sang, and no breeze reached the hiding spot.

He thought of chasing Jem through the pine forest on Ergh as Jem desperately ran away from Cador and Delen, terrified of what he'd heard. The agony of watching helplessly as Jem leapt from the Cliffs of Glaw as Cador's own brother tried to cut him down.

Now here they were a world away, Cador's bollocks tender from spending so fully. Where had the blood come from? He wanted to ease Jem into his arms and coax the truth from him about the strange wounds, but Jem stood stiffly with arms crossed, his gaze on their boots.

"Are you all right?" Cador asked quietly.

A nerve twitched in Jem's cheek as he clenched his jaw. "The marauding woodsman doesn't—"

"I'm your husband. No more games. Who hurt you?"

"No one," Jem muttered, eyes still downcast.

"Why won't you tell me? Who are you protecting?"

He shook his head, curls waving. "No one, I told you. Are you going to accuse me of infidelity? When would I have had the time to find a lover at the castle?"

Cador breathed through the surge of frustration. "I'm not accusing you of anything. But I know you're lying, and I want to understand why."

Jem's sharp gaze pierced him. "Oh, you know, do you? How? You lied to me for months and I was none the wiser."

"Because you're good and trusting. And not a convincing liar. I wish I hadn't been able to deceive you. All I can do is promise I never will again. You are my greatest joy. If you let me, I'll spend the rest of my life proving my devotion."

Jem's throat worked as he swallowed with a *gulp*. His honey eyes lit up with hope even as he clearly tried to fight it.

Cador sank to his knees, leaves rustling beneath him. Branches scratched his bare back and shoulders. He kept his arms at his sides even though he ached to pull Jem close.

"Please believe me." He peered up at Jem as he had on the cliff top. "My love—my little prince."

"I did it," Jem blurted. His lips trembled, his eyes filling with tears.

"What?"

Jem motioned to his head. "I did it."

It took a few heartbeats like Massen's pounding hooves to understand. Cador shot to his feet, ignoring the scrape of branches. He fought to keep his hands steady as he gently parted Jem's thick hair. Jem dropped his head, apparently surrendering.

Some scratches were almost healed. Others were scabbed with dried blood and a few were fresh marks. It *hurt* to see, and

Cador wished he could heal these wounds with touch and kisses and promises. He could only whisper, "Why?"

Head still bent, Jem was silent so long it seemed he wouldn't answer. Then he did. "I'm not really sure. It's bizarre, I know. But I kept thinking about the sack suffocating me and the cliff and Bryok cutting off my head. The pain...cleared my mind somehow. It became a strange habit when the memories struck, and I could barely breathe. When the nightmares wouldn't stop."

Cador wanted to scream his fury to the fickle gods. He cursed Bryok's name in his heart. He cursed Tas and Delen and most of all himself for being part of the terrible choices that led Jem to Ergh.

He wanted to hunt down Jem's pain and tear it to pieces with his bare hands. But he could only caress Jem's head with the gentlest of touches and wrap him in his arms, Jem's tears dampening his bare chest.

"I'm sorry," Cador croaked. "If I could go back and change it all, I would. I'd never stop until I could keep you safe. I swear it. And I swear I'll never let anyone hurt you again. *I'll* never hurt you again."

Jem sobbed against him, his words almost lost. "I believe you."

Cador longed to hear the words more clearly. Was he forgiven? At least partly? Was there hope to win back Jem? Was it true? Jem had to hear the thunder of Cador's heart under his ear.

For now, Jem was folded into his arms, allowing Cador to comfort him, and it had to be enough.

Still, after long minutes passed and Jem's tears slowed, Cador found he was greedy for more. A kiss wasn't too much to ask, was it? Merely a peck—the feel of those perfect lips against his. He'd been so deeply inside Jem's body, his seed surely still wet in Jem's arse. Yet the thought of a simple kiss seemed so much *more*.

"My little prince," Cador murmured. He drew back only enough to lift Jem's chin with his fingers. Jem slumped against him bonelessly, his tear-streaked face open and vulnerable. Cador traced Jem's full lips with his thumb.

Dipping low, Cador slowly brought their mouths together, only a breath between them—

The onslaught of footsteps through the trees and bushes were too loud to be only Pasco, and as the guards took shape, rushing out with swords drawn, Cador only had time to think that he should have known better than to trust the bastard before he launched into battle with only his bare hands.

Chapter Nineteen

WITH A ROAR, Cador ordered Jem to run, barreling into the oncoming royal guards. Heart in his throat, Jem stumbled back, tripping over one of the legs of his ruined breeches that he couldn't remove without taking off his boots. How had neither of them noticed the guards' approach?

Because they'd been blind to everything but each other and the promise of their lips meeting, of the kisses Jem craved like water for his dry throat. Now, Cador toppled three guards but it was no use. More streamed through the leafy branches, trampling the delicate blossoms that grew in the shadows of the forest floor.

What was happening? Jem had been blind in so many ways. Now had Pasco turned on them? Though why he was taking Cador prisoner was a mystery. Had he truly been concerned that Jem was hurt by his husband? Jem shouted at the guards to release Cador, who kicked and spit and snarled.

"Go!" Cador shouted at him, but even if Jem thought he could outrun the guards, he wasn't leaving.

"Unhand him!" Jem commanded, his voice hoarse.

They ignored him, and his blood boiled.

After clambering up to a low branch of a tew tree, he shouted again. "I said *unhand him!*"

This garnered the attention of the half-dozen guards. They surrounded Cador on the leafy ground, his hands bound with rope behind his back, two men holding down his thrashing feet, a leather gag in his mouth. They looked up at Jem where he stood balanced on the thick branch.

Where he belatedly realized the shirt he wore like a skirt gaped at his hip. He clutched it shut, their eyes on him like ants over his skin. He was supposed to be their prince, and what a spectacle he must look. He expected them to burst into gales of laughter, but apparently they were too well trained.

"Prince Jowan, we have our orders." The woman in charge bowed to him swiftly, her tall hat under her arm, leaves and twigs clinging to her red uniform from the scuffle. A light rain that was more of a mist filled the air.

"I don't care what my brother told you! I'm well, and this is my husband. Release him!"

She shared a glance with another guard before saying, "Your brother, sir?"

"Prince Pasco. I don't know what he said, but I'm ordering you to release my husband."

"We follow the orders of your mother the queen, Prince Jowan. We haven't seen your brother."

Dread sank its claws into Jem. "My mother? But why?"

"I don't know, sir. We do not question the queen's commands. She ordered us to bring your husband back to the castle."

"As a prisoner? This is preposterous! I won't allow it!"

With a flick of her head, the woman apparently gave the order to take Cador away, and he shouted around his gag as they dragged him out of sight. Pasco appeared holding dark breeches for him, and the remaining guards departed.

Jem tugged off his boots and redressed eagerly. "Why did Mother have Cador seized? What the fuck's happened?"

"Never heard such language from you, brother. Damned if I know."

"You're saying you had nothing to do with this? It isn't because Cador hurt me?"

Pasco's gaze narrowed. "You insisted he didn't. *Has* he hurt you? Tell me the truth."

"No! I meant that you'd thought he had. But he didn't."

"Jem, he's not here. He's a barbarian, and you never should have been traded off to him. I did my best to dissuade Mother, but her mind was set."

Jem examined his brother's serious, pinched expression. Pasco seemed sincere. "You seemed amused by my predicament at the time. Nothing more."

He held up his hands. "I tried to make light of it, yes. The deal had been made—there was no sense in worrying you even more. I told you on your wedding day I thought you and Prince Treeve of Ebrenn would be far better matched. Mother wouldn't hear of it."

Jem did faintly recall it. "Oh. Yes. She hates the West."

"That old son of a bitch on the throne won't live forever. It was shortsighted." Pasco sighed with a shrug. "But Mother knows far more than either of us about ruling."

"Well, at least Treeve is trying to stop his father from attacking us."

Pasco stood straighter. "What? How do you know that?"

"I met him at the Holy Place."

"Treeve?" His voice rose. "When?"

"Like I just said, at the Holy Place. He helped Cador and me escape his father."

For a moment, Pasco seemed truly flummoxed. Jem marched in the direction of the trail back to the castle, but Pasco reached for his arm.

"Wait. Tell me truly—has that stone-headed beast hurt you?"

Jem had to answer truthfully. "Yes." He quickly added, "Though not in the way you think. He's never raised a hand to me. It was ages before we actually…" He motioned vaguely with his hand, cringing to discuss this with Pasco of all people. "And it was good. Very good."

Pasco's brow furrowed. "I admit, he does look at you as if… Well, similar to how you once regarded your precious books. But I saw blood. Vigorous bed sport—even in the woods—is one thing, but—"

"It was a scratch I already had. I'm telling you, it wasn't Cador."

"All right. Then how did he hurt you?"

"I'll explain it all, but I must go to him first." Jem took off at a run.

"Hold on!" Pasco grumbled.

Jem knew the valley's nooks and crannies far more intimately, and he left his brother behind, not willing to wait and not needing to stick to the path to find his way to the dungeon below the castle.

He was out of breath when he skidded to a stop before the young male guard he recognized, the ground soft with steady rain now. The guard shot to his feet from where he crouched by the dungeon entrance to stay out of the rain, protesting only slightly when Jem shoved past him into the dank tunnel. Grabbing a rusty lamp from a hook on the wall, Jem rushed to the cells. Voices rose behind him.

Yet Cador wasn't there. The lantern cast long shadows over the miserable stone walls and iron bars as he hurried along the row. As he neared the end, a terrible cry echoed, familiar from Jem and Cador's imprisonment.

"Prince Jowan, please!" The young guard was at his heels, others coming as well. "You're not supposed to be here."

Jem spun. "Why not?" A horrible thought gripped him. "Who is that prisoner?" Oh Gods, he should have found out. What if...

Yet when he thrust the lantern between the bars of the final cell, he didn't recognize the crumpled man in the corner. It wasn't Kenver. For an instant, he'd been sure he was about to discover a vital piece of the puzzle, and disappointment settled through him, the heady rush of his dash from the forest dissipating. He still had to find Cador. The prisoner wailed, holding up a trembling hand to the invasion of light.

"Who is he?" Jem demanded.

The guard said, "I don't know his name. He's from a village near the coast. Won't stop drinking too much ale and beating his wife. The magistrate has decreed he stay here until he regains his senses."

"Oh. Did the healer see to him?"

"Yes, but they said there's nothing to be done until he adjusts to the lack of ale."

"You haven't seen my husband today?"

The young man blinked. "The Erghian? No, Prince Jowan." He seemed sincerely confused.

With a curt nod, Jem ran, almost ending up on his sore arse, his boots slipping on the damp stone floor of the tunnel, his lantern light swaying madly. He shoved the lantern toward another confused guard at the entrance, ignoring the chief guard's shouts as he veered toward the stable.

There was no time to climb back up the winding drive to the

castle, and it would take too long for a carriage. Jem raced into the barn, ignoring the surprised rumblings of the grooms. There was Dybri, the mare who'd bore them from the Holy Place. His heart thumped. He'd struggled to mount her before, but he'd do it now.

Could he?

Yes! He'd do it. He'd worked hard on Ergh to learn. Thoughts of Austol and betrayal intruded, and he shoved them away, blinking up at Dybri. She was so big, and falling off her back would hurt and—

He paused, attempting to banish the fear and uncertainty. He could ride! He'd done it before. Why was he so afraid now? He took a run of a few steps, desperation fueling him.

"There you are! Darling, what are you doing?"

At his mother's familiar voice, Jem's timing went off, and he yanked on poor Dybri's mane as he slammed down on his arse on the hay-strewn floor. Dybri whinnied, other voices rising. Pain radiated up Jem's spine as embarrassment flushed him.

"Jem!" Mother was there reaching for him.

He scuttled back out of reach, jumping to his feet and ignoring the ache in his backside. "Where's Cador? Why did your guards take him?"

"Darling, calm down. I'll explain everything when—"

"*Now*. You'll explain now!"

Eyes widening, she stared at him. The grooms went silent. She addressed them sharply. "Leave us."

As they scurried out into the rain, Dybri stamped and snorted, and Jem pet her neck, murmuring to her. "It's all right. I'm sorry, girl." To his mother, he demanded in a hard tone, "Tell me where Cador is."

"He's perfectly safe, I assure you."

Gods, how Jem longed to be assured. This was his mother, after all. She'd always taken care of him. Well. Until she hadn't. But it'd been time for Jem to do his duty by marrying Cador.

Everything was so muddled now, but he could still trust her. Couldn't he? There had to be an explanation for her knowledge of the sevels and Cador's arrest.

Yet dread roiled in Jem's stomach, his life feeling dangerously out of control. He was home, and home was supposed to be safe. His mother should have been safe. Part of him wanted to throw himself into her arms and be comforted, but he realized with a pang of sorrow that those days were over, no matter what was actually going on.

Jem cleared his throat. "Tell me."

Her mouth tightened into a smile that was mostly grimace. "There's been an...incident. I felt it prudent to take Cador into custody to prevent any unpleasantness. I'm sure it will prove to be unnecessary, but I refuse to take chances with your safety."

"Cador wouldn't hurt me." Yes, he had, but Jem grew more and more certain with each word. "I trust him completely. He's my husband. My partner. We take care of each other. We've had our struggles, but he won't hurt me now."

She regarded him silently for long moments. "I truly hope that's the case, my dear."

"Where is he? What happened?"

"Come. Let us discuss this in privacy. Have you eaten breakfast? We can—"

"Stop! I'm not a child! Stop coddling me." He could admit he'd been eager to return home and nestle under his mother's protective wing.

No more.

She stared at him wide-eyed. "Jem. You're still my baby, no

matter how old you grow.

"Tell me!" He flung out his hands, knocking over a broom resting against Dybri's stall and sending a bucket rolling and clattering to the next stall. Cursing, he went after it without thinking, plucking the bucket from the floor, another horse snorting and likely expecting some feed.

As Jem turned back to his mother, he opened his mouth to once again demand answers. Then he stopped. He looked back at the other horse, this one a huge stallion. He stepped toward it tentatively. Another step when the beast made no move. Reaching out, he scratched its muzzle and peered closely at the white speckles splashed over the gray horse's face.

"Lusow?"

The horse whinnied, rubbing its muzzle into Jem's hand.

"Why is Jory's horse here?" Jem spun to face his mother, who watched him warily. Perhaps Lusow had been exhausted by the journey south. That was plausible. Jory could have taken another mount when he left with the chieftain to search for Cador and Jem...when? Gods, what day was it? How long had they been at the castle? On the mainland? It had all blurred into a jumble.

"When did Kenver leave with Locryn to search for us? Why didn't Jory take his horse? He loves Lusow. Why aren't they back yet? Surely if you sent a rider after them, we should have heard a message by now?"

There. Most people wouldn't have noticed the flicker on his mother's face before her expression smoothed into the familiar comforting, calm visage.

Jem was not most people.

"Where are they?" Gods, poor Jory, who'd only been kind to Jem. His voice rose. "What have you done?"

Her jaw clenched. "Jem. Calm yourself. This isn't like you."

"Where are they? Where's Cador?" What if he'd been hurt? What if… His heart thudded, clammy sweat breaking out over his body. "Tell me the truth!"

"I will, but you must calm yourself. Cador is perfectly safe. They're all safe."

For the first time in his life, Jem wasn't sure if he believed his mother, and he hated it more than he could bear. He hardened his voice, though it trembled. "Where?"

"In the castle."

"The chieftain and Jory? Cador?"

"Yes. And his sister and the others. They haven't been harmed, but they've needed to be…contained."

The fist of fear and tension in Jem's chest loosened a fraction. "Cador is unharmed?"

"Of course."

"You say that as if I'm being unreasonable for fearing otherwise. Why did you tell us his father and Jory had left to find us?"

She glanced around. "This isn't the place for this discussion."

Jem planted his boots on the dusty floor, ignoring the stench of fresh shit. Lusow and Dybri snuffled and shifted. "I'm Neuvella's emissary on Ergh. My husband is next in line to be chieftain. You married me off to him for the good of Onan. You said it was time to grow up and do my duty, and you were right. Tell. Me."

Crossing her arms, bracelets jangling, Mother said, "I received word from the Holy Place that you'd arrived. That you'd tried to flee your husband, but he'd caught you and spirited you away on a horse to gods-knew where."

"Because King Perran and his soldiers showed up!"

"Yes, but why were you running from Cador in the first place? No one knew."

"I wasn't! Well, I was, but…" He could see how the snatches of information could be misleading. He *had* run from Cador and the Erghians, and Cador had hunted him down. Loudly.

"I wasn't about to take any risks, Jem. If Cador were holding you captive, I would have leverage. I received a confusing message shortly before this Jory arrived, so I tucked him safely away with the chieftain until I had more information."

"*Tucked* them away? Where? I've been in the dungeon."

She wrinkled her nose. "Of course I wouldn't put them *there*. The north tower has a suitable set of chambers. They're perfectly comfortable."

Jem wanted to scream. "But Cador and I have been here for days!" Yes, it was surely days at this point. "Why did you lie to us?"

"I had to discover Cador's intentions." She smiled softly. "He does seem to truly love you. I'm glad of it. Surprised, but glad."

"Why surprised? You don't think I'm lovable?"

She huffed, lips pressing together. "Don't be ridiculous. I simply didn't expect a barbarian of Ergh to appreciate your worth."

"Yet you forced me to marry him anyway."

"Yes. It was your duty—as you now agree. We all must do our duty to our people. As regrettable as it can be at times."

"Yet now you've locked up Cador with his father? I don't understand any of this! And I heard you and Tregereth—how did you know about the sevels and this horrible disease? How is Hedrok? Have you imprisoned him too?"

clerics or belief in the gods. "How long have they known about the disease?"

She shrugged. "Who can say? Years, I'm sure."

"*Years*?" he shouted.

"Shh!" His mother's eyes blazed. "Jem, this is a dangerous business. Keep your voice down." At his nod, she added, "As I said, the clerics are patient."

"But innocent children suffer." He shuddered, thinking of Eseld and Hedrok and so many more.

"What better way to gain followers on Ergh? People desperately want to believe the gods can fix anything."

"But you knew too?"

She sighed. "Ysella came to me two years ago, shortly after Ergh attended the peace summit for the first time in forever. Her loyal spies on Ergh had informed her well. There seems to be a link between the sevel drought and the disease; therefore Ergh needs our sevels at any cost."

"'Our'? Ebrenn is the only place the sevels grow."

"Yes, but Ebrenn is part of the mainland, and control of the sevel crop must remain here. As much as I hate Perran, we've always been able to reach a bargain without bloodshed. Ergh might be vastly outnumbered, but never underestimate barbarians. Nor desperate, grieving parents. The sevels are more valuable than we could have guessed, and the mainland must control the crop."

"Even as children die in agony?"

Her face pinched. "It truly is a terrible thing. Most regrettable, but as a Neuvellan territory, we will soon provide assistance."

Regrettable. Assistance. Neuvellan territory?

Jem's throat was so dry he could imagine he'd swallowed

dust or ashes. "For two years we could have at least shipped all our sevels to Ergh."

"And leave none for our own children? A balance must be struck. We will send our best and brightest to help Ergh grow sevels again."

He nodded dully. "In return, you'll mine Ergh's distant mountains, hoping to strike a new source of the oil you depend on Ebrenn for."

"Exactly. And if Ergh can grow sevels, all the better. Even less dependence on the West."

"And what does Gwels think of this?"

"They'll think whatever I tell them, Jem. They are our closest allies. They're family."

Family. A word that had never seemed so very complex before. Jem asked, "What do the clerics get?"

"They'll build temples and schools across Ergh. We might not share all their beliefs, but the gods do bring comfort and meaning to many."

He thought of the crude altars to the gods in Rusk. Creeda and her bundle of twigs, her child dying in agony. They'd all been pawns in a much bigger game. Jem's marriage, even if—

A thought so hideous struck him with the force of an angry stallion's kick. Shivering, Jem could feel the blood drain from his face.

"Darling?" His mother reached for him. He stumbled back, thudding into the stall. Suddenly, the least frightening option was to mount Dybri or one of the other horses and gallop far, far away.

Yet he had to ask. "Did you know?"

She shook her head. "Know what?"

The words were like shattered glass on his tongue. "Did you

and Ysella know about the chieftain's plan?" They seemed steps ahead of the Erghians at every turn. "Were you going to let him go through with it?"

Her gaze sharpened along with her voice. "What plan?"

"To kidnap me. To, to—" He clenched his fists, the outline of the brand on his right hand feeling fresh and searing. "Cut off my hand and send it to you. Framing King Perran for it. So you would join Ergh in war against him."

For an endless moment, Jem's mother only stared, a chasm of despair yawning open inside him. Then fury erupted, her brown eyes flashing and her face flushing as she too clenched her fists. Relief flowed in Jem. She hadn't known.

"Kenver planned this?" She bit out the question through gritted teeth. "He'll pay for it. Oh, how he will pay."

"No! Please. Enough. We must come together. Ysella and the clerics are right in that at least. I can forgive Cador and the others for what they did. Unity is the way forward."

Perhaps it should have been a more complex process to reach forgiveness. Perhaps he should have exhaustively debated it with himself. Yet as the leaden grief and sorrow in his heart lifted free, he understood how very heavy it had been.

Jem didn't want to carry it a moment longer. He wanted to run to Cador and finally—finally—kiss him again. It was difficult to breathe with the yearning.

"Jem?" His mother watched him with furrowed confusion and an impatient shift of her silk slippers in the hay.

"Yes." He reluctantly refocused. "I forgive them. And after what happened with Bryok…"

"Tell me everything."

It was a command, and Jem did as he was told, relaying the horrible, sad story. From the chieftain's plan to Cador's change of heart, to Bryok's betrayal that would have seen Jem lose his head. He didn't forgive Bryok, and that was all right. He didn't have to. Bryok was at the bottom of the Askorn Sea, and he'd terrorize Jem no more.

His mother engulfed him in a fierce embrace, and it was a wonderful luxury to relax against her and breathe in her lavender scent. Only for a minute, he could take comfort. But a minute only, for a hue and cry rose above the drumming rain.

"Western soldiers approach!"

Chapter Twenty

I F THIS WOULD be his end, Cador wished he could have kissed Jem one last time.

He kicked and thrashed, but he was bound, his arms wrenched painfully behind him. It was humiliating to be hauled like a felled boar, and he gnawed on the leather gag, mumbling the crudest curses he could think of.

It was hard to see where he was being dragged, and he expected to go down into the dungeon again. He had no idea what the fuck was going on but assumed it was Pasco's doing. Perhaps the man thought he was genuinely protecting his brother, but Cador still wanted to rip out his flimsy spine.

Instead of down, they seemed to be taking him up into the castle. Not by the massive staircase off the entrance, but a narrow, twisting passage lit only by the flickering glow of lamps. Cador bumped up the stairs, rough hands on his arms, barely able to get his thin, useless boots under him.

What if Jem was in danger? The guards hadn't seized him but who knew what the fuck was going on. He growled around the smooth, damp leather in his mouth, ready to chew through it—then the throats of anyone who tried to keep him from Jem. He didn't need his spear or sword or his hands at all. He'd kill them all. He'd—

A door opened, and he stumbled into a room headfirst, barely able to gain his footing before crashing onto his chin.

Angry voices rose. He braced, expecting kicks and blows or worse, but then Tas was hauling him up, Tas was there, and Delen and Jory, and what the fuck?

The room shook with a mighty thud, and Cador blinked in the lamp light, the windows here narrow and high. It took him a few moments to realize that the sky beyond was also unnaturally dark and gray. It made him think of Ergh with a pang of longing so powerful he almost wept as Tas hugged him.

"My son, my son," Tas muttered, and Cador leaned into him gratefully. He was about to disappoint Tas beyond the telling, and he let himself enjoy the moment of peace.

Cador's hands were freed, and he shook them gratefully. Delen was there pressing fabric to his chin, saying something he couldn't focus on. Jory hugged him as well, and there was a terrible keening that make him want to clap his hands over his ears.

Creeda wept, huddled on the stone floor, Delen going to her side and cradling her. The chamber—for it was a chamber with an ornate bed in the corner—was crammed full of Erghians. How were Tas and Jory here? Had they just returned? Had they been taken captive? Where was Jem?

There was apparently an adjoining chamber, this one also with an ornate bed, though not as fancy as Jem's. Cador allowed himself to be steered into this room with Tas and Delen, Jory trying to soothe Creeda now, her wails louder.

Tas shut the door, leaning back against it with a weariness Cador had never seen in him before. His light hair was wild, and his pale skin was smudged dark beneath his eyes. He looked as though he'd been wearing his leathers for days.

Creeda's cries were muffled, though Delen paced, shooting worried glances to the door as though she could see through it.

"We have to get out of here. She must be allowed to return to Hedrok."

"*Allowed*," Tas spat. "We must take what is ours! That bitch of a queen will not hold me another day."

"Hold you?" Cador's mind raced as he tried to make sense of it. "You've been here? Prisoner?" Dread seized him. He'd believed without question when Jem's mother said Tas and Jory had gone looking for him. "How long?"

"A fucking week. That bitch locked me up and threw in Jory when he arrived. Guess her spy was able to ride ahead of him. Probably knew a shortcut." Tas paced the way a boar did when captured. Cador wouldn't be surprised if he snorted the same way. "She said it was 'merely a precaution.' Been bringing us their fancy food and pretending to be hospitable. She's lucky Bryok isn't here. Where is he? Why did you and the prince return?"

Here was the moment, thrust upon them with no warning. Cador and Delen shared a glance. Sweat glistened on her face, and her arm was wounded, blood seeping through a makeshift bandage. She had the wild energy of the hunt, and if only they were home with spears in their hands and horseflesh bearing them through the winter forest.

"What the fuck is going on?" Tas demanded. Not in a shout but a whisper, which sent an icy coil through Cador.

"Bryok's dead." Cador's own voice sounded strange. "I'm sorry. It's my fault."

"Bullshit!" Delen hissed.

Tas echoed, "Dead?" He rocked unsteadily like he might topple over despite his sturdy boots.

Cador nodded. "I'm sorry," he repeated. As Delen opened her mouth, he held up his hand. He took another breath, gathering his courage. "But it wasn't my fault. Or Delen's. It was Bryok's. No one else's. He betrayed us all. He would have cut off Jem's head rather than his hand. He thought you weak, Tas. He insisted murdering Jem was necessary, but he wanted more than the sevels. He wanted to conquer the mainland for his own greed."

Cador thought of Jem on the edge of the cliff, terrified and betrayed, utterly alone. Brave and beautiful. He loved Jem so much he almost couldn't bear it. Almost.

"Bryok's right. I was too weak. Too willing to be merciful when mercy will be the end of Ergh." Tas snarled. "I'd cut off the prince's head right now and feed it to his mother if that's what it takes."

"No!" Cador's heart raced. "Jem is innocent. He wants nothing more than to help us. Help Ergh."

The grim focus of Tas's eyes on him had Cador stepping back. He suddenly felt raw and exposed with his bared torso.

Tas asked too calmly, "What is that you call him? 'Jem'? Don't tell me Prince Jowan has made a fool of you?"

"Tas, please," Delen said. "Jem is a good man. Brave and honorable. He might be tiny, but he is worthy of Cador's love."

"*Love?*" Tas shouted, his voice going hoarse. "He has made a fool of you all right. I should have listened to Bryok. You're too weak to do what's necessary. *Love?* With that sorry wisp of a boy?"

"My husband is not pathetic!" Cador clenched his fists, blood-red rage surging. "And I wouldn't change anything. I'd marry him again tomorrow. And the next day and the next. I'll spend the rest of my life treasuring him above all else."

"Even your duty to your people?" Tas demanded.

"Yes." It was simple. He didn't have to weigh the options.

"You chose Prince Jowan over your brother?"

"Yes!" Again, Cador didn't hesitate. He repeated, "Yes. I'd choose Jem again a thousand times. As would you have if Father had ever been threatened like that."

Tas gaped. "You dare compare your father to that pathetic mainlander? You dare put him above your own brother?"

"Jem has my heart. Bryok is at the bottom of the Askorn Sea where he belongs."

Now Tas's eyes widened. "You killed him, didn't you? You killed Bryok to protect that—"

"Yes!" Cador willed Delen to stay silent. "Bryok was a liar! Dishonorable. He betrayed you and us all. When did you start hating Jem so much? Didn't you pity him?"

"That was before his mother locked me up!" Tas screamed, spittle flying from his lips, teeth bared. "I don't give a fuck about these people, only Ergh's suffering!"

"But that isn't the way forward," Delen said calmly. "And *I* killed Bryok. He would have murdered Cador and Jem, and I have no regrets. Creeda has no regrets. Only for her children." She glanced to the shut door. "I must go to her. Then we will ask for an audience with the queen, and we will discuss the way forward. We are vastly outnumbered. Ergh's future hangs in the balance. Anger will not triumph, Tas, and you know it."

He slumped against the tapestry-covered wall. "Leave me," he muttered.

Part of Cador was eager to get away from Tas and his anger. Worse—his disappointment. Cador had meant what he said about choosing Jem. He'd never take it back. But he'd never disappointed his parent like this. He felt so *small*.

Should he beg Tas to understand? To release him from his role as the next chieftain—though he hoped that wouldn't need to be hashed out for years. First things first. So much was happening, and Cador didn't know where to start. Oh, to be home with Jem in the peace of the forest away from politics and betrayal.

Neither he nor Delen left. They waited as Tas closed his eyes, leaning against the tapestry of the castle in which they stood, silence heavy but for his ragged breaths. "Bryok is truly gone?"

"Yes." Delen lifted her hands. "I'd say I'm sorry, but I'm not."

Tas jolted, eyes opening. "Not weak like your brother. You should be the next chieftain, my daughter."

"I agree!" Cador exclaimed. If Tas thought it would wound him, his spear had gone far wide of the mark. "The last thing I want is to lead Ergh. I don't care if I'm next in line. I don't want it. I never have, and I never will. I want to return to my cottage. Hunt boar and fuck my husband and raise a family with him in joy and peace. Delen will be the leader we need. The leader we deserve."

Tas seemed truly shocked now, hurt and anger and confusion creasing his pale, drawn face. Cador immediately wanted to apologize, to earn back Tas's favor, to be his faithful and obedient child as always. But he couldn't. He wouldn't.

To Delen, Cador said, "Forgive me. I was a pisshead when we parted."

Delen smiled. "You were." She hugged him tightly, whispering, "We must stand united. Tas is not himself. He will understand in time."

Cador could agree Tas was not himself, though perhaps it was wishful thinking. To plot to kidnap Jem and sever his hand in the first place meant this part of him had always lurked. It didn't matter now. Hedrok was dying, Jem was at risk, and it was time to meet with the queen and tell the fucking truth for a change.

IT WASN'T LONG before the outer chamber door swung open. Cador wanted to raise his fists in a mighty cheer when Jem walked in, but Jem only gave him a nod, his expression cool and damn confusing. Cador almost strode over and swept him up into a kiss anyway.

Dripping water all over the stone floor as if he'd gone for a swim, Jem stiffly approached, the guards watching warily from the doorway. He bowed to Tas and said, "I apologize for your confinement." His gaze flicked to Jory. "And yours. All of you."

Tas snorted. "How generous."

Cador's instinct was to defend Jem, but he'd spent his life obeying Tas. Seeking his approval. Clearly he'd lost that now, but he still hesitated. He looked to Delen, who sat in the corner with Creeda's head in her lap. Delen watched Tas closely. Creeda had finally wailed herself into exhaustion, passing out more than falling asleep.

Though he looked like a tiny drowned boar as he wiped his wet curls off his face, Jem stood straight. Unbowed. He said, "When I left Ergh, seeing you and your children locked away in the dungeon was my greatest wish."

Not a surprise, but it still gave Cador a sick jolt to hear Jem say it. Delen watched silently, stroking Creeda's tangled mess of hair, and Tas glowered.

Jem continued. "I imagined I would return home and tell my mother what you'd done. How you'd planned to maim me at the very least and see me suffer to manipulate her. Then she'd throw the three of you in the dungeon, and I'd be safe. She'd take charge and fix everything. Make this all go away so I could return to my sheltered little world of books and privilege. Find a way to heal the sick children without war. Somehow. It didn't matter as long as all was right in the world once more."

He met Cador's gaze, and Cador could hardly breathe. Jem said, "But I can't go back. None of us can. Our world is changed, and we must band together to build a new future."

"Why should we believe a word of this? Where's the queen? Why isn't she apologizing?"

"Why aren't *you*?" Delen hissed. "Jem didn't deserve any of this."

"And our children did?" Tas roared. "Hedrok did?"

Creeda stirred awake, and Delen petted her as she said to Tas, "Of course not. But Jem's right. We must work together for all our children. You and the queen have both made a mess of things trying to protect your people. Who knows what the West will do, but—"

"Perran's soldiers are less than an hour away." Jem grimaced as thunder boomed so loudly the windows rattled. "And it seems Glaw has finally decided to make up for lost time with the late-summer rains. My mother is preparing for the West's arrival. Hopefully it won't be an invasion. The army that approaches is small, so we'll see."

"Let us fight!" Tas shouted. He quickly added, "As you said, we must be allies."

"We hope to avoid any fighting, but yes, you are all released. I will take Creeda back to her son."

Creeda, who shoved herself to her feet with Delen following, wasted no time in barreling out the door. Jem hesitated, blinking at the floor. Cador followed his gaze to the bundle of twigs Creeda must have dropped.

For a moment, Jem looked like he might vomit. Then, with a deep breath, he crossed the room and picked up the talisman. Giving Cador another calm nod, he left.

Tas was saying something, but Cador raced after Jem, soon dizzy in the tight circular tube of stairs. From below, Hedrok's screams echoed, Jem staying just out of reach as Cador struggled to stay upright on his ridiculous boots, his chin throbbing.

It seemed like chaos in the sickroom, though really it was still aside from Hedrok's thrashing arms. The healer stood nearby with hands clasped, Creeda on her knees by the bed and Delen hovering near.

Jem extended the twig talisman to Creeda, a tremor in his hand. She tore her gaze from her son, poor Hedrok writhing though his tortured body could barely move now aside from his arms. Creeda snatched the twigs from Jem but only stared at them, not launching into one of her prayers.

Cador dropped to his knees across the sickbed from her, taking one of Hedrok's hands. It was hot and sweaty, trembling and weak. What could Cador say to provide any comfort? What could anyone say or do? The tendons in Hedrok's neck were surely going to burst through his papery skin, and the screech of his cries would haunt Cador's nightmares.

"Can't you do something?" he demanded of the healer—what had Jem called them? Tregereth?

Tregereth stepped forward. "The only thing any of us can do is ease his journey to the gods."

Jem seemed to brace, inching back from Creeda to the foot of the bed. Delen too seemed to ready for a battle. But Creeda only stared between the bundle of twigs and her boy. She placed her hand atop Hedrok's head and looked not to the healer, but Jem.

"What do you think?"

Jem actually glanced behind, clearly surprised she was asking him. He stepped forward and kneeled beside her. "I think Tregereth is right and you should allow them to end Hedrok's pain." He looked to Cador, raising his eyebrows in question.

"Yes," Cador rasped before clearing his throat. "You've done everything you can. Bryok..." He wished he knew what to say about his brother.

Creeda gritted her teeth. "Bryok should be here with his son, but he never had the kind of strength that matters." She pressed the talisman to her dry lips. "Will you pray with me?" She looked to Tregereth and nodded in one sharp motion.

As the healer went about their work, Hedrok seemed to sense relief was coming, his cries calming to pitiful whimpers. Cador held his hand as he choked on Tregereth's potion, Creeda murmuring her prayers, her palm anchoring her son's head as he passed from this life to what Cador sincerely hoped would be a place of peace.

It happened shockingly quickly, Hedrok's hand going cold and clammy in Cador's grip in only a few heartbeats. He was so very small, and Cador could imagine him simply withering into dust now that the pain had vanished along with his life. Hedrok was empty, and Cador felt the same.

Creeda prayed and prayed, all of them witnessing her pleas with heads bowed until she fell silent. Delen gave Cador a little nod, and he and Jem slipped out with the healer, who went on their way without another word.

Cador and Jem were finally alone again in the hallway, rain lashing the windows under a stony sky. Had it only been hours since Cador had fucked him roughly and spilled inside him? He was still shirtless and Jem was sodden and shivering.

Before Cador could think of the right thing to say or take Jem into his arms or do anything other than stand there uselessly, that fucker Pasco strode down the hall. Cador growled with a sudden burst of rage. He wanted to punch and spear and scream, for Hedrok was dead and it wasn't fucking fair.

Jem grabbed his arm. "No. It wasn't Pasco who took you to the tower."

"I don't care." But he didn't fight, eager to feel the touch of Jem's small hand.

Pasco raised his hands. "We have bigger foes to face."

"Perran's army?" Jem asked sharply.

"I assume the rain has slowed their approach at least." Pasco peered out the windows, forehead furrowing. "These rains are heavier than usual. I suppose it's better than wildfires, but Glaw is overdoing it." He turned his frown on Jem and Cador. "You two better clean up. How is the boy?"

"Dead," Cador answered flatly.

Pasco's mouth turned down. "I'm truly sorry. We must cure this terrible disease."

Cador had to agree, so he nodded, the restless, bloodthirsty energy fading. "You will help us fight King Perran for the sevels if need be?"

"If need be," Pasco agreed easily. "You two must make yourselves presentable."

Cador scoffed. "I can run King Perran through on my sword naked if I have to." Too bad he'd left it behind at the Holy Place.

"As...*impressive* as that might be to watch, let us hope diplomacy will be attempted first." Pasco turned on his heel and left them.

Jem released Cador's arm, walking toward the grand staircase. Cador followed, for what else could he do? He wanted to be at his side. Yet at the door to Jem's chamber upstairs, Jem turned to block him, saying, "You need to change. Your clothes are in there." He nodded to the marriage chamber.

"Yes, but—"

"Please. We must join my mother and ensure whatever negotiations happen are in Ergh's best interest. Everything else can wait."

"We don't even know if there will be negotiations."

"No, but let's hope for it. Whatever happens, we must represent Ergh with honor."

He was right, and Cador loved him all the more for caring about Ergh's best interests. So he nodded and retreated to the other chamber instead of carrying Jem to his bed and stripping off his wet clothes to warm him with kisses. It would have to wait. Jem might still reject him, so at least Cador could live in hope for a little while longer.

He pawed through the clothing hanging in a wardrobe, pleased to see the seamstress had already finished true Erghian-style clothes including leather trousers and vest. He hesitated. If a fight did break out with the Western soldiers, these clothes would be far more practical. But would it be more...political to wear the fancy Neuvellan things?

Tas would hate it. But would it please Jem and the queen? What mattered most was coming to an agreement with King Perran. Reluctantly, he picked a green silk shirt and clean breeches. He was still struggling with the shirt's fine, smooth buttons when Jem knocked.

"Come in!" Cador called, annoyed that Jem had knocked at all. They were still married. This was their wedding chamber, wasn't it?

"Are you ready?" Jem remained in the doorway. His curls were still damp, but he looked every inch the mainland prince in a fresh purple shirt and fawn breeches and boots.

"If I could just… Why do you mainlanders insist on wearing such ridiculous garments?" He was ready to rip off the damn buttons.

"Here, let me." Jem joined him by the wardrobe, easily closing the row of buttons. Jem peered into the wardrobe. "Wait, why don't you put on the leather?"

"I wasn't sure if—I thought you might like me more in this." He hadn't meant it to sound so damn needy. "Not—I don't—" He grunted in disgust, not knowing what the fuck to say or do.

Jem watched him silently before reaching into the wardrobe and pulling out the stiff new leather clothing. "Neuvellan clothes don't suit you." He frowned. "Your chin is bleeding again." He disappeared into the bathing room.

He wasn't wrong that the thin, fancy clothes didn't suit Cador. They made him uncomfortable, and obviously he should wear the leathers. It shouldn't have fucking wounded him to hear Jem say what he did.

Stop being pathetic.

Whether he was a mighty hunter of Ergh or a marauding woodsman or whoever he had to be for Jem to forgive him, he wouldn't win back his husband with childish sulking and hurt feelings.

Cador yanked on the black leather trousers and laced the vest over his bare chest. There were even boots that had clearly been modified from a tall Neuvellan pair, but they'd do.

He sat on a stool to tug up the boots, raising his head to find Jem watching. Silently, he approached Cador and dabbed at his cut chin with a damp cloth. Though Cador still sat on the stool, Jem didn't have to bend far to tend to his chin. He leaned close between Cador's legs. Holding his breath, Cador wanted to wrap his arms around Jem's middle and never let go.

But he kept his hands at his sides as Jem dabbed a stinging ointment on his chin before saying, "That'll have to do. We should find my mother." He paused, his hand coming to rest on Cador's bare arm. "I'm sorry about Hedrok. I wish there was more we could have done."

"At least he's not suffering any longer." Without warning, tears pricked Cador's eyes. He had to breathe deeply before he could say, "We must help the other innocents before it's too late." He pushed to his feet before he started weeping.

Worse than being pathetic and weak was the fear that if he allowed himself the grief and tears, Jem wouldn't offer comfort, and that would hurt even more.

Chapter Twenty-One

THE KNOCK CAME before Jem could find the words to comfort Cador. Cador strode to the door, throwing it open to reveal a quaking servant girl who squeaked, "Your father is looking for you!" and gave a lightning-quick bow before disappearing.

Kenver filled the doorway, barging inside with Jory on his heels. Jory flashed Jem an apologetic smile even though Jem's mother had just kept him locked up for days. Kenver spoke to Cador, ignoring Jem.

"Where's Hedrok? Now that I'm free to roam—for the moment—I would see him."

Jem stifled his groan. Cador's tas had the bearing of a caged mountain bear from Ebrenn Jem had seen as a boy at a summer fair. He'd changed into the fur-topped cloak he'd worn at the Holy Place all those months ago.

It seemed another life.

"He's gone," Cador told him bluntly. "I'm sorry. But he only knew pain at the end, so it is best."

Kenver nodded, seeming to lose a few inches of height. "I would see him anyway. And his mother." He turned and strode away without a glance at Jem, clearly expecting Cador to follow.

Cador hesitated. "Jem..."

"Go on. I owe Jory an apology."

Frowning at that, Cador left. There was so much more Jem

should say to him, but he didn't know where to start. At least he knew with Jory, who was opening his mouth, holding out his hands in likely protest.

"I'm sorry," Jem said. "You've only tried to be a friend to me since I first journeyed to Ergh, and I rebuffed you. I was jealous."

Tucking his wild ginger hair behind his ear, Jory smiled softly. "There's no need to apologize, but I accept."

"Just like that?"

Jory seemed genuinely puzzled. "Of course. I only want you and Cador to be happy. For *everyone* to be happy and well." His pale face flushed. "A childish wish."

"No. It is a simple wish, but we share it. I'm not sure how to achieve it, though. Seems that will be frightfully complicated."

"Indeed. What of you and Cador?"

Jem smiled wanly. "More complications. By the way, I saw Lusow in the stable. He seems no worse for wear."

"Ah. Thank the gods. May I see him?"

"Of course. Let me ring for a servant to escort you."

When Jem was alone again, he retreated to his childhood chamber, Jory's wish echoing. Surely that was a shared goal of them all, even King Perran? For everyone to be happy and well. For children not to be stricken by a deadly disease that should be avoidable.

Was there a way to remind his mother and Perran and the chieftain that they should unify—and not because of the gods or whatever the clerics preached. Simply because it was right.

Curled in his old bed, Jem blinked at the familiar walls. The tapestry was faded since he refused to shut his drapes in his chamber no matter how much the housekeeper scolded him. What was the sense in shutting out the sunlight for the sake of wool and cotton, no matter how fine the needlework? Though now there was only murky light from the rain-dark sky.

Even though the seascape had indeed faded over the years, Jem still loved the sweep of golden sand between azure blue sea and cloudless sky. A mermaid frolicked in the shallows, the foamy splash of her tail rendered in delicate silver. He'd liked to pretend she was the sister of Morvoren's merman lover.

Jem had named her Wenna and imagined adventures for her just as grand as Morvoren's. Wenna's skin was brown like his own, her scales and fins a shimmering gold and ruby, long curls flowing over her bare shoulders.

This had been his chamber all his days. His sanctuary along with the aviary. If he did remain in Neuvella and Cador went back to Ergh, what would his life be like? More years of quiet solitude here with his books and imaginings? There were worse alternatives, that was certain.

Yet as much as he'd longed to return home, now sadness filled him at the idea of staying. More than sadness—a hollow ache. Was it possible he missed *Ergh* of all places? The thought of Cador returning to the cottage in the woods without him had him choking down a lump in his throat.

According to their initial agreement, they'd both be free to take lovers. Jem hated the notion more than he could express, hot jealousy, anger, and denial battling his empty sadness. He'd told his mother he trusted Cador completely.

Even if he trusted Cador not to hurt him or conspire against him again, could he really flay open his heart and soul and love him unconditionally? Make a life with him?

Jem stared at Wenna glumly, envious of her carefree smile. Which was ridiculous given she was made of woven fabric. She and Morvoren would never be real. Jem was home—in his chamber, in his bed. Yet he felt like a ghost haunting his own life.

His mind returned again and again to the cottage in the forest so far away on Ergh. He imagined snuggling under furs, fresh-baking flatbread filling his nose, Cador clomping around in his muddy boots.

And gods, if he could have a simple wish granted, he would return there in a heartbeat.

Jem sprang from his bed. He had to see Cador. No more wallowing in hurt. No more stubbornness. He trusted his husband. He loved him more than he'd thought possible.

This love wasn't simple as it was for Morvoren and her merman. It was messy and imperfect and *real*, and it was Jem's and Cador's. It was worth rescuing. Worth battling for.

He rushed down to the sickroom, his heart skipping at the claps of thunder that seemed impossibly close now. The army must be too. Would the West truly attack? All Jem's life, his mother and Perran had growled and sniped at each other, but the idea of an actual battle was utterly foreign. Especially here in the place where he'd only known peace.

The sickroom was empty now, and he raced around, barely resisting shouting for Cador frantically. He needed to see him *now*. They had to speak. They had to touch. Gods, they had to *kiss*. Nothing else seemed as important though he knew that wasn't true with soldiers bearing down and sick children and the diplomatic disaster between his mother and Kenver, resentment surely poised to boil over.

But where was Cador?

At the landing atop the grand entrance, Jem skidded to a stop, his attention catching on the view from wide windows over the valley. For a moment, he blinked and squinted, unable

Chapter Twenty-Two

G OOD THING CADOR could swim.

For the moment, he could still wade through the swirling, swiftly rising tide, the shockingly cold water around his thighs. Rivers poured into the valley.

It rained and snowed often on Ergh, but if he believed in the gods, he'd be certain Glaw was furious. First the mainland was ablaze, and now it seemed in danger of sinking beneath a new sea.

Doryty squawked where she was bundled inside his vest. Her beak tapped below his throat, and he murmured encouragement as he would to Massen or the goats at home. He'd wrapped her in the scraps of cloth from her nest, trying to keep her from drowning or being crushed. He might fail, but at least he'd try.

Jem's book was damp, but the pages inside had been dry when Cador had squeezed it into the waist of his leather trousers. It rested against his belly under his vest, and he kept his arms wide for balance as he fought the current of floodwater.

Roots and floating debris threatened to trip him as he slogged his way along what he hoped was the path back to the castle. The rain was so thick and sky dark that he couldn't see past the treetops. He was sure this was the right way, though.

Wasn't it?

Doryty cried as he stumbled and grasped a low branch. "It's

all right, little one. I'll keep you safe."

He should have been preparing for battle, but he'd imagined it wouldn't take long to fetch Doryty and Jem's beloved book. He'd been powerless to go back and change his actions when he'd dumped Jem's books on the side of the road, but he would return Morvoren to Jem now, damn it.

Unless he, Doryty, and Morvoren were swept away and drowned, a possibility becoming more likely by the minute. "Nonsense!" he shouted. "You are a mighty hunter of Ergh." Who was talking to himself.

He plowed on through the murky forest, the water rising impossibly fast. The roar of rain drowned out his own harsh breathing, and he considered climbing a tree to wait out the worst of it.

Then a uniformed body swept by in the current. He didn't recognize the uniform, so this had to be a Western soldier.

Doubling his efforts, Cador strode in wide steps, his boots sinking into mud. He was still in the lowest part of the valley, and it seemed rivers came from all sides. He had to get to higher ground.

Why was the water so cold? The mainland had been on fire, and after the stinking heat this rain made him shiver down to his bones.

He could hear distant shouts above the drum of rainfall. A crack of lightning lit the sky, surely hitting the castle since it stood so tall. Was Jem frightened? Cador had to get to him. The trick would be not drowning on the way.

The floodwater's current yanked at him as he fought for elevation. He wasn't sure even faithful Massen would get far against the growing force. He thought he heard horses, but perhaps it was wishful thinking. Cador panted, downed branches clawing at him as they swept by.

As the water rose to his hips, genuine fear took root. Someone was screaming, and Cador watched in amazement as a man caught in the flood slammed into a tree trunk and disappeared. There were shouts and cries all around now, and he had to get the fuck out of here or he'd be next.

The horse appeared so suddenly from the curtain of rain and leaves that Cador shouted in surprise, shielding Doryty with his hand as she trembled against his skin. Somehow, it was Jem holding down his hand to Cador, the horse whinnying and fighting the current.

A sob choked Cador to see his brave, beautiful little prince atop the stallion. He'd surely pull Jem right off if he took his hand and tried to swing up, but he loved Jem so much for trying.

He wordlessly eased Doryty from his vest and handed her to Jem before reaching around to grab the horse's mane and mount. The horse—Lusow, Cador was almost sure—withstood it valiantly, accepting his weight with only a snort. Cador settled behind Jem, one arm locking around his waist, relieved to feel his body close.

He kissed Jem's wet curls, praying Jem would not object. Jem gripped Cador's arm, but he didn't shove it away. Instead, he gave a squeeze that had Cador's heart soaring.

"Jem—"

"I know. We must get to safety!"

Cador wanted to demand—beg—for an answer of what exactly it was Jem knew, but it would have to wait.

With Doryty now tucked in his shirt, Jem took the reins and guided Lusow through what seemed a labyrinth of trees. Lusow struggled against the flood but had the strength to carry them toward the castle, the land sloping upward.

It was when they broke through the trees that they could see the disaster of King Perran's army on a distant hill across the valley.

"Gods!" Jem exclaimed. "They must have been on the road we took here."

And it seemed the flooding had carried soldiers and horses down the hill and crashing into trees, people and beasts littered across the valley. Many riderless horses galloped aimlessly. There were likely many bodies under the water now, the rain and flood relentless.

Shielding his eyes from the rain with his hand, Cador peered up to the castle. He could see the queen's people in their bright red uniforms though they looked like insects. The castle appeared well protected, especially with Perran's soldiers felled by the flooding.

"Your local village is above the valley?" Cador asked.

"Yes, thank the gods. Or whoever decided to build the village on higher ground. Though I'm sure the flooding has still ravaged their homes. I've never seen anything like this. I've read ancient tales of the lake in this valley rising to great heights, but I thought that was merely a story."

"Let's get back to the castle before it becomes even more real." He leaned around Jem, peeking down at Doryty. "Is she well?"

"I think so." Jem opened the collar of his shirt to pet her trembling head with his fingertip as Cador tried to block the rain. "Thank you for saving her. And my book. I assume that's what's jammed into my back at the moment."

Cador had to laugh, the feeling unexpected and very welcome. It was all right. Jem had rescued them. Ebrenn's advance seemed a failure. And though poor Hedrok was gone, Cador was allowed to laugh. He was allowed to joke.

"It feels so good to have you close that you might feel something else as well." He rolled his hips.

"You're incorrigible!" Jem laughed too, his smile flashing bright amid the gray. That smile! How Cador had missed it. "You're…"

Heart racing, Cador leaned closer, rain pelting his head. He lifted his other arm, trying to shield Jem as best he could. "Yes?" He held his breath. Rain clung to Jem's thick eyelashes, and he blinked up at Cador.

"Cowards!"

They jerked toward the distant voice. Reluctantly, Cador spurred Lusow. "The water's still rising."

"Yes." Jem faced front, Doryty cradled to his chest. "It sounds like someone needs help."

As they found the slope leading up to higher ground around the castle's base, the voice grew louder. It sounded like an old man ranting and raving, the words lost in the rain's drone. Out of the flowing water now, Lusow still struggled on the muddy trail, and they dismounted, practically crawling at times, Lusow faring far better without them on his back.

Atop a ridge, the castle looming high above in the unnaturally dark sky, they came face to face with the man still shouting. He was indeed old and covered in mud, bloody scratches and wounds on his pale face and hands. His filthy cloak over fine mainland clothing must have cost a fortune.

And surely did, since King Perran of Ebrenn would insist on the best.

His crown was missing, and considering how large he'd loomed in Cador's mind—how much power he wielded over

Ergh's future—it was bizarre to see Perran so diminished. At least some of his soldiers had been lost in the flooding but where were the rest? Who was this pathetic king shouting at?

The rain was finally easing, though the floodwaters showed no mercy. Perran caught sight of Cador and Jem, Lusow snorting restlessly. Cador let go of the reins, letting Lusow continue up the trail. He was a clever horse and would surely find the stable or other shelter himself.

"King Perran?" Jem asked uncertainly.

"Cowards!" the old man screamed. "I said attack!" His boots were so deep in mud it could have been quicksand. He didn't seem to recognize Jem and Cador.

"King Perran, there will be no fight today." Jem gave Cador an uncertain glance before clearing his throat and speaking more confidently. "Come with us to the castle and we can discuss our differences peacefully. Please."

Perran practically growled. "*You.*"

Cador itched for his spear or sword, but he would snap Perran's neck with his bare hands if the bastard threatened Jem.

"I said attack!" Perran shouted to no one.

"Father!" Treeve appeared on the far side of the ridge, soaked and muddy as well. He had no weapon Cador could spot and dragged his left foot as he stumbled toward them. "The gods have made it clear what they think of your warmongering. I've gathered the rest of our people in a safe place atop the other side of the valley. They refuse to follow you to their doom. This is madness. Let us go with Prince Jowan and find the queen. We must—"

"If that bitch thinks I'll give her an inch of land in the Valley of the Gods, I'll—"

"Forget about the valley!" Treeve shouted. "You'll ruin eve-

Pasco waved a hand toward Treeve. "We thought you two would be a good match. Strengthen the bond of our family."

To Treeve, Jem said calmly, "You told us it was your father's idea."

"It was." He shrugged. "But Pasco and I had discussed it as well."

"You think Mother would want me to marry Perran's son?" Jem asked Pasco.

"If it served Neuvella. And Mother won't be queen forever, Jem." Pasco still gripped the bloody sword, Perran's body face down in the muck between them. "Treeve and I are forward thinkers."

Cador hoped the queen slept with one eye open.

"I didn't realize you even knew each other except by name," Jem said.

Pasco shrugged. He narrowed his gaze on Cador. "If you'd step aside, I'm sure we can convince the clerics of an annulment. We'll make it worth your while, of course."

The fucking nerve of this pompous ass to talk about Jem and Cador's marriage as if it was nothing more than a transaction. An inconvenience! With effort, Cador loosened his left fist and spread his fingers wide, displaying the dillywig brand. "Jem is my husband until I die."

Mud squelching under his boots, Jem returned to Cador's side, clasping their branded palms tightly. "Cador is my husband. Ergh is my home."

Pasco tilted his head, brushing rain from his eyes. "Huh. You really mean it." To Treeve, he shrugged carelessly. "I suppose we'll have to adjust the plan."

"I suppose we will," Treeve agreed carefully. His gaze slid to his father's corpse. "I should be sorry, but…"

They stared at the body in silence but for the rain until Jem said, "Now tell us everything you know about the sevels and the disease."

Lightning flashed, the storm seeming to gather force again. Cador shifted uncomfortably. "Maybe not *everything* right this moment."

"No," Treeve agreed, eyeing the dark clouds warily. "I can tell you I've learned much in the past year about our methods for farming the sevels."

"Have you?" Pasco's gaze slithered to Treeve like a sarf. "How fascinating."

"I believe the shallow soil on Ergh can be strengthened by growing another simple crop that will nourish the sevel roots."

Cador frowned. "But sevels grew on Ergh for countless generations."

"Yes, weakening the earth over time. Slowly, slowly, until the roots withered. On the mainland, we have many other crops. Whatever it is the sevels contain must also be present in those foods. On Ergh, the diet is limited. The balance much more fragile. I believe Ebrenn can help."

"As can Neuvella," Pasco insisted. "After all, we've already formed such a strong bond between our people." He motioned at Cador and Jem.

There was a determined lift to Jem's chin. "Indeed. Though with Ebrenn's generous assistance, Ergh will have no need to disturb its pristine mountains mining for oil to trade with Neuvella. I'm sure Ebrenn will be happy to continue supplying what Neuvella needs. Seeing as you are such a forward thinker, Prince—or make that *King* Treeve."

Treeve gave Jem a bright smile. "Of course, Prince Jowan. Why, I'd hate to think of Ergh's way of life being altered by mainland interference."

Pasco laughed sharply. "Perish the thought." He shook his head. "Fine, I'm sure there will be negotiations to be made between our families. And the clerics, who only have power if we give it to them."

Treeve grimaced, glancing to the sky as the rain increased. "This weather will be seen as an omen. A judgment."

"Yes, so we'll have to decide exactly what the judgment is and how it can benefit us," Pasco said. "Of that, I'm sure my mother will agree." He gazed down at Perran's body. "Now what do we do with this?"

What might have been grief flickered over Treeve's face. "Will you help me carry him to the castle?"

Cador released Jem's hand. "Of course." He still didn't know what the fuck to make of Treeve, but the man shouldn't have to haul his father's body. He tried not to, but he thought of Bryok on the end of Delen's spear before tumbling into the black. "What about his wound? It's clear he didn't drown."

Pasco easily said, "Killed by one of his own soldiers after he stubbornly led them into a deadly flood. Cursed by the gods for his warmongering and hubris." He still held the sword, the blade washed an innocent silver again in the rain.

Keeping distance between himself and Pasco's blade, Cador grunted his agreement. How he detested these games of politics. Not to mention the murder.

The idea that he would one day be chieftain and have to negotiate with Treeve and Pasco and the fucking clerics made him want to snatch up Jem and run far, far away. He bent to heave Perran over his shoulder.

"Doryty!"

Cador spun to see Jem with hands outstretched, the little

bird apparently ready for freedom and valiantly flapping her wings. But the rain was still heavy, and she floundered toward the mud. Where Jem followed, lunging to catch her—and slipping down the slick incline headfirst as though it was ice.

From the corner of his eye, Cador thought he saw Doryty gain her strength and fly as he dove. He caught Jem around one ankle, gripping the soft leather of his boot. Now they were both sliding until Cador lurched to a stop, holding on to Jem's foot with all his might.

Behind him, Treeve grunted, yanking on Cador's boot, Pasco helping to drag them back to solid ground. Or at least slightly more solid ground. Cador hauled Jem safely onto his lap.

"Did she fly?" Jem asked.

"Yes." Cador wasn't positive, but since he couldn't see her anywhere in the muck, he'd rather believe she flew than drowned.

"It's all very touching, but let's get the fuck back to the castle, hmm?" Pasco crouched by Perran's body, tugging the dead man's arm.

Jem nodded, and Cador reluctantly let go of him. With Perran slung over his shoulder, they trudged up past the dungeon, the queen's guards soon arriving to help. Pasco ordered them to take Perran's body, and Cador was glad to be rid of the awful weight.

In the grand entrance, they dripped mud over the colored tiles. The queen embraced Jem tightly, apparently not caring how dirty her fine dress became. She held him, and held him more before giving his father a brief chance. With Delen, Tas appeared, striding toward Cador and eyeing Treeve suspiciously.

Cador braced, half expecting Tas to shout at him again. But

perhaps the visit to Hedrok's deathbed had calmed him in some way. He only clasped Cador's arm, giving him a nod Cador wasn't sure how to translate.

Treeve raised his empty hands. His breeches and white shirt clung to his body, the filmy shirt translucent over his tawny skin. "Your highness, I want no fight."

"The gods show their anger!"

They all turned at Ysella's proclamation, the old woman descending the stairs with surprising speed given her wizened body. Cador swore they all groaned in unison under their breath as well. Before Jem's mother could respond, Treeve did.

"Yes, I think the gods are clear. First fire, now flood. We must come together in these dark times. Unify Onan." Treeve sighed heavily, clasping his hands before him. "My father is dead."

Tension rippled through all in attendance. Then Tas barked, "The fucker's dead?"

Cador had to credit Treeve with the smooth calm he showed. "He is. I'm afraid his mind was gone. It is a comfort to know he's at peace now."

Another silence before Jem's mother murmured, "Indeed. A comfort for us all. I fear he suffered too long."

No one asked precisely how he died. They murmured vague agreement and pretended Perran hadn't been a threat to them all.

"Hail the king of the West!" Ysella proclaimed.

Treeve bowed to her. "I humbly request your blessing." To the queen, he added, "Ebrenn's soldiers have no wish to fight. I've stood down my father's—*my*—remaining troops on the far side of the valley with strict orders of a truce. I'm sure they can be of assistance once these rains stop and we assess the damage to the area. I also ask your help in tending to our injured soldiers and horses."

The queen nodded, giving quick orders to her staff.

Treeve said, "Thank you. And we must discuss the sevels. There's no time to waste."

Unspoken tension rose to new heights as thunder rumbled, the drone of rain unrelenting. The queen seemed about to reply but then turned to Tas. To him, she said, "I'm sorry. I did wrong by you and Ergh. I hope in time you can forgive me and that we can truly unite our people." Her gaze slid to Jem, softening. "And our families."

Standing rigid, Tas said nothing. Cador willed him to make the right choice this time. They wouldn't win a war against the mainland. More than not winning, they'd *lose*. They'd lose so fucking much. The queen and clerics had been a step ahead of them all along. Tas had to choke down his pride.

Cador and Delen shared another worried glance. Tas had to make the choice Delen surely would as leader. They'd just watched Hedrok die. No more. *No more.*

Finally, Tas nodded. He looked to Cador and Jem at his side. "We have all made mistakes."

"Let us sit together briefly as these rains cease," the queen said, motioning toward one of the long corridors off the entrance. "After you and King Treeve. Perhaps our children should join us also."

Pasco was already walking at Treeve's side. Cador ached all over, and the thought of more politics and having to be careful with his words was exhausting. Jem sagged against him. Cador realized Tas was watching them, and he stood straighter. He would do his duty.

"I think Cador and Prince Jowan need to rest," Tas said.

Chapter Twenty-Three

J EM ONLY BROKE the kiss when he was forced to gasp for
breath. Cador kicked the door shut, and they stumbled to the
carpet beside the bed. Jem inhaled Cador's mossy scent deeply,
elation and desire blossoming.

"You're my husband, and I'm no virgin," Jem mumbled
between kisses, spreading his legs for Cador to rut against him,
welcoming his crushing weight. No more games or denial.

But he could feel the book still wedged in Cador's vest, and
he pushed against his shoulders. "Wait, wait."

Sitting back on his heels, Cador panted, rubbing himself
through his sodden leather trousers. "Will you punish me now
by waiting?" He smiled, but it was strained—as if he truly feared
Jem would deny him and made a jest of it.

"No." Jem sat up and kissed him. "I forgive you. No more
punishment." He squeezed his hands into Cador's vest, carefully
easing out the soaked book.

"Fuck, did I ruin it? I'm sorry."

"You rescued it! Thank you." Jem gingerly set it on the table
before snagging the vial of oil.

"After what I did before, tossing away your books... I had
to." Cador's face flushed, and he let his arms hang at his sides.

Jem crawled into his lap. "I forgive you. That seems like a
lifetime ago now."

"It does. I can barely imagine a time when I didn't care for you. When I didn't love you so much it hurts."

They lost themselves in kissing again, the fervor flowing into long, slow slides of tongues and exploration as they caught their breath and peeled off ruined clothes.

When Jem sank down, sheathing Cador's cock inside his slick, tender arse, they groaned and kissed messily. They were bedraggled and mud-streaked, Jem's thighs spread wide over Cador's, facing him this time. Had it been only hours since they'd rutted like beasts in the forest? At least now, Jem's wardrobe of breeches was close at hand. He laughed.

Cador spread his hands wide over Jem's ribs, a quizzical smile on his kiss-slick lips. "What?"

"I don't know." He couldn't stop laughing. It all felt like a strange dream to be back in Neuvella, and now so much had happened he wasn't sure what to think about anything. "Perhaps I've gone mad. Will you still have me?"

Cador flashed a deliciously feral grin before kissing Jem with deep sweeps of his tongue. He thrust up into Jem's sore body. "I'll take you in every way you can imagine."

"Mmm. I can imagine so many scenarios."

Cador took Jem's face in his hands, blue eyes searching. "You truly forgive me?"

"With all my heart. If I hide away and never give you a second chance, what good will that do me?" He squeezed around Cador's cock seated deep inside. "What good would it do me to still love you and deny ourselves a future?"

"Your face is meant to smile, and I will see you smiling for the rest of our days."

Jem could only kiss him, their movements suddenly frantic with lips and hands insatiable. "Fuck me. Hard. The way I need. Give me your seed and—mmph!" He laughed again as Cador tumbled him back on the carpet.

Though he covered Jem with his big body, thrusting into him with long strokes, Cador took care. "Tell me if it's too much."

"Never too much," Jem moaned, though his arse *was* sore. "More."

"My insatiable little prince." Cador pressed kisses to Jem's face. He rocked into Jem with slow, sensuous movements.

Jem was pinned the way he loved. He let himself go lax, taking every inch of Cador's shaft with joyous shouts and mumbles, his knees high and wide, reveling in how Cador mastered his body and soul.

He wasn't a fictional prince and Cador was no woodsman. This was his husband, and even if they'd had little say when they married, they chose each other now.

"I wouldn't change it," Jem gasped, grasping for Cador's branded hand and pressing their palms tightly. "I'm so glad you're mine."

Cador squeezed his hand as he angled his hips to rub the perfect spot inside Jem. "Mine forever."

Jem could only cry out, a wildfire of ecstasy deep inside him. While the pleasure had been undeniable when they'd been playacting, it was all the sweeter now.

After Cador filled him, he sucked Jem to release, white drops escaping his lips and clinging to his new beard. He nuzzled low between Jem's splayed legs, and Jem didn't squirm away from his gentle inspection of his stretched hole.

He only flinched when, his head resting on Cador's broad chest, hair tickling his cheek, Cador traced one of the fresh scratches on Jem's skull. They were still on the carpet, the bed seeming impossibly high and far away.

"I'll try to stop," Jem whispered. In time, he was sure the compulsion would fade.

Tension rippled through Cador's body beneath him. "I failed you. But I swear I'll never let you be hurt again."

Jem had to laugh. "You can try, at least."

"I will!" Cador sat up suddenly, bringing Jem with him, his handsome face so earnest. "I give you my vow."

Curled in his barbarian's lap, Jem made his own pledge. "I love you. Always."

They could have kissed for hours, and perhaps they did before a rapid, familiarly insistent knock interrupted. Cador groaned, "What now?"

"It's Santo." Jem called out, "Coming!" before groaning himself as he heaved to his feet, muscles protesting, and fetched a silky robe. He tossed a blanket at Cador, who'd flopped back down on the carpet. Jem opened the door, Santo practically tumbling in.

"Oh, Jem!" They hugged him close. "Mother and Father insisted you were unhurt, but I had to see for myself."

"I'm fine, yes." Jem squeezed them affectionately. "You and Arthek are too?"

"Yes, we were busy helping—" Their gaze found Cador on the carpet. Dismay creased their face. "Oh! You're napping. I didn't mean to..." They frowned at Jem. "I hoped you were reconciled?"

"We are," Jem assured them.

Cador said, "We were fucking. Couldn't make it to the bed." His hands were folded behind his head, the blanket haphazardly covering his midsection, his hairy thighs poking out.

"Oh!" Santo grinned. "I'm very glad to hear it." Toying with their braid, they gave Cador an approving nod. "You've proven yourself worthy of my baby brother."

"Thank you." Cador said it solemnly, which made Jem smile.

Santo cheerfully added, "And don't forget my husband will have you killed if you mess up again. Now, there's much work to be done. I'd say you two need a bath, but all hands are needed in the village after the flooding. We must help our people."

Cador stood, apparently uncaring that the blanket pooled at his feet. "I'm ready."

"That you are. Still, there's time for trousers." They mock sighed, winking at Jem. "Sadly." Their smile faded. "Do you think we can trust Prince Treeve? I suppose it's King Treeve now. Well, it will be officially after the ceremony at the Holy Place. Who knows when that will be. First fires, now floods! I hope Ergh fares better." They grimaced. "Aside from this terrible disease. I'm so sorry about your nephew, Cador. Gods, everything has become so complicated."

"Yes," Jem said. "But we'll manage. We'll have to."

Santo's dear face brightened again. "Indeed. What would Morvoren do?"

"She'd get on with it," Cador answered. "While fucking her merman every chance she gets."

Santo winked. "As ever, let Morvoren be our guide."

THE HOLY PLACE still needed seat cushions.

Jem shifted restlessly on the hard stone chair. Ysella was on the raised dais in the courtyard's center, droning on and on. Jem would have thought she'd said all she could possibly say at Treeve's coronation the day before, but apparently the Feast of the Blood Moon came with its own set of sermons.

Across the way, Santo gave Jem a wink. They wore tight breeches and a flowing silk shirt with billowing sleeves, their hair twisted into fine braids that were surely Arthek's work. Beside them, Arthek sat peacefully, his little finger linked with Santo's.

The rest of Jem's family stretched across the front row of Neuvella's side, his parents appearing to listen attentively to Ysella. Pasco and Locryn and their wives were there too, the children mercifully spared the boredom.

How strange to be back at the Holy Place but be sitting in Ergh's section. Beside Jem in full leather, Cador seemed unbothered by the ridiculously hard chairs, but he was undoubtedly bored senseless and hot. Jem wore leather trousers as a nod to Ergh, along with a fine purple silk shirt in the Neuvellan style.

His cousins from Gwels were resplendent in their brightly colored clothing, Treeve and the Ebrennians wearing more sedate styles since of course they were officially mourning for King Perran.

In truth, Jem had never seen them looking so cheerful, and he couldn't blame them one bit. Perran's crown that had been lost in the flooding hadn't been found, and Treeve wore a new headpiece of many emeralds that didn't quite match his mourning garb.

Cador leaned low and whispered, "When does the actual feast begin?"

Jem didn't answer, stifling a chuckle. On his other side, Delen hissed, "Can't be soon enough."

Kenver ignored them, though he'd taken off his curved tusk headdress an hour earlier when it seemed clear Ysella was

in the past months, but as Jem glanced around in the night, he realized this was the first time they'd spoken alone. Cador was nearby in their room, fast asleep after indulging at the feast, but he'd come running at a shout.

Not that Jem needed rescuing. He could speak to Kenver alone. Though this man had coldly plotted his kidnapping, there was nothing to fear now. He didn't imagine they'd ever be close or grow fond, but they could be civil.

"I…" Kenver swore under his breath. "I owe you an apology."

Jem dropped his hand suddenly, realizing he'd reached up to scratch his scalp, his fingernails scraping. He breathed deeply to calm his thumping heart. "You do. Yes."

"I'm sorry. I thought of you as nothing but a pawn."

"Thank you?" He cursed himself silently for his tentative nervousness, clasping his hands behind him and standing taller. "I mean to say—you did. And you should be sorry."

Kenver nodded, shifting uneasily, his gaze on his boots. He was clearly not accustomed to issuing apologies. He gruffly added, "You make my son happier than I knew he could be."

"I'm glad you recognize it. He makes me extremely happy too. The happiest."

"Good. I will see my children and grandchildren happy if I have anything to say about it." He suddenly smiled with a softness Jem had never witnessed. "My husband would have liked you very much."

"Cador says he was a great hunter." Jem wasn't sure what he would have had in common with the man.

"Oh, yes." Kenver gazed out across the moonlit field, the grasses a harvest gold. "But he was so much more. A wonderful father. Our Cador was always such a good boy."

He was silent for long moments before seeming to snap back to attention, peering intently at Jem. "He has grown into a man to make his parents proud. You are a good match. We return to Ergh with the mainland's finest agricultural minds and healers thanks to your mother. Thanks to you."

"Tas?" Cador approached swiftly, wearing only unbuttoned trousers, his feet bare. "Jem, I woke alone."

"I'm well." Jem instantly reached for Cador's hand, their branded palms meeting like second nature. "I wanted some air. Nothing to worry about."

Still tensed, Cador looked between his tas and Jem. "If you're sure."

"I am," Jem said. He squeezed Cador's fingers.

"I drank too much mead," Tas said, backing away. "Makes me fucking sentimental. We all need sleep or we'll be dragged by the horse tomorrow." He disappeared around the building.

Cador watched him go uneasily. "What did he say to you?"

"It was an apology. Nothing to worry about." He glanced down at Cador's bare feet in the grass, knowing he must have almost run from their chamber naked in concern for Jem. "Come, my love. Let's get back to bed."

Cador nodded, then groaned. "Too much mead. Why does it taste so good?"

Laughing, Jem led him inside and made him drink a whole pitcher of water. Then another. And one more for good measure.

IN THE DAWN's light outside the stable, Cador was surprisingly chipper. "Would you like your own horse?" he asked.

Dressed for travel in leather, Jem hesitated. "No, but…" He backed up, took a deep breath, and skip-hopped into the air and over Dybri's back, fingers tight in her mane as he muscled all the way across, fighting through the moment when he might have crashed back down to the ground.

Though if he'd fallen, Cador was there to catch him.

Grinning, Cador mounted easily behind him, tucking Jem comfortably between his thighs and back against his body. Kenver, Jory, and the others had already started north, the dozens of carts of sevels—and one with Jem's books squeezed in—creaking to life.

"Ready?" Cador asked, one arm snug about Jem.

Channeling Morvoren, Jem cried, "Onward to the ends of Onan!"

They laughed and rode into the future, ignoring any curious glances, lost in their own world.

Epilogue

Five Years Later

SHIVERING AT THE icy bite in the so-called spring breeze, Jem let Nessa nose at the tentative buds on the shrubs lining the trail to the cottage. He was glad of his red, fur-lined cloak, though the clasp at his throat was worn and would need replacing.

In his wildest imagination, Jem couldn't have fathomed how truly freezing Ergh was in the dark of winter. Yet Cador assured him it was typical. Fortunately, after the bizarre summer of fires and floods, the weather on the mainland had returned to its normal rhythms. The gods were apparently appeased.

As Nessa investigated, Jem took the opportunity to listen for any hatchlings in distress despite having his hands full the past week with three adult askells with broken wings. They'd been snared in the nets protecting the surface of the sevel roots as the shoots fought their way deeper into Ergh's hard earth.

The chief farmer from Ebrenn would be returning to Ergh with Jem and Cador after this year's summit to check in on the progress, and Jem hoped they could come up with new strategies to protect both the askells and the precious trees that were due to grow fruit after these years of careful cultivation.

"All right, come on." Jem clucked his tongue and spurred on Nessa, his patience waning. His husband awaited.

And even though Cador was so familiar to him now that Jem could imagine every nook and cranny of his muscled body and dear face—right down to the faint new creases at the corners of his eyes—Jem's stomach still fluttered to see his silhouette beyond the aviary's barred glass walls.

It had been backbreaking work to expand the cottage's clearing, though dozens of neighbors had helped. The aviary was unique in that its iron bars were fused with thick blown glass to keep out the bitter cold, the bars keeping the birds from attempting to fly through the opaque walls.

In fact, even with the sun a rare visitor in the long, bitter winters, the rectangular building could be surprisingly warm. Well, *warm* was perhaps an overstatement, but keeping out the wind was half the battle.

The Erghians first found Jem's desire to heal birds curious but had accepted it in time, now bringing any and all injured birds to him and often asking for stories in return. Though not an official part of Jem's duties at the stable, he still hosted a story hour several times a week for people of all ages.

He left Nessa to graze with Massen, greeting the goats and chickens in their expanded pen as he passed by. The aviary door was ajar, and he peeked in, surprised to see a trio of hatchlings trembling in a nest. Cador knelt by them, his big body low, fingers dirt-encrusted and worms in his mouth.

Gods, Jem loved him. "Who do we have here?" he asked.

Cador startled, choking and coughing, spitting madly into the nest. "Fuck!" He swiped his mouth with the back of his hand. "I almost swallowed them!" He coughed again.

Jem had to laugh. "Apologies. I wasn't trying to sneak up."

"So you say." Cador mock glared at him, then grinned mischievously, standing. Dirt smeared the corner of his beautiful mouth, caught in his trimmed beard. He towered over Jem. "Come closer for a kiss."

"Not before you rinse your mouth!" Jem giggled, backing

out of the aviary as Cador stalked him.

The chase was merry and lasted longer than it should have considering Cador could have snatched Jem up into his arms in a heartbeat.

Instead, he let Jem escape around the cottage, which was now three rooms. Jem traced his fingers across the thick glass window that sat over the massive bed that dominated their chamber as he paused, trying to guess if Cador would come around from left or right.

Though windows weren't particularly practical on Ergh, Jem loved to wake with even faint, watery light illuminating the bookshelves that lined the walls of their chamber.

Of course, Morvoren's complete collection of adventures held a place of honor, the pages worn and well-loved. Jem had brought numerous copies to lend out. The original stained and misshapen tome Cador had rescued from the flood sat in its own special place, too fragile to actually read.

Jem did miss the brilliant sunshine of Neuvella, but this was home now. He crept to the right, sticking close to the outer wall of the other room they'd built, which would be a nursery come autumn.

Butterflies flapped as Jem imagined the infant he and Cador would adopt. Jem would miss his work at the stable with Jory and Austol and the horses, but eventually he'd return. In the meantime—

"Got you!" Cador wrapped his arms around Jem from behind, lifting him off the muddy ground and pressing kisses to his cheek and neck as Jem squirmed and kicked, laughing too hard to put up a real fight. Cador nuzzled Jem's curls, which grazed his shoulders.

He would cut his hair short again before the journey to the mainland but each winter let his curls grow. It was long ago now

course meant Ergh had no need to mine for oil in its northern mountains to trade to Neuvella.

Jem suspected his mother hadn't given up on striking a deal with Delen that would stop Neuvella's economic dependency on Ebrenn's oil, but with the sevels growing and the disease halted in the afflicted children, her designs for Ergh were thankfully scuttled.

Cador sighed. "Yes, Delen will accompany us to Neuvella. At least she can deal with politics, and hopefully we can have some peace. But of course I know you're eager to see your mother."

Jem traced a mindless pattern on Cador's leather-clad thigh. "Yes. Though it's far more complicated than it once was, I'll always love her and miss her. She's still my mother. It's difficult to turn away from family even when they gravely disappoint us."

Cador made a low sound of agreement, likely thinking of Bryok. Jem nuzzled his neck and murmured, "At least we have peace now and my family is across the Askorn Sea."

Cador groaned. "A blessing but also a damn curse. I hate to even think of the weeks it will take to get there."

"I'd better kiss you properly to distract you."

"Mmm. You'd better. But only a kiss? I think I need to fuck you to really clear my mind."

Jem yelped as Cador swept him into his arms without warning and kissed him fiercely, sparking lust in a blink. Reaching below his knees where Cador held him aloft, Jem pressed Cador's wrist the way he faithfully did at sea on every journey.

His husband carried him home. Under Jem's fingers, the powerful rhythm of Cador's heart matched his beat for beat.

THE END

I hope you loved reading Jem and Cador's epic romance as much as I loved writing it! I'd be grateful if you could take a few minutes to leave a review on Amazon, Goodreads, BookBub, social media, or wherever you like. Just a couple of sentences can really help other readers discover the book. ☺

Wishing you many happily ever afters!

Keira
<3

P.S. Keep reading for a sneak peek at *Kidnapped by the Pirate*, a swashbuckling "breeches-ripper"!

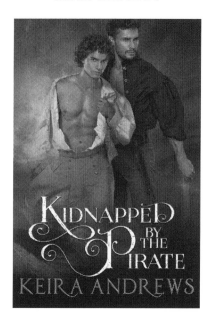

1710

I F PIRATES WERE to be the bloody, savage end of Nathaniel Bainbridge, he wished they'd get on with it.

The windswept deck was damp beneath his bare feet, prompting thoughts of the dewy grass of home. What he wouldn't give for the freedom to run across the fields of Hollington Estate, wind rushing in his ears over the steady thump of his heart, the world falling away in his wake.

Instead he was confined by an endless, restless sea taunting him with its wildness. In England, he'd heard countless tales of villainous pirates and their dastardly deeds. People spoke as if the ocean teemed with the brigands, but the voyage had been mile after mile of...*nothing.*

Nathaniel shook his head at his foolishness. Not that he actually wanted pirates to attack their ship and massacre them. If only he could *move,* he would keep boredom at bay.

He gripped the railing, longing for dirt beneath his nails, scratches on his palms from tree bark as he climbed and explored, wonderfully aching muscles from hours in the lake. If he could only run a simple mile. Hardly any distance at all, but trapped on the ship, that much clear land would be a marvel.

He wiped sea spray from his eyes. If only the ability to run and jump and swim was worth anything at all in his world instead of being childish folly he was supposed to have out-grown. Men did not climb trees or swim for hours, and certainly they didn't *run* for the sheer pleasure of it the way he had at Hollington.

Of course, the estate wasn't theirs anymore, sold off to pay debts, so even if he made his way back to Kent one day, he would never return to those rolling hills. Its verdant trees and round, tranquil lake would now be home to another family.

No, for the foreseeable future, home would be Primrose Isle, a new colony his father desperately wanted to see flourish. Walter Bainbridge had found his fortunes in England not the least bit fortunate, and as a governor in the New World had the thing he loved most dearly: power.

Nathaniel's future bride waited there. Elizabeth Davenport stood to inherit quite a fortune, and for the colony—and Walter—to thrive, alliances had to be made. So Nathaniel would do the only useful thing he could and marry.

He brushed a fresh spray of briny seawater from his face as he stared out at the endless night, keeping a firm hold on the rail. His untucked shirt flapped in the breeze, the lower fastenings on his breeches unbuckled under his knees.

In the dark, there was no one to comment on his state of undress, and he supposed the crew didn't care a whit anyway. His trimmed hair curled at the ends in the dampness, and he tucked a lock behind his ear. It had been his little act of rebellion to cut it much shorter than most gentlemen. He certainly wouldn't be wearing dreaded wigs, either, if he could help it.

Clouds conspired to hide the stars and razor-thin crescent of moon. He shivered in the late September night's chill; he really should have worn his hated shoes and jacket.

At least the wind was no longer the bitter cold of the mid-Atlantic as they neared the West Indies. He shifted back and forth on his feet, lifting them like a racehorse stamping at the starting line.

The *Proud William* was fairly large, a merchant ship carrying a cargo of salt fish and forged metal tools to the colonies. But when he'd attempted even a light trot around the main deck, the crew had reacted with consternation at best, hostility at worst.

Running was his very favorite activity and the thing he excelled at most in life—much to his father's disgust. Swimming in the lake in summertime, cutting through the placid water with sure, even strokes, was a joy as well.

To be surrounded now by endless water but unable to dive in and soothe his cramped muscles was the worst torture. He'd asked the captain if he could at least climb the mast or sail rigging and had been flatly refused.

So he stood by the starboard rail and sometimes paced, careful to stay out of the crew's way. At least he had been told their progress was swift, and that after a month's voyage—thirty-one days and some thirteen hours since they left England, to be exact—they would reach the island in a fortnight if the wind held.

He was informed that some ships took several months to reach the colonies. Ships could leave London the same day and arrive weeks or more apart. Such was the way of the sea.

Staring out at the nothingness, he stopped his restless shifting and squinted. The weak sliver of moon had valiantly escaped the clouds for a moment, and Nathaniel thought he spotted a strange kind of movement. The night took on shape before becoming uniform once more.

Perhaps it had been a great ocean creature surfacing—a whale or giant squid, or some kind of mysterious monster.

He chuckled. Earlier that evening, Susanna had read aloud fables from one of the old leather-bound tomes they'd brought from home, and his imagination was clearly running wild.

She'd always been the far more indulgent of his two older sisters, and he knew she'd packed books he'd favor, although she certainly had a taste for adventurous tales rather than the sentimental stories ladies were supposed to read. They'd both enjoyed the diary of a naval captain who'd served on several ships of the line and described life aboard in vivid detail.

Although the cabin Nathaniel and Susanna shared was tiny, at least they had privacy. He really should rejoin her in their cabin to sleep and end another interminable day, but the walls closed in on him, and it felt like a prison. Susanna's thunderous snores didn't help matters, but he couldn't begrudge her anything.

For the hundredth time, he wondered what his life on Primrose Isle would be like. The colony was only a few years old, and there had been whispers of struggles with agriculture and trade, rumors of corruption and settlers packing up already.

He'd be forced to work for his father or at some other respectable job procured for him, like Susanna's husband, Bart. Handsome Bart was thirty and penniless, but of good breeding and an agreeable disposition. He and Susanna had insisted on

on the cot, her book thudding to the floor. One hand pressed to her round belly, she cried out, "What is it?"

"I think it's pirates." He could hardly believe the words as he uttered them. Had he wished them into existence by grumbling over boredom? Oh, what a fool he was.

The blood drained from Susanna's sweet, round face. "Pirates?"

"I don't know what else it could be." He threw open a trunk and dug for his sheathed dagger, cursing himself for not raising the alarm sooner. His mind raced, thoughts jumbled as he grasped the hilt of the weapon and tossed the leather scabbard aside.

The thunder of the crew's footsteps shook the ceiling, dust motes shaking loose and shouts filling the air. Susanna looked down at her nightgown, despairing.

"There's no time for petticoats or any of that nonsense." She threw her flowing green gown over her head, her voice muffled by it. "My God, it really is pirates, isn't it? Oh, I think I'm stuck."

Nathaniel helped tug the material down over her swollen belly. She emerged from the folds of soft fabric and peered up at the ceiling, as if she could see through the hull. Footsteps scuffled and thumps reverberated, tense voices shouting commands too distant to make out clearly.

Susanna whispered, "No gunshots. Must be too many. The crew isn't fighting them. Help me pin this shut." She had stopped wearing her corset, adopting what was apparently a new French style while she was with child.

After he'd pinned the material enough that the robe-like gown would stay put, drawing a prick of blood from his fingertip in his haste, Nathaniel yanked on his stockings and refastened his breeches below his knees before jamming his feet into his buckled shoes. He wouldn't face these brigands in a state of undress.

He tucked the dagger into the back of his trousers and whipped on his sleeveless waistcoat, fingers clumsy on the buttons. But there was no time for his cravat or jacket. Raised voices already echoed down the corridor. He spun about, belatedly hoping to find something to bar the door.

Susanna had apparently had the same thought. "The trunks aren't heavy enough. Besides, it will only anger them. It's no use."

"Get behind me." He urged her to the back of the cabin, which was barely wider than the breadth of one's outstretched arms.

"Be sure to mind your tongue," she said. "You know how thoughts can sometimes go right from your head and out your mouth without pausing for assessment."

He huffed. "What exactly do you think I'm going to say to *pirates*?"

"Shh!" She slapped his shoulder. They waited, listening.

More pounding footsteps, and shouts that possessed an undeniably feral quality. The hair on Nathaniel's body stood on end, his mouth going dry. Perhaps the pirates would pass them by. Perhaps they'd plunder the cargo and be done with it. Perhaps—

The door burst open, almost flying off its hinges, and Nathaniel barely held in his yelp. His heart drummed so loudly he was certain the two invaders could hear. One of them brushed matted hair from his eyes. They both wore ripped and stained trousers as baggy as their shirts, and their boots were worn out.

The long-haired man's beady gaze raked them up and down,

and he asked his squat companion, "You ever fuck a bitch with pup?"

Nathaniel's stomach swooped. *How do they know?* Susanna was hidden behind him. He lifted his chin, forcing strength to his words. "You shan't lay so much as one filthy finger on my sister."

Ignoring him, the squat man leered, baring snaggled, yellow teeth. He answered his friend's question. "Good and juicy, I tell you."

Behind him, Susanna dug her fingers into Nathaniel's shoulder. Heart in his throat, he yanked the dagger from the waist of his breeches, brandishing it toward the pirates. "Stay back!"

The two blinked at Nathaniel, then each other, before bursting into raucous laughter. The long-haired man said, "Oh no, we're done for, Deeks!"

Heavy footfalls sounded in the corridor, brazen and commanding. Spines snapping straight, the pirates stepped aside as a man filled the doorway, shoulders almost brushing the frame. He was tall enough to duck slightly as he entered, and his sharp gaze swept the cabin, which had never seemed quite so small.

He wore black from head to gold-tipped toes—open-collared shirt, trousers tucked into knee-high boots, and a long leather coat that flared out behind him. A pistol was tucked into his wide belt, and a cutlass winked from his hip. Gold gleamed on the belt buckle, matching the small square earring in his left ear, rings on his fingers, and the tips of those black boots.

The ends of a red sash dangled over his hip, the only splash of color aside from the gold. He had to be twice Nathaniel's age, his face weather-worn, a scar jagging across his left temple. His dark hair was cut fairly close to his head, a surprise since

Nathaniel had expected all pirates to have long, unruly hair like the animals they were.

His trimmed beard shadowed his strong jaw. In the low light, the color of his narrowed eyes was impossible to ascertain, but Nathaniel imagined they must be as black as the pirate's soul.

He might have been the very devil himself.

Nathaniel's palm sweated around the handle of the dagger, and he hated the tremors in his outstretched arm. His throat was painfully dry, and he croaked, "We—we don't have anything of value. No gold or jewels worth your effort."

Susanna added, "Even my wedding ring is plated."

Tully, one of the *Proud William*'s young crew, had entered the cabin. The man—the pirate captain, undoubtedly—glanced to him. Tully nodded. "'Tis true. Only clothin' and trinkets in their trunks." He sniffed dismissively, tossing his reddish hair. "Nothin' hidden anywhere in here we could find since we left London."

Nathaniel had thought better of the crew, but saw now how naïve he'd been. It must have been Tully who had informed the pirates that Susanna was with child. "What a coward you are, Tully."

He snorted. "As soon as I got a good look at the flag, I knew we were done for. Everyone knows the Sea Hawk will gut you from stem to stern once you're in his talons. I ain't dying for cargo I don't give a fuck about and a captain who treats us like garbage."

"Your destination is Primrose Isle?" The pirate—this Sea Hawk—demanded, his tone low and calm.

"Yes," Nathaniel answered. "It's a new colony."

Tully nodded. "Her husband's there. We're to drop them off

with their father. The old man's the guvnor or some such thing."

At this, the Sea Hawk seemed to jolt, but a moment later the ripple had vanished and he was still again, fearsome and dispassionate. Nathaniel thought he must have imagined the hiccup.

Yet a gleam entered the captain's devilish eyes, and dread slithered through Nathaniel. The Sea Hawk loomed nearer and demanded, in the same deliberate but undeniable manner, "Your name, boy."

Heart hammering, all he could manage was, "Uh…"

"This one's called Bainbridge," Tully offered.

"Bainbridge," the captain repeated, barely a whisper now. "As in Walter Bainbridge?"

Fingers going numb around the dagger, Nathaniel nodded. He'd have bruises where Susanna clung to him, her sharp exhalations ghosting over the nape of his neck. There was no sense denying it. "Our father."

"You're the son Walter Bainbridge killed his wife to achieve?" The captain's focus sent chills down Nathaniel's spine.

He couldn't hide his wince, and had to nod. His mother had never even held him before the rest of her lifeblood drained away. Susanna had been but six, spying through the keyhole, and she'd confessed it all after Nathaniel's endless badgering when he was a lad.

Strange how he could experience the aching, hollow absence of a touch he'd never had, even after eighteen years.

The captain's eyes glinted. Good God, the man was enormous. Nathaniel was tall enough, five feet and seven inches or so, but this monster towered well over six feet. It was all Nathaniel could do to hold his ground and not stagger back against Susanna. The tip of his blade quivered mere inches from the villain's black heart.

The Sea Hawk gazed down at them as though they were prey he was most eager to consume. "Your father is a liar. Corrupt. An evildoer in silk stockings and a curled wig."

Nathaniel swallowed hard, hand shaking. Could he lunge and push the dagger into this vile man's heart? Not that he had much love for his father, but who was a *pirate* to talk of evildoers?

The Sea Hawk's eyes glowed with hatred. "Your father cheated me. He was tasked with justice, with fairness. Instead he conspired to steal from me. He branded me a pirate when I was a privateer."

"Aren't they the same thing?" Nathaniel blurted. As the Sea Hawk's nostrils flared, Susanna dug her nails into Nathaniel's shoulder.

"No, they fucking are not," the pirate gritted out. "Privateers are licensed. Legal. Privateers follow rules. Laws. Just as your father was supposed to as a judge in the Court of Admiralty in Jamaica. Your father tried to strip me and my men of everything we'd worked and suffered for. We escaped him, but in the years that have followed, he has never paid the price."

Dread consumed Nathaniel. His father's greed and avarice would once again bring suffering. If not for Walter's mounting debts, Nathaniel and Susanna would still be safe at home, waiting until she had her babe before making the journey. Hollington wouldn't have had to be sold at all, and now they faced God knew what at the mercy of pirates.

Oh Lord. Please spare Susanna and her child!

Bile rose in his throat at the thought of any harm coming to his sister, terror clammy on his skin. Sweat slipped down

Nathaniel's spine. "I…" He racked his brain for something—anything—to say, some means of escape. His dagger shook, and he licked his dry lips. "I'm sorry." He had to *fix* this.

A slow, ghastly smile curled the devil's lips. "You will be."

**Join Nathaniel and Hawk on a steamy,
swashbuckling pirate adventure!**

Read more age-gap romance from Keira Andrews!

The wedding is off, but the love story is just beginning.

Betrayed the night before his wedding by the supposed boy of his dreams, Ethan Robinson escapes the devastating fallout by going on his honeymoon alone to the other side of the world. Hard of hearing and still struggling with the repercussions of being late-deafened, traveling by himself leaves him feeling painfully isolated with his raw, broken heart.

Clay Kelly never expected to be starting life over in his forties. He got hitched young, but now his wife has divorced him and remarried, his kids are grown, and he's left his rural Outback town. In a new career driving a tour bus on Australia's East

Coast, Clay reckons he's happy enough. He enjoys his cricket, a few beers, and a quiet life. If he's a bit lonely, it's not the end of the world.

Clay befriends Ethan, hoping he can cheer up the sad-eyed young man, and a crush on an unattainable straight guy is exactly the safe distraction Ethan needs. Yet as the days pass and their connection grows, long-repressed desires surface in Clay, and they are shocked to discover romance sparking. Clay is the sexy, rugged *man* of Ethan's dreams, and as the clock counts down on their time together, neither wants this honeymoon to end.

Honeymoon for One is a gay romance by Keira Andrews featuring a May-December age difference, a slow burn of newfound friends to lovers, first-time m/m sex, and of course a happy ending.

Read now!

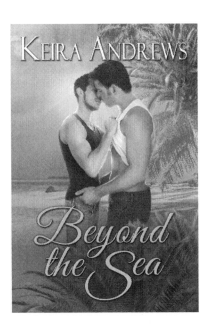

Two hot guys. One desert island.

Troy Tanner walks out on his boy band's world tour rather than watching his little brother snort his life away. Screw it. He'll take a private jet home and figure out his life away from the spotlight.

But Troy doesn't make it home.

The plane crashes on a jungle island in the South Pacific. Forget dodging the paparazzi—now Troy's desperate for food and water. The turquoise ocean and white sand beach looks like paradise, but danger lurks everywhere. Thank God the pilot survived too. At least Troy's not alone.

He has Brian.

Brian's smart and brave and strong. He doesn't care that Troy's famous. Brian's *real*. As days turn into weeks with no sign of rescue, Troy and Brian rely on each other. They make each other laugh. They go from strangers to friends.

What happens when they want more?

Although he and Brian both identify as straight, their growing desire burns hotter than the tropical sun. If they explore their sexuality in this private world a thousand miles from anything or anyone, can their newfound love survive when they're finally rescued?

This slow-burn LGBT romance from Keira Andrews features bisexual awakening, scorching exploration, an age gap, and of course a happy ending.

Get swept away with Troy and Brian as they explore love in ways they never expected...

Join the free gay romance newsletter!

My (mostly) monthly newsletter will keep you up to date on my latest releases and news from the world of LGBTQ romance. You'll also get access to exclusive giveaways, free reads, and much more. Join the mailing list today and you're automatically entered into my monthly giveaway. Go here to sign up: subscribepage.com/KAnewsletter

Here's where you can find me online:
Website
www.keiraandrews.com
Facebook
facebook.com/keira.andrews.author
Facebook Reader Group
bit.ly/2gpTQpc
Instagram
instagram.com/keiraandrewsauthor
Goodreads
bit.ly/2k7kMj0
Amazon Author Page
amzn.to/2jWUfCL
Twitter
twitter.com/keiraandrews
BookBub
bookbub.com/authors/keira-andrews

About the Author

After writing for years yet never really finding the right inspiration, Keira discovered her voice in gay romance, which has become a passion. She writes contemporary, historical, paranormal, and fantasy fiction, and—although she loves delicious angst along the way—Keira firmly believes in happy endings. For as Oscar Wilde once said, "The good ended happily, and the bad unhappily. That is what fiction means."

Printed in Great Britain
by Amazon

74166984R00189